HEART OF THE DRUAE

HEART OF THE DRUAE

Dana Lyons

Black Lyon Publishing, LLC

HEART OF THE DRUAE
Copyright © 2008 by Dana McEndree

Our books may be ordered through your local bookstore or by visiting
the publisher:

www.BlackLyonPublishing.com

Black Lyon Publishing, LLC
PO Box 567
Baker City, OR 97814

This is a work of fiction. All of the characters, names, events,
organizations and conversations in this novel are either the products
of the author's vivid imagination or are used in a fictitious way for the
purposes of this story.

ISBN-10:   1-934912-00-X
ISBN-13:   978-1-934912-00-3
Library of Congress Control Number: 2007942743

Published and printed in
the United States of America.

**Black Lyon
Ancient Times Romance**

To my two greatest loves:
For the love of my heart, my husband, Randy,
and for the love of my soul, Mother Earth.

Special Acknowledgements:

To Wayne Herschel, www.thehiddenrecords.com and his fascinating research, which gave me the idea for the Star Children and the references to humankind's home before Earth.

My sincerest gratitude to Grace, for gracefully showing me it wasn't perfect—yet.

- Dana

CHAPTER ONE

An unexplained vibration rose from the ground and tingled through archaeologist Eric Beck's body, fanning his unease. He studied the small scruffy hill, wondering what created this phenomenon—and why was he the only one who detected it? The mystery disturbed him, causing a wave of goose bumps to sprint across his neck in spite of the hot afternoon sun warming his bare head.

Every new dig site held the potential for discovery and produced a raft of thrills and excitement, but this location presented certain anomalies that eclipsed both science and sanity. He closed his eyes and rocked back on his heels.

"What is this power?" he whispered. "Why am I drawn here?"

The answer came in an instant, moving from the shadows of his mind to replace the vibration in his body with the smoke of desire. *A fall of silken hair, dark as midnight, graced the soft curve of a bare shoulder. Above the gleaming flesh, gold beckoned with a wink ...*

"Damn," he groaned, running a hand through his hair. "Where in the hell am I getting this stupid vision?"

Sudden pain erupted in his ribs as if he'd been jabbed by a sharp elbow. "Oww," he cried, rubbing his side. He spun to catch the culprit but no one was there. "What the—" he muttered, as concern for his mental health enveloped him.

And yet, he could not walk away.

Less than a mile distant, Stonehenge stood majestic and commanding, with the tallest stone trilithon just visible. Tomorrow, at precisely 6:18 PM, when the sun reached the exact moment of the much celebrated solstice, he would be here, toiling with this unique yet ignoble little hill that no other archaeologist saw as interesting.

There was other physical evidence, admittedly a brief collection: a scrap of iron, some pottery shards, a few arrowheads. Certainly nothing conclusive. But as sure as his heart beat steady in his chest, he knew a tribe once lived and breathed within the shadow of Stonehenge—a special people, undiscovered, with precious few remnants left behind to identify them.

He propped his chin on his palm, pondering the site and its mysteries. As disturbing as his questionable emotions and these unfounded convictions were, what bothered him even more was he didn't understand how he knew all this with so much certainty. The unscientific nature of it was driving him—

"You crazy American," came a shout. "Where is your hat in this sun?"

He turned to see his friend, Cedric, at the edge of the field, hands cupped to his mouth. "A hat," Cedric cried, "Do you hear?"

Eric smiled and waved back, muttering, "What is it with these Englishmen and their obsession with covering their heads?" Reluctantly he turned from his dig site, glancing at his watch to mark the time. "Cedric," he called, "come save me from this place."

He walked towards his friend. "What brings you here?" he asked, grasping Cedric's hand in a hearty shake. "I know you care nothing for this madness of mine."

"Just watching out for you, ol' chap. God knows you need it. Where's your team? Surely you aren't here alone?"

"Andre was called home on a family emergency," Eric said. "And Mason has gone back to the university for additional equipment. He should return by tomorrow." He glanced back at his meager site, suddenly sheepish about the little hill that was his fascination.

Cedric gazed across the field. "That's it? That's your answer to the lost tribe?" His incredulous face expressed far more than his words dared.

"I know there's not much to see," Eric said, "but there's evidence that calls for me to be here." He shrugged, unwilling to divulge the more mysterious aspects of his dig site. "My primary consolation is that no one has excavated this particular hillock, which means my theory has a chance."

Cautious skepticism colored Cedric's face as he studied the pile of raw earth sitting beside the hill. Motioning to the opening, about four feet from the hill's base, he asked, "Your entryway to this lost tribe?" He paused to dramatically wave skeptical brows. "I do wonder, what is your inspiration?"

Eric put his hand in his pocket and touched the artifact he found during the preliminary boundary excavation. "Yes, that's where I'll enter tomorrow. But, it's getting late and your timing is perfect. I'm closing up for the day. Give me a hand, will you?"

He unfurled the protective tarp and Cedric helped him settle it down over the small opening in the hill. They set the stakes marking an archaeological dig site and encircled the area with red tape.

"So, your site is ready for you to begin tomorrow," Cedric said, brushing his hands together. "This means you're free to join me in a pint at the Weary Traveler, am I correct?"

Eric chuckled and sniffed the wind. "Do I detect some ulterior motive within your precipitous arrival, Cedric? What manner of reform have you come up with now?"

"No reform, I assure you," Cedric protested. "However, considering your loss of one assistant, I do have some good news you may appreciate. Perhaps to the point of purchasing that aforementioned pint?"

Eric eyed Cedric closely. "Hmm. Let's see, you've mentioned money and alcohol in the same breath. The unstated element lends me to surmise your assistant is … a woman. Am I right?"

Cedric pulled his chin back, indignant. "My good man, you are ever the suspicious type. It must be all that digging around in past lives. I insist you search where there is naught." His chin pointed to the tarp-covered hill. "I hope you're more successful with your lost tribe than you are at ferreting out my simple little secrets."

Eric burst into laughter and clapped his friend on the back. "Cedric, you give yourself away. I was only fishing, but with that response, now I'm sure. I'll buy you that pint, and you can try again to introduce me to one of your endearing lady friends. I just hope she isn't like the others."

∞

The Weary Traveler was packed with the strange and the curious, all come to celebrate tomorrow's solstice at the henge. Eric led the way, elbowing through the boisterous crowd, seeing many a pint find thirsty throats on this unusually warm June afternoon.

"Molly," he called out, tugging Cedric along.

"Eric, I saved you a table in the side room," she said. "I figured you'd not want to be in the middle of that racket." She nodded to the happy crowd in the front room and winked at him before leading them to a table by a window.

"Two pints?" she asked, casting a brief glance at Cedric.

"Please," Eric said, settling into the corner seat. "And see it goes on my tab."

Cedric took the other seat, tossing his cap on his chair back and propping himself against the wall with an indignant flop. "Well, it's a good thing you're here," he mumbled, "or I'd likely never get a glass. It's clear that the lovely Molly has the eye for you—as they all do."

Eric tucked his chin, pretending to fuss with the condiments on the table. Before he could voice his defense, Molly returned with their glasses. She served Cedric with a bare nod, then graced Eric with a blinding smile. He took his drink and tried to smother his grin. Across the table, Cedric mimed the lone man with his pint.

"You'll call me, won't you," Molly purred, her eyes locked on Eric. "When you're ready for … more. I'll be waiting." She dosed him with a long, suggestive look before walking off, her exit alive with rolling hips.

Eric felt his cheeks flame and took a gulp of his ale. Before Cedric could start, he blurted, "It's the American thing, you know. They think … Well, I honestly don't know what they think. Maybe you should give up the cap, Cedric?"

Cedric burst with a gasp of laughter, blowing foam from his top lip. Hastily he wiped at his moustache. "Handsome, lone wolf archaeologist finally discovers lost love. News at 11:00."

Eric drew back, a sudden hammering uncomfortable in his chest. "What's that supposed to mean?"

"What it means," Cedric said, "is you provide the irresistible challenge and it works damnably well. You can have any girl that lays her eyes on your handsome face, yet you hold yourself aloof and thereby, irresistible. It is the call to arms for all women, surely you know."

Eric shook his head, not wanting to hear Cedric's answer, even as he asked, "Know what? What are you saying?"

"That your heart is taken," Cedric replied. "You just don't know it."

Eric stared remotely at his glass, his thoughts a maelstrom. Cedric's statement held a grain of truth, and yet he was unsure exactly what that truth was. A sudden sense of terror slid through his belly. In his mind, a daring precipice opened, offering him a taste of something unknown.

A hum filled his ears, and he frowned as his glass slid through his fingers and clunked onto the table, splashing its contents. The tavern noise telescoped into the background, disorienting him further. Detached and with mouth agape, he stared at Cedric's face as more startling words tumbled forth.

"When you are at your sites," Cedric said, "you get this possessed look on your face. It is as though you are searching for your love—a lost love. You're not looking for the remains of some anonymous primitive, Eric. You're looking for your heart."

At these bizarre words, the mental fright and physical disorientation of the abyss evaporated, leaving him in a vacuum. Unseen tumblers fell into place, echoing deeply within—

He blinked, terrified, and barked with choked laughter, "What complete nonsense. That's the most ridiculous thing I've ever heard. You're kidding, right?"

He looked about for a distraction, found Molly watching, and waved to order two more drinks.

Cedric eyed him sharply. "If you attempt to tell me you know nothing about this, you will have to buy my dinner."

"I'll be glad to buy your dinner," Eric protested. "But your theory is invalid. The only thing lost in my life is a lost tribe. As for this business you propose that I am looking for my heart—"

Molly reappeared with their drinks, clearing away the old glasses from Eric's side of the table. He asked, "What's the special tonight, Molly?" As soon as he saw the sultry look in her eye, he regretted his words.

"They've got sweet little hens drizzled with honey," she said in a seductive whisper. Her eyes hooded with invitation as she drew her tongue across her top lip and inhaled, presenting an ominous display of cleavage.

Cedric cleared his throat loudly and waved his hand until Molly finally glanced his way. "We'll take two, thank you, and another round with the meal."

She gave him a slanted look, but didn't comment. Collecting the glasses with a sigh, she left.

"That's what I'm talking about," Cedric said. He leaned across the table, nodding at the receding curvaceous form. "You're saving yourself, and they know it. Women have been throwing themselves at you ever since I've known you, and you do nothing to encourage them. Your dark good looks, granted, are responsible for some of it. But they are drawn to your aura—that of one somehow doomed. They all want to be the one you are searching for, so they can save you."

Eric sat back. The hum in his ears was a buzz, irritating and uncomfortable in the back of his head. He wondered if he was going to pass out.

Maybe tomorrow I'll wear a hat.

He licked his lips, thinking of the vision that had haunted him since he first laid eyes on the scruffy little hill, long before the ground penetrating radar showed its possibility. His heart began the now familiar crazed pace, instantly alive with the passion in his mind. He rested his head against the wall and closed his eyes with sweet anticipation, eager to see—

Her hair was a cascade of silk, dark, yet full of light. Her smell, so fresh and wild, was unlike anything he had ever known—and yet, oh, so familiar.

"Eric, did you hear me?"

Cedric's voice pierced Eric's senses, pulling him from the seduction in his mind. He opened his eyes and his belly suddenly swooped, as though he'd fallen off a carousel. Clutching at his seat, he turned his head slowly. "Say again?"

"Old man," Cedric intoned plaintively, "you really do need someone to save you. Wear your hat tomorrow, will you? I said, what is the latest on your lost tribe?"

Should I tell him?

The iron artifact he found appeared to be the crosspiece of a pair of scissors. He immediately recognized the incredible workmanship that matched the other pieces in his library of artifacts. It was his best piece of evidence, and oddly, he was reluctant to share it.

"No, nothing new," he answered. "The ground radar does show some interesting potential, though. Tomorrow is the longest day of the year, and I'll be on site before sunrise. With a little luck, I'll be inside the hill by the afternoon." He leaned across the table and lowered his voice. "Ced, there's something else—something different about this site. It sounds crazy, I know, but I feel … like I know these people. Bachofen says the scholar must be able to renounce the ideas of his own time and transfer himself to a completely different world of thought, and ultimately that's the greatest challenge for the scientist."

He hunched his shoulders and pegged Cedric with a direct look. "I'm just saying I feel—a connection, a bond—" The words were absurd, and he clamped his mouth shut. The utter implausibility of the statement rang so senseless to his own ears he dropped the subject, refusing to look Cedric in the eye. Thankfully, Ced offered no rebuttal.

Their food arrived and Cedric attacked his honeyed hen with gusto, while Eric found his appetite oddly lacking. As a bachelor, he possessed nothing in the way of culinary skills, and would probably starve to death if he didn't have a microwave. Being able to eat out while working on a dig site was heaven. He poked at his hen, knowing if he didn't make some attempt, Cedric would stab the food off his plate.

Cedric paused between bites. "I have found someone who wants to help you on this project."

Eric groaned, sensing this was the original plot and purpose of Cedric's appearance today. In reflex, he searched for an exit, glancing to the front room. The rowdy, Stonehenge revelers were gone, replaced by a quieter, sleeker crowd of tourists and couples. He glanced back at Cedric and opened his mouth, but not fast enough.

"Yes, yes, we all know you have your own hand-picked assistants," Cedric said. "But this person is uniquely qualified. Her particular expertise—"

"As you said, I have my assistants. I don't need some bumbling archaeologist-wannabe trashing my delicate site."

"Really," Cedric argued, "you're being unreasonably judgmental. I think you should at least take a look at her. She has the most—"

Through the archway, Eric noticed the front door open. An older woman entered, elegant in all black, carrying a basket of roses tied with ribbons. As she made her way around the room, she turned, and a flash of gold caught Eric's eye. She wore earrings of long gold loops, shiny against her faded red hair. He struggled to bring his attention back to Cedric, but in his mind he saw a similar flash of gold.

What did I just see?

He craned his neck to look for the woman, and was startled to find her staring at him from the arched doorway, not ten feet away. The hum scrambled through his ears again and he gulped, reaching for his drink. When he set the glass down, the woman was at his side. He wiped his mouth hurriedly and gave a shaky smile—when the gold fired up the vision in his mind.

The smell of her hair and the feel of her skin were like nothing he had ever known—and yet it was so sweetly familiar. He brushed her hair aside to expose the curve of her neck. Tangled loops of gold lay against her skin, entwined with the dark silk of her hair. He kissed her neck, and against his lips, the gold was warm—

He blinked, jolting into reality, and gripped his chair. Before him, the mysterious woman studied him intently. "Do … do I know you?" he stammered. He shot a sideways glance at Cedric, who had set his fork down and was staring with bulging cheeks and eyes.

The woman's face held an unfathomable expression that scattered goose bumps down Eric's arms. She unlatched one earring, then the other. He lifted his hands in silent protest, not understanding the carousel in his belly, the sensation in his ears, or the soul stirring vision that disrupted his heart and mind. Now this.

The woman pressed her earrings into his open hand. When he tried to say no, she leaned forward and whispered, "Save us."

The buzz hissed louder, threatening his eardrums. He blinked hard, scrunched his face and swallowed to release the tension. When he opened his eyes, she was gone.

His stomach lurched, so that he was afraid to move. The scent of roses wafted lightly, then faded.

"Good Lord, what was that all about?" Cedric asked. He peered over the table at Eric, reaching for his glass. He took a healthy gulp, asking, "What did she say?"

Trouble danced across Eric's nerves, for the earrings seared his hand and his mind with a startling familiarity. He frowned, certain he had never seen the woman before. And he had no idea what she meant by—

"Well, as I was saying," Cedric announced, clearing his throat, "I have someone to help you, and it appears you need all the help you can get." He pointed to the mysterious woman as she slipped out the front door without any further explanation. "I believe I can rest my case on that subject. In fact," he went on, "this woman I mentioned wants to come by and see you."

Eric stood and dug several pound notes from his pocket, laying them on the table.

"If you'd just take a few moments," Cedric protested, "to talk with her. Really, she has the most striking—"

"I have to go, Cedric. Tomorrow is going to be a long day and I have a lot to do." He reached for his satchel. "Send your candidate out to the site tomorrow."

"But she said—"

"Good night, Cedric," Eric called over his shoulder. He clutched the gold earrings and passed through the arched doorway into the front room.

"She says she's been looking for you," Cedric finished, frowning at the empty seat.

Outside in the parking lot, Eric paused in the twilight to stare at the earrings.

These are a part of the vision.

The need for answers was becoming more and more critical, especially with this latest addition. He slipped the earrings into his satchel and glanced at his watch. "Dammed early for a grown man to go to bed," he muttered as he turned towards his car.

∞

By the time the sun cleared the horizon into a sharp cloudless sky, Eric's site was ready. He had carefully expanded the opening into his hill and placed the freshly excavated material off to the side, ready for sifting. His journal lay open and the camera waited with a new memory card. Beside these items, the scissors artifact sat as mute witness.

Everything was waiting. Even the subtle vibration he detected in the ground seemed charged with expectation.

While the sun colored the sky brilliantly, he paused to wipe the sweat from his face. He felt the gold earrings, heavy in one of his cargo pockets, and mumbled, "Cover your head today, old man. If you pass out and someone finds these earrings, you'll be known as the lone wolf, cross-dressing archaeologist." With a chuckle, he settled his worn hat firmly on his head.

"6:10 AM," he said, marking it in his journal. "About twelve hours until the Solstice." He adjusted his flashlight and peered into the hill. "Let's see if I can find that lost tribe before the afternoon shadows strike the altar stone in the henge."

The ground radar report showed two separate depressions below the surface. The first one lay right below this opening, through two-and-a-half feet of soil. He followed the flashlight beam to the floor eight feet below, and a slow exhalation hissed through his teeth. Moving the light around the walls and floor of the cavity, he hummed. "So, my little hill is actually a hollow."

He spotted several unnatural straight lines peeking out from the dirt. "Yes," he said with a self-satisfied nod. "And the hollow is artificial, built of masonry walls." He grinned, and rubbed his hands together. "Lost tribe, here I come."

His cell phone rang and he fished it from a pocket. "Hello. Mason, where are you? I'm here doing all the work." He frowned. "Are you hurt? Good Lord, man, what hospital are you in? Have you notified the university? Can they send another assistant?" His frown deepened, remembering how quickly he rejected Cedric's proposed assistant the night before.

While Mason explained, Eric picked up the scissors and turned them over, finally setting them on the table with a sigh. "No one you say? Well, I don't want to leave the site today. I've already found promising signs. Look, I'll come see you next week, and don't worry—I'll find another assistant." He tossed the cell phone on the table and eyed the opening in his little hill. "So, it's just you and me."

Several backbreaking hours later, he stood within the cavity to examine the masonry. Bricks made of soil had crumbled with age, losing their corners and leaving the occasional straight line as the only sign of their presence.

"Masonry that rejoins the earth over time," he mumbled. "An interesting way to build, if you want all trace of your presence to eventually disappear." He pulled out one of his fine brushes and gently swept the edge of a brick; the shape disintegrated.

"Okay," he breathed lightly. "I understand. You just don't want me to know you were here." He put the brush away and shone his light around, examining the roof and the floor. All he saw was dirt, caked and crumbling.

"Damn," he grumbled. "There has to be something more." A small growl of disappointment stirred in his throat as he ground his teeth. "If you think I'm giving up this easy, you don't know who you're dealing with."

He went back outside and began the laborious task of rough sifting the excavated soil. High noon came to a still cloudless sky and he paused to take lunch in the shelter of his car. Sweat plastered his shirt and his hair was soaked. In spite of the hat, the skin at his shirt collar was sunburned.

"All right Cedric, where is this expert of yours to help me out?"

The time was 1:45 and he returned to work. He stared at the results of the rough sift. While incomplete, the material had produced nothing so far, so he was tempted to leave it for Cedric's candidate to finish. Whenever she might— "Or might not," he complained, "show up."

"So, what have I missed?" he asked. He crawled through the opening and descended the short rope ladder, easing a sigh of relief at the cool temperature.

The interior was roughly eight by ten feet. On the northeast side, a stack of flat rocks called to him. He sat and tossed his hat to the floor. Resting his elbows on his knees, he pondered the tops of his boots. "Where is your lost tribe, Eric?" he asked.

He snorted instantly, a sound of derision and disappointment shooting from his nostrils. "Give me a minute, will ya?" he answered. He let his head fall into his hands and stared at the ground, his heart sick at the thought of failure.

If I quit, I can walk over to the Druid ceremonies.

Unwilling to give up so easily, he refused to move. A bead of sweat slipped through his soaked hair and fell, disappearing into the soil. A second drop followed, and simple curiosity tinged with desperation prompted him to dig at the spot with the toe of his boot. Earth gave way to rock. He scraped again—and suddenly, the cooled hairs on the back of his neck lifted.

He dropped to his knees and pulled a brush from one of his cargo pockets. Gently, he swept the dirt away to reveal symbols carved in the stone. "EB 62108," he read. His heart stuttered in his chest and he skewed his face in disbelief. "What the—"

Lunging to his feet, he jumped back, getting his boots tangled in his hat. He teetered, wind-milling his arms wildly before crashing back into the wall. "Oomph," he grunted as his rear hit the ground and his hand plunged through the ancient brick. He cringed, recalling his crisp, arrogant words to Cedric last night about amateurs.

He glared at his hat wrapped around one boot, and kicked the offending object loose. Reluctant, he slowly turned to see a finely decorated piece of iron embedded in the broken wall.

He struggled to his feet and stared back and forth between the ironwork piece in the wall and his initials in the rock. Pointing an accusing finger at the rock, he said, "How are my—"

His heart jigged, suddenly wild and insane, just as a similar madness skittered through his subconscious. "No," he said, as his educated mind shouted, *Yes! Finally, something tangible.*

But the absolute impossibility of it …

"Today's date." He snorted and shook his head in disgust. There was so much he had hoped for with this excavation, not the least being answers to his questions about the vision in his mind that called so strongly to his heart. He closed his eyes and cried, *Who is she?*

No answer came in response to his demand, leaving cold reality to flood his belly. The carving with his initials—

Will invalidate any work I do at this site, and destroy any hope of proving my theory of a lost tribe.

Eyeing the relic exposed in the wall, he felt his joy wither and join the dust on the floor.. He turned away and kneeled before the initials, sweeping the area with a brush until he saw the letters and numbers without a doubt. "EB 62108," he read, rubbing the marks with his fingers.

His chest was rigid, forgetting the need for air. "Breathe," he commanded, and drew several deep inhalations, pinching the bridge of his nose. At last he stood and backed away, making the sign of the cross as he went.

He wiped his face and brought his thoughts to bear on his new physical evidence. "Yes, my friend," he hissed, for the exquisite work was quite familiar. The iron was layered with hammered copper and silver, and covered with artistic detail. He peeled away the dry, crumbling brick to reveal the piece solidly set into a stone foundation. "3:00 PM," he said, to mark the discovery in his mind.

He examined the wall, first needing to clear a working space around the artifact. Even though the brick was fragile and came away easy enough, it took him two hours to haul all the debris outside. "Something more for the candidate." He sniffed, wiping the sweaty grime from his face.

Back inside the hill, he brought out the fine-haired brush to examine the stone base surrounding the iron piece. Fresh chills raced down his sweated back as a foundation slab was revealed beneath the soil, indicating the presence of another chamber. "So the second depression comes on board," he muttered. "But how do I get in?" He stared at the mysterious iron. Below it, the adjacent floor slab gleamed out of place in the dark soil.

Examination of the ironwork showed it to be finely decorated. The copper and silver were covered with delicate Celtic knots interspersed with the sun, moon and stars—all surrounded by the distinctive curving spirals seen in the goddess cultures.

He wiped the sweat from his palms. "You are so close ... but where? And why is this beautiful piece here sticking out of the stone?" He touched it gently, hesitant to use any force on the brittle metal. He examined the base with his flashlight and the magnifying glass. "You're in there. But what do you do?"

Sitting back on his haunches and bringing his arms to cross over his knees, he said, "Ockham's razor says reduce this to its simplest components." He looked at the iron and shrugged. "Damn if it doesn't look like a switch to me, but to what? And if I call it a switch, then how does it work?"

There seemed no way of moving the lever either down or sideways, but an impossible thought in the back of his mind begged for attention. He reached out and pushed the iron from the underside. It glided, clicked, and stopped.

A quick shiver dropped down his back. The low level hum filled his ears and rocked through his bones. "No way," he whispered as he reached out and nudged the lever again.

The iron clicked, sliding, and the stone floor began moving with a loud grinding shriek. Several feet below, a dark compartment opened.

With no time to think, he grabbed the lantern and jumped, landing on the balls of his feet on the lower floor. The error of his actions was evident immediately. "Idiot," he barked, smacking his forehead. "How many mistakes can you make in one day?"

He looked up.

The tail of his ladder waved, several feet out of reach, while a quick glance around showed him no way to climb out. "Great," he muttered, setting down the lantern. "Lone wolf archaeologist spends night alone in dig site." He looked at his watch. "Twenty minutes to the solstice. Well, at least I have found my tribe."

The dust settled as the moving stone disappeared. He looked around and his concern over the ladder evaporated in the rush of a new discovery. "Now, this is more like it," he said, forgetting about the initials up above. He gazed around the compartment, fresh wonder quickening his heart. "This is what I expected from the radar."

Stone slabs fit perfectly into the earth to form a circular chamber. Behind him, rising stone steps disappeared into the dark soil. Ahead lay a room with a mosaic floor; in the center was a pedestal holding a crystal.

The floor mosaic was made of what appeared to be crushed bluestone and pieces of chalk covered with a sealant. A prancing bull was etched into this hard surface, and on the pedestal, the coconut-sized, blue crystal winked in the sudden lantern light.

He stared at the pedestal with longing, but the perimeter came first. He walked around the edge of the room. Here the pulverized rock produced a glinting dark background. More chalk the size of golf balls was placed strategically, forming a recognizable pattern. First he walked through the three stars in the belt of Orion, then across the tips of the bull's horns. Next came the Pleiades cluster, and then back down to the bull's hooves.

"The constellation Taurus," he said, his voice shaking with amazement. Glancing at his watch, he noted the time. "6:17, almost solstice." Then he saw the second hand on his watch twitching around the dial. He tapped the watch face, but the second hand continued to bounce erratically.

The hairs on his arm rose and he looked up, startled. His ears picked up a hum again, only this time the vibration accelerated quickly to pain.

He pressed his fingers over his ears and turned to the pedestal. The crystal had come to life, glowing, and in short seconds, the chamber was brilliant with blue light.

The hum moved through his body and shook his insides. The light from the crystal was fracturing into piercing bright beams, so he threw his arm up across his eyes. He spotted his watch face. The second hand was stopped at exactly 6:18. Beyond the watch, his fingers thrummed like a tuning fork.

Teeth grinding, he fell to his knees and clamped his arms to his body. The pitch went higher, driving him to the floor. Curled into a ball, he hung on as his atoms rattled, and the intense pain begged for relief through oblivion.

Too late, he opened his mouth to scream.

Chapter Two

If I could only stay here . . .

She sighed and snuggled down into the bedding, her mind at ease in the netherworld—where dreams were real and reality nonexistent.

She was content, warm with the soft slide of fox fur gliding against her bare legs. Long and lazy, she stretched and drew her hand in a slow path along her warm belly, across her ribs and up to her breasts. Her long dark hair tickled her back and she arched against the furs, wiggling her rear to displace the tickling when another warm hand slipped around her waist.

This hand moved gently up her ribs, following the same recently traveled path to her breasts. There it stopped and cupped her, palming the soft flesh.

Her peaks stiffened and she pressed her rump into the stirring hardness that nudged behind, offering another more delightful tickle—

"Aydyn." A voice came from the real world. "Wake up, little sister. The stones are stirring. Someone comes. The elders are calling for ye."

The words moved through her ears and stirred in her mind, but she turned her back on the sound of duty, wanting the delicious, exciting sensations of her dream world. She hunched her shoulders and pulled the furs over her head.

"Sister, I say waken," came the persistent voice. "The circle stirs. The stones are speaking."

This time, the words were followed by a rough shake of her shoulder, shattering her dream. She pushed the furs from her face and her eyes shot open in the dim morning light. "Ye say the stones have awakened?" she croaked in a rough morning voice. "Someone comes?"

Finn, her older brother by two summers, handed her clothes. "Aye," he hissed. "Someone is coming, and they want ye there."

Her heart pounded. She was fully awake now and … frightened? Thrilled? She didn't know how to feel. This was the first time the stones had sent someone in her lifetime.

She scrambled to jump up and slip on her tunic and leggings, running a frantic hand through her hair. Sweeping the long ebony mass from her face, she tied it in a knot behind her head. From the pitcher, she poured cool water and dashed the sleep dust from her eyes. She smoothed her hair again and ran her hands down the front of her linen tunic.

She was tall, almost as tall as her brother. She glanced at his large, broad shouldered form where he stood facing the door, politely waiting for her while she dressed. When she stepped to his side, he peered at her.

"Ready?" he asked.

Aydyn lifted her chin and gripped her staff. A symbol of her position as Ovate, the seasoned oak was covered from the base to its cap with an intricate design of an endless weaving vine. Within the vine were snared various important symbols of power. The cap was solid gold and added killing weight; it, too, was carved with magical symbols and stars. She regretted leaving behind her sword and bow, but the chamber where they were going was too small.

I hope whoever is coming is not better armed than this.

She gave the staff a solid shake and shrugged, not knowing what to expect. *Maybe it's one of the Star Children*, she thought. The unknown thrill brought goose flesh to her arms and she stamped the earth with her staff. "Let us see," she said, "who comes to see the Druae."

∞

"Do you reckon he hurts?"

"From the way his face is all mashed up, I think so."

Eric stirred from a world of pain and sweeping blackness, his consciousness rising to follow the sound of voices. He mumbled, "Thank you, God—"

Cedric's candidate has finally shown up and found me.

Whatever horrible thing had knocked him out was gone, and he was never so glad to see people in his life. He opened his eyes and strained to focus on who was rescuing him. In his thrashing, he had rolled onto the pocket with the earrings. Feeling them dig into his leg, he chuckled weakly. It seemed he had just missed his opportunity to be the cross-dressing, lone wolf archaeologist.

"His eyes are opening. Help him sit up. Bring water," a strong female voice commanded.

Eric's ears perked up at the sound of this voice. He thought she would be Cedric's candidate and what a fool he must look.

He touched her smooth flesh and the gold at the same time. "I will be yours forever," she said, her voice deep and husky.

The vision careened through Eric's belly and he gasped, falling off the damn carousel again. He lurched and struggled into a sitting position with the help of a strong arm. Grabbing that arm, he looked into eyes of the most striking turquoise color. He blinked and squinted, bringing his full focus on the woman's face.

At last, I have found you.

An intense sensation of joy bolted through his being. He blinked again, and the joy was eclipsed by a shadow of foreboding that waved from the back of his consciousness. He frowned and glanced around, seeing another man and woman in very peculiar clothing. His heart began to pound in time with a ringing pain in his head. His eyes crossed, loosing his hard-earned vision.

Where am I?

He hated to ask, because he knew where he was, of course. And yet something wasn't right. His eyes snapped back into focus and he looked at the woman crouched before him. She wore an outfit of linen ... leggings? On the floor beside her was a staff with astonishing carvings and what appeared to be a solid gold cap.

He frowned.

Why, that must have cost a fortune.

His eyes slid back to her face, beautiful with those brilliant blue eyes and—

"Oh!" he gasped, pulling back as his brain finally registered her tattoos. Two copper teardrops graced her right eye, one above the brow and one below the eye. They were like nothing he had ever seen and the ringing in his head peeled a little louder. He shot quick glances around the room and his heart took off again as his unease increased.

Hysteria and laughing oblivion argued over him.

"You are going to lose him again."

Eric turned to this new voice, a man's, and saw more linen leggings and a leather breastplate. He felt his eyebrows creeping higher, notch by notch, as his brain tried to assimilate this overload of anomalies. When he saw a sixteen-inch knife in the man's belt, his racing heart hitched to a stuttering halt.

Newly forged iron, delicately shaped, with hammered copper on the handle and chased silver …

Eric's eyes strained in their sockets. He stared at the man's face and thought, *I know you.* But the man wore his hair long, braided behind each ear, and his face was blue. Eric gulped as he took in the entire bizarre sight with fresh trepidation.

The knife was new, yet made like the ancient iron.

Eric's head was beginning to spin. He made a feeble sign of the cross, desperate to conjure up Cedric's comical face in this strange crowd.

Too much, too much.

He turned back to the woman and his eyes caught the stairs behind her—stone steps graced with daylight and shadows. His unease had become an elephant on his chest and he shot a glance at the stone slab ceiling. Where is the curved underside of the dirt hill? Panic began to unfurl and he tapped his heel into the hard mosaic floor of the chamber, the chamber he just discovered—that much he remembered.

He looked back into the beautiful turquoise eyes and opened his mouth to speak. But before the words could formulate, his overloaded brain finally crashed. And darkness took him again.

∞

"Put him here," Aydyn commanded, throwing back the covers of her recently vacated bed.

Finn laid the man down and Aydyn drew the skins back over him. She poured water from her pitcher into a small basin and began wiping the dirt from his face. With a clean cloth, she drizzled fresh water onto his lips. As she wiped his mouth, her recent dream surfaced in her mind with a searing flash that sweated her palms.

"He looks to be clean out," Finn said, coming to her side.

Aydyn tucked her head, feeling the heat come to her cheeks. "He is not bad to look at," she said. "His eyes, what little I saw while they were open, are green. I wonder where he comes from." She picked up the traveler's hand and noted the evidence of recent hard work. She shook her head, examining the long fingers. "But I don't think he is a warrior." She frowned, looking up. "Where are they? They should be here by now. What is taking them so long?"

"Tend the traveler. I'll see what is happening," Finn said as he ducked out the door.

Aydyn stared at the stranger, afraid to touch him again. There was something about him that drew her, yet she knew not how. She looked at his hand and the long fingers.

The hand in my dreams has such fingers.

She brought the damp cloth to his neck. The fabric of his clothing was different, but the fastenings were simple to figure out. I must try that with my leggings, she thought, opening and closing the hard round disk through a slit in the cloth. She opened the garment around his neck and bathed his sunburned flesh.

"Ye have worked hard to get here," she said, pushing the hair from his face. He seemed to be sleeping with ease and for a moment she wanted to crawl in next to him.

"Who are you?" she whispered. She brought her lips to his face, hovering just above the skin. Her breath blew against him and she drew his scent into her flared nostrils with short bursts. Sudden warmth uncoiled in her belly and she closed her eyes as delicious sensations spread out from her core. Desire twitched in her loins and she tingled from her woman's core to her breasts and out to her fingertips.

"Oh," she gasped in a throaty whisper. The sensations ignited by his scent spread throughout her being and she burned with a primal fire. Wildly, she wanted to return the favor by stripping off her loincloth and rubbing her moist heat on him.

"Ssss," she hissed, pushing away from him and standing up. She rubbed her hands against her leggings, wiping the tingling sensation from her palms. "Who are you?" she asked again, backing up and shaking her head. She glanced at her staff and picked it up, even though he was no real threat.

Or is he?

The door opened and in stepped Finn and Uncle Talie. Last was her mother in full ceremonial robes. Aydyn shot a glance at her brother, but he kept his eyes from her. She frowned and peeked at Uncle Talie. His face held a distant look, as though he were somewhere else.

An annoying chill flooded Aydyn's hands. "What? He is not one of the star people, I know that." She looked in fleeting glances to all three, but none would give her a clue.

"Tell me," she whispered, straightening her back to stand tall, even though the chill had moved from her hands to her heart.

Her mother raised her head and pierced her with dark eyes ringed with trouble. "He is the traveler in the prophecy, Aydyn."

"No!" Aydyn blurted in a strained shout. She glanced at Finn, and when he finally looked at her, she saw the truth.

"No, you are wrong. They have been wrong before. This cannot be the end, not now," she cried. She pleaded, knowing her face was stricken with grief, but she was unprepared for this.

Not after what I just—

"Tell me he is not the end of the Druae," Aydyn demanded. She clenched her staff and held on to it as she reeled from the devastating message. She looked at her mother; her eyes had changed back to a lighter turquoise as the effects of the seer-ceremony herbs wore off. She dropped to one knee in front of her mother. "Tell me you are wrong."

Cayri rested her hand on Aydyn's head, stroking, soothing. "I am afraid he is the one. He is here to help us see our final day. We must take care of him."

"Take care of him?" Aydyn shouted. She stood and stepped away from her mother. Picking up her staff, she raised it over the man in her bed. "I say we send him back."

"It is too late, my daughter." Cayri reached a hand to Aydyn's shoulder. "Cease, Aydyn. He is here and the prophecy is so. Will you take care of him?"

Aydyn shrugged from her mother's touch and whirled to stand by the door. "I will not welcome him. He is here to destroy all that is my life."

"It is not his fault," Cayri pleaded. "He is just a sign sent to tell us the end is near."

Aydyn gave a hard look at the man in her bed. The wonderful sensations he pulled from her just moments ago were gone. She shook her staff at him. "Get him out of here by the time I come back," she snarled. Turning on her heel, she bolted out the door.

∞

The shouting and troubled words came from far away, but Eric heard them. Angry words, words of denial. He wanted to stand up and shout too, but he didn't have his legs with him.

Prophecy? Druae? What's not my fault?

He thought he knew the answer, then oblivion closed the drapes and he slipped away again.

∞

Eric opened his eyes in a sudden wakening. He stared at a tightly thatched roof, sensing it was morning. The smell of something he would like to eat wafted to his nose and his empty belly rumbled. He sat up and stared into the clear gray eyes of the man with the iron knife. He cleared his throat. "Hello?"

The man looked back as though pondering a new species. He pursed his lips and returned, "Hel-looo." Working the syllables, drawing them out. Then he grinned and held out his hand. "Finn is my name. How are ye called?"

Eric's hand was grasped in a surprisingly modern shake. "Eric— is my name," he stuttered. He looked around the wood and thatch construction. "Where is she?"

"Ah, Aydyn, she threw ye out, ya know," Finn answered. He gave a conspiratorial grin and spread his arms expansively. "Not to worry, ye can stay here, I have plenty of room." His grin broadened. "Besides, I want to know everything about where ye came from." He leaned forward in his seat with a child-like expression of glee. "So, tell me, where did you come from?"

"Aydyn, you say," Eric said. The sound of her name rolled across his tongue all the way to his heart. "The woman with the—"

"Blue eyes and the big stick?" Finn responded. "Aye, my sister. I guess ye never got the proper introduction, what with coming to us out of thin air and then passing out. So there ye have it. Now, where do ye come from?"

"She—" Eric pressed, uncertain. "I heard angry words, about me. What's going on?" He pulled his legs around to the floor, hoping they would support him when he stood.

"Yea, brother, and that is a long story ye might not want to hear just now. Ye were telling me where ye came from?" Finn prodded.

Eric stood and took a step, glad to see that both his legs worked. He looked at Finn, whose persistence reminded him of Cedric. "First, you must tell me where I am now. Who are your people? Are we within sight of the great henge?"

"The circle, ye mean? Yea, brother, the stones are just beyond the village." He stood and pointed over his shoulder. "And we," he said, tapping his leather clad chest, "are the Druae of the great stone circle of the Western Isles."

Eric took a long breath and eased back onto the bed.

This is my lost tribe.

He felt an incredible relief to know that his suspicions about such a people were correct. He smiled, his lips tremulous with pride, knowing he had been right, but the pride and smile soon faded with a wilting thought.

Good God, how am I here?

"The Druae," he whispered, clutching at the bed furs. "I think this is about 1600 BCE. And you—you are the ancestors of ..." He stopped, a whirlwind of emotion threatening to overwhelm him.

He stared at the primitive man with a face painted blue and a sixteen-inch knife in his belt. He didn't understand how he came to be here, but the scientist within him was screeching a warning. Idly, he stroked the lush fox pelt as more insistent alarms started to fire.

Suddenly he shuddered with a new thought and his breath slammed against his ribs. "I ... I cannot be here in the past," he struggled. He looked up as panic filled his chest. "What have I changed by being here?"

Finn stood and stepped closer, comprehension dawning in his eyes. "Ah, so, ye are from the future. Then tell me, brother, where or rather *when*, are ye from?"

Eric shook his head, unwilling to speak even though he knew it was pointless. By his mere presence here, something must be altered. "Good Lord," he muttered, running his hand through his hair. "I think I am from 3600 years in the future." He rushed on. "I need to go back quickly, before I—"

Finn chuckled and sat back down. "Well, ye better relax then. For there is no going back. Many great-mothers have prophesied yer coming here. We need ye to stay with us until the day we fall, so ye can show us how to destroy the stone circle." Finn waved his hand as though such calamitous events were of no consequence. "But, that is a story that can wait," he said, smiling.

Eric felt his head bobble. "You have a prophecy," he said. He waved his hand back and forth in a weak effort to negate the words.

"And I'm going to help you destroy—" He stopped as hysterical laughter clawed through his dry chest. "I'm going to help you—" He shook his head. "No. You see, I can't be here. And I am certainly not going to help to you destroy Stonehenge."

"Stonehenge, aye, so that is what ye call the circle," Finn said. "Would ye like to see—"

Eric threw his hands into the air and cried, "Aren't you listening to me? I said, I have to go back, I can't be here!" He clutched the fox fur in his hand and a tiny voice whispered to him of desire, fox pelts and long legs …

"Aye, I hear ye, brother," Finn said. "But the truth is, yer with us now and from what I understand, yer here to stay. So relax and try to—"

"I study the past," Eric said, shaking his head. "I study the remnants of lost civili—" He stopped mid-syllable as a new shiver of horror skittered down his spine.

I can't even light a fire in a fireplace.

He slapped his hand over his wide-open mouth and stood, his angst erupting. "I have to go," he said. "You have to tell them I can't stay, and they have to do whatever they did to cause me to be here. And—and reverse it."

He stepped to Finn and grabbed his shoulder. "I cannot stay," he said, shaking his head back and forth to emphasize each word.

Finn's bright gray eyes sobered. He reached up and grasped Eric's hand with camaraderie. "I will talk to the elders and see if there is anything we can do, but then we will talk. Right, brother?"

Eric nodded weakly and Finn responded with a mighty crushing squeeze of his hand before turning to dart out the door. Alone, his heart began to thud with growing excitement as he looked around. The archaeologist within finally stirred.

The hut was surprisingly solid with walls of great wooden planks reinforced with mud. The roof was thatch, woven tight enough to keep out the worst elements. Everything was made of wood—the chair frame, a bedside table, the bed supports, a cup and comb. His hand rested on one of the bedposts—hard oak, carved with intricate swirling designs. He remembered the big stick Aydyn carried.

"She's why I'm here," he whispered, not understanding how he knew this, or what that meant. When he thought again of the ramifications of his presence here, his chest drew tight all the way up into his throat. "Breathe," he whispered, slipping into the chair. He eased himself onto the leather wrapped wood and sighed. The simple design was surprisingly comfortable.

With an effort he controlled his breath, closed his eyes and leaned back. The pounding of his heart slowed and faded from his hearing, allowing him to notice his surroundings and hear that one aspect of his study he always missed: the sounds of life.

The leather creaked as he slipped deeper into the chair, listening to this world. Soft footsteps ran nearby. Beyond that, the dull thud of wooden utensils. He heard women's voices, and someone sang a light tune. In the distance, dogs barked and he heard children at play. He smiled, suddenly relieved by this addition to the picture.

He sat forward with his elbows on his knees and his face in his hands. He remembered sitting like this in the chamber. Was that yesterday? He had no idea how long he'd been unconscious. The air felt cool and damp and he was sure the hour was early morning. He dared not look out the door to learn more, for fear of changing events any more than he already had.

A distant cook fire teased his forgotten stomach, eliciting a rumble of complaint. "Yes, a meal would be a good thing," he muttered, thinking twice about following his nose in search of food. Hesitant, he rose and stepped to the door. Suddenly, the quiet was replaced by sounds of alarm. He peeked out, his heart hammering.

A handful of children clustered around a girl child on the ground. A woman wailed and threw her fists to the sky, but the child lay still at her feet. A young boy sobbed next to her.

Eric pulled back and shrank against the wall. "No," he whispered. He squeezed his eyes cruelly tight and then looked out the door. The child remained still on the ground.

"Damn," he cried through stiff lips. He threw the door open and ran out.

∞

"Send him back right away," Aydyn said, "and it will be as though he never arrived." They stood in Cayri's hut and she glared at Finn, wanting to bang her staff against his hard head.

"Aye, and he wants to go back," Finn said, eyeing her with a piercing look. "But now that he is here, we need him."

Aydyn turned on her brother and lifted the edge of one lip. A feral noise came from deep in her throat as she spit, "So, whose side are you on, brother?"

Finn pulled back in the face of her threat. One eyebrow shot up as he asked, "Well, sister, as I recall, when ye first got yer hands on him, ye said he was not bad to look at." He peered into her eyes, "What happened to turn ye against the man?"

She pushed Finn out of her face and glared back. "Nothing happened, you fool. He is the prophecy. What else is there to know." She turned to her mother and let the pleading fill her face and her voice. "He must go back, Mother. I have never asked anything of you. Please, you must send him back for the sake of the Druae."

"He is part of the Druae's path," Cayri answered. "We cannot change what is meant to be, what will be, or what has already been. You know this, daughter. Yes, we can send him back, but now that he is here, he must stay to help us, for the prophecy is set in motion by his arrival."

Aydyn felt her face flush with the heat of her anger. On one side, Finn watched her with a heavily hooded stare. On her other side, Cayri sought to capture her understanding. Aydyn exhaled and rolled her eyes before dropping her gaze to the ground. She was unwilling to give her mother or Finn the chance to look too deeply.

The traveler has changed me by his scent, by the mere touch of his hand. What else will he change if he stays?

She raised her head and met Cayri's look. "Must it be like this?" she whispered.

Cayri put her arm around Aydyn's shoulder and squeezed. "I know this change is difficult, but we must fulfill our destiny. We have prepared for this time since the Star Children last walked the stone circle. We will bear this change and prosper."

Aydyn saw the truth in her mother's eyes. Even though she wanted to scream, to voice her objections to the heavens, she knew protest was pointless. As always, duty was her first command.

What was, will be again. What is, shall pass.

Her eyes watered and she glanced away while she wiped at the wetness. "I do not do this willingly," she ground through tight lips. Finn's elbow dug into her ribs and she gouged him back in a lightening flash strike. She looked up, making her reluctance clear in her face and her stance.

"We must learn from the traveler while he is here," Cayri said. "He will bring much to share with us that is good. Give this time, you will see." She turned with the familiar look of the dreamer in her eye, gazing sightless into the distance beyond the door. "Even now," she said, her eyes lit with the glow of second sight, "he returns to us one of our own."

Aydyn had long ago learned to be wary of that look, for it meant her mother had one foot in the world of visions. She turned on Finn. "What do ye—"

"I dinna know what she—" He shrugged with a hapless expression.

They heard the shouts, and a shiver brought bumpy flesh to Aydyn's arms. "Where did you leave him?" she cried to Finn as they ran outside.

"He was in my hut, refusing to come out." Brother and sister stared first at a group gathering around the shouts, then at each other. "I canna wait to hear his stories," Finn said, teeth flashing.

Aydyn stared at the crowd and a wave of dread flooded her heart in spite of her mother's words of comfort. Finn pulled at her arm, but she snatched it away from him. She didn't want to see the traveler.

"Eric," he said. "His name is Eric."

Cayri, Finn and Talie led the way with Aydyn plodding along behind them, even though her feet threatened with each step to turn and bolt in the opposite direction. "Eric," she snipped, silently mouthing the name with venomous intent.

When they reached the murmuring crowd, the group parted to reveal Anna kneeling on the ground. Beside her, Eric held her four-year-old daughter, Maisy, in his arms.

A silence settled over them as Aydyn pushed to the front of the crowd. Maisy's pale blue eyes glittered with glee as she stared up at Eric. "I knew you were coming to save me. I dreamed about you last night." She pointed several feet over their heads. "And I saw you, from up there, when you made me spit out the berry. A pretty lady was with me. She told me not to be afraid."

The traveler smiled and pushed the hair back from Maisy's eyes. Her bright face turned serious and she gave him a stern look, her baby brows pinched together. "The lady told me to tell you not to be afraid." She smiled and crooked her finger, calling him closer. With her lips cupped to his ear, she whispered. And Aydyn watched as his face turned pale as moonlight.

Maisy then kissed him on the cheek, a child's kiss smacking of sweetness. "Remember what she said," she repeated. She turned and held her arms out to Anna. "Momma, I saw the pretty lady."

Anna, tears streaming down her face, took the child into her arms. "Thank you," she whispered to Eric, clutching Maisy to her chest.

Finn stepped in, grinning ear to ear. He pulled Eric to his feet, asking, "Brother, does this mean ye have decided to stay?"

The traveler stared at them, his green eyes lost and helpless. Color flooded back into his cheeks with a bright stain, but his soundless mouth continued to work like a landed fish.

He does not wish to be here, Aydyn thought. Suddenly, his green eyes found hers, and she could not look away.

Help me.

She stepped back.

Finn clapped him on the back with a hearty chuckle and pulled him into the crowd. He eagerly introduced Eric to Cayri and the many children as others streamed in. More and more faces came to greet the silent stranger.

Aydyn edged out of the crowd. She watched her people accept the man who brought their destruction, and was struck with choking disbelief. Yet the pain in his green eyes reached out to haunt her. She shook her head and turned away.

Like a shadow, she was gone.

CHAPTER THREE

Alone, leaning against a large log before a campfire, Eric stared at the flames. He held a sodden, sticky berry in his palm, the obstruction that flew from Maisy's throat when he performed the Heimlich maneuver on her.

I couldn't stand by and let her die, not when I knew how to save her. I could never live with myself if I had.

But saving her life was not what knocked the bottom from his stomach; it was her words.

"Did you bring the pretty gold?"

He stared at the berry, struggling for understanding. Since arriving, he had been in a constant state of emotional agitation, desperate for something to hang onto in this world of startling abnormalities. Did he believe Maisy gave him the earrings in the future so he would come back and save her in this life? The conundrum of time travel offered him no comprehension.

"Where's a travel guide when you need one," he whispered.

He chuckled with poor conviction. Since 6:18 PM yesterday, everything in his life had changed, and not just his location in space and time. What he once stoutly believed and thought he knew with certainty was fast proving to be an illusion. Only the earrings, heavy in his pocket, were evidence he could hold.

Were they my ticket onto this crazy carousel?

The concept of time travel was well discussed in the dormitories of archaeology, as was the theory of affecting the future by altering the past. He had undoubtedly changed the future now by changing the path of Maisy's life. He shivered, thinking about the possibilities of what that meant, then just as quickly wondered if his being here was not an accident—that he was here because there was something he was meant to do.

Or, as the Druae say, something I have already done.

He looked up at the sky. The major constellations showed little change, but some differences were visible in the night sky. With everything around him different—the sky, the earth, the people— did that mean he was different, too?

All things considered equal, I must be.

He looked at his hands. The long fingers were brown and calloused, the same fingers he woke up with yesterday, 3,600 years in the future ... give or take a century. He prodded a small laceration from yesterday that was healing nicely here in the distant past.

Was he just someone in the right place at the right time? Or was he chosen for this specifically? Did he really have something to give to these people during the greatest challenge to their existence?

That morning he had met many of the Druae. A surprisingly intelligent and beautiful "primitive" people, they possessed an amazing faith in infinity.

He shook his head again and shrugged, open-mouthed.

I can't even conceive infinity. And yet these primitive people have grasped the concept well enough to structure an entire belief system around it.

"Now, brother, that is a serious face ye have," Finn said, arriving as silent as the moon. "The night is fine, what worry can there be? Here," he said, handing Eric a cup. "'Tis a sweet brew with honey and grain."

Eric took the cup and sniffed cautiously. He tasted the beverage and smiled. "You remind me of a friend I have," he said.

"Ah, from the future. Now that is why I am here. I came, hoping to begin that talk ye promised," Finn said.

Eric gazed up at the sky and pointed. "When I was a child, the stars were my first love, long before archaeology. I wanted to travel and see life from all around the universe. Then I went to school and I was taught we were the only life there was." He stopped to sip his beer, eyeing Finn who gazed at him with rapt attention like a child hearing some famous, fantastic tale.

"I don't believe," Eric finished, "I was taught the truth, the whole truth and nothing but the truth." A raw chuckle strangled his words. "I have been here about—" He paused to look at his watch. "This damn thing hasn't worked since—"

Finn leaned in to see. "What does this do, brother?"

"This is a watch, a device that tells me the time." At Finn's blank expression, he added, "The hours of the day."

Finn grinned and pointed to the great henge beyond the village boundary. "We have something similar, only we do not need help with the hours of the day. Our watch, as ye say, tells us the path of the moon and the sun. The stone circle works verra well, but ye canna put that on yer arm. So, tell me brother, why are ye so concerned about the hours of a single day?"

"Time is money, they say, and so we watch every minute that goes by," Eric said, feeling that "his people" were very foolish. "Your watch—how did the stones come to be here? Did you build the—"

"Oh, no," Finn answered, drawing back. "The elders say we started the circle, for the Druae have been here a verra long time. We were drawn to the power. Ye can feel it, can ye not? Long ago, the early ones came and marked the circle on Mother. They dug the ditch and brought in the bluestones. But, no, it was the Star Children who built the circle."

Eric felt his throat go dry in a breath. He set his cup down, wishing he'd examined the drink more closely. "The Star Childr—" He stopped to cough and clear his throat. "Finn, who are the Star Children?"

Finn threw his head back and pointed to the night sky. "There," he said, "see where the bull dances? Follow the stars in the belt, across the bull to the cluster of the gods. They point the way home."

He gazed to where Finn pointed. The belt stars Finn referred to was Orion, and what he called the cluster of the gods was the Pleiades. "Home?" Eric asked. "Home for who? The Star Children?"

"Aye, and us," Finn answered. "Ye know we come from there, brother? So far from the future, ye must know this?"

Eric sagged back against the log and clutched at the ground. "No, I didn't know that," he said. He stared up at the twinkling night sky and fingered the gold in his pocket—his ticket onto the carousel of time.

He recalled the Brookings report from the 1950s. The study determined if a primitive society were suddenly exposed to a highly advanced culture, the lesser society would be destroyed.

How will I survive exposure to these primitive people?

He wasn't so sure anymore who was the primitive. The precipice opened in his mind, daring him to approach once again the ominous unknown. He shuddered as a sinking sensation flowed from his scalp all the way to his rump. The ground felt ready to swallow him up.

"They are planning a special ceremony for ye," Finn said.

"A ceremony for me?" Eric groaned. A new trepidation stirred in his belly and he reared back, feeling his cup of life way over-filled.

Now what?

He stared at Finn, his new friend in this strange world, and wondered at the openness of that man's facial expression. Eager anticipation of Eric's every word filled his face. Eric squirmed, his butt wriggling into the bare ground, unsure his words warranted such devotion.

"And what sort of ceremony are they planning?" he asked. Surely if they were intending something dire, like a sacrifice, he would see it in Finn's face. "Is this ceremony because of the prophecy?"

"Aye," Finn answered. "Now that the prophecy has been set in motion, we must let all the Druae know, for we canna say how much time we have. Tomorrow night, the Goddess moon will rise through the great circle. We will light the crystals and send the message to the heavens before releasing the messengers to the four corners."

Eric stared at the fire. He was beginning to understand he would be here for some period of time. But no one had answered his other questions.

How long? Will they be able to send me back to my time? And what about Aydyn? What was her part in all this? That she was important to him was the only thing he knew for certain in this new world.

He had not seen her since he saved Maisy that morning. Just thinking about Aydyn made his heart thud as if it suddenly possessed some new purpose besides driving the blood through his body. This startling physical reaction to her reminded him of the throbbing drums of the jungle tribes, a single beat sending a message over long distances.

Will she be at this … Goddess moon ceremony?

Finn rose and stretched. "Aye, you will see her there," he said with a wink.

Eric hunched his shoulders. Finn had a habit of answering his questions before he could speak them. "She seemed to object to me being here. She—"

"Aydyn will do as she must," Finn said. "She is a Druae warrior and Divination Ovate. Her life is not hers to command. She may swing a big stick, but she will do as she is told."

Finn reached down and grasped one of Eric's hands in what Eric had learned was the Druae greeting and parting. "Ye have the bed tonight," Finn said, nodding to his hut. Eric followed Finn's gaze across the camp of fires to a hut in a far corner. "Yer arrival has been most advantageous. My talents are needed elsewhere." He grinned and bowed, leaving without a sound.

Eric sighed and rubbed his face. Earlier, he was served a bowl of delicious stew and flat bread for the evening meal. His stomach was full and, in spite of the chaos of the last twenty-eight hours, he was content. The night was fair and the fire alluring, drawing him deep.

He stretched his legs out and settled back against the log. Even though he was exhausted, he felt sleep would be elusive. The flames took his gaze and worked their magic. He was captured, content to burn.

Like a moth, he thought, and smiled.

Above him, the stars winked.

∞

Aydyn watched him from the sheltering shadows of the great forest. The trees covered the land for as far as the eye could see, surrounding the village and the great circle. She loved it here; the forest was home. There was not a trail, a tree or an animal she did not know.

She straddled a large limb in the upper branches of her favorite tree, a great oak. The giant tree was alive with the wisdom of Mother earth and Father sun, and she admired its steadfast dedication to just being … being alive and being free. No one told the oak what to do, where to go, or how to act.

The oak has a life, I have another.

Tomorrow she would command the crystals, for she was taking on a new duty—that of teaching the traveler, Eric, the ways of the Druae, so he would tell them how to destroy the stone circle when the time came. She watched him, curious.

How his world must have changed in the blink of an eye.

She shuddered. She, too, was going to lose her world, but she had time to prepare. He did not.

Perhaps he is a warrior, after all. Or at least a very brave man.

His scent, how he affected her, the strong calloused fingers that touched her so intimately—all burned deeply in her memory. She was certain he was the man from her dream.

She exhaled sharply, pushing the air from her chest along with the thoughts from her head. "Who are you?" she asked, challenging the man from another time and place. "I understand who you are to the Druae. You are the prophecy. But who are you ... to me?"

∞

Eric never heard her footsteps, only his accelerating heart told him she was near. He looked up from the fire and she stood above him. He scrambled to his feet, rising from a rump gone numb on the ground.

"Hello. Umm," he struggled. "I'm sorry I didn't rise sooner, I didn't hear you." His nervous words faded and he didn't know what to say. His heart had gone wild, taking his breath away. All he wanted to do was stare at her. "Turquoise," he said, drowning in her brilliant eyes. "Do all the Druae women have this color of eyes?"

"It is called the Druae blue," she said. "And yes, this is the eye color of Druae women only." She stepped up to him. "I am Aydyn."

He noticed she did not extend her hand for the greeting so he stuck his hands in his pockets. "I'm Eric. Eric Beck," he said, feeling awkward. He shuffled his feet and stared at his boots, afraid to look into her eyes again. Afraid he might never return.

His initial glance took her all in. She was tall, about six feet, and well formed—muscular, yet lean and beautifully shaped with vigor and a deadly vitality.

She carried a staff and he eyed the intricate carvings, finding himself easily captured by the beautiful work. He was trying not to stare at her face and the teardrop-shaped tattoos; the copper coloration was stunning against the blue of her eye. In his pockets, his hands grew warm with a tingling. He wanted to touch her face and stroke the copper tattoo. He jerked his eyes back to the carved oak. "Your staff is incredible. May I?"

She didn't answer right away, and he feared he had breached some protocol. He tensed, afraid to breath. Finally, she released a hiss and lifted the staff into the light as though nothing bothered her.

"This has been a source of power and wisdom used by the Druae women for longer than anyone knows," she said.

She motioned to the ground beside him and he realized she was asking him for permission to sit. "Please," he said, stepping out of the way. His heart stuttered and he felt as though all his molecules were sliding to a stop.

She is going to sit. What if I say something stupid?

As lithe and graceful as a wild cat, she dropped to the ground with her legs crossed. She looked up at him and frowned. "Will you sit with me?" she asked, indicating a place next to her.

Relax, you are an educated man. You can do this.

He sat in stages, bringing his tall body to the ground with somewhat less grace than she did. His face burned as he worked to arrange himself next to her.

"You are not used to sitting on the ground, are ye?" she asked. "We have seen people who live so."

She smiled, and he swore the stars spun through his soul and the ground pitched beneath his folded legs. He was thankful he wasn't standing.

"Your body will adjust. Just give yourself time," she finished.

He shifted, squirming to gather some equilibrium. Smiling lamely, he prayed he didn't look like a clown. "The staff." He pointed, "Please, tell me about it." When she turned towards him, the firelight glinted off the copper on her face.

She held the oak up, turning it slowly. "This is the staff of an Ovate, a staff of Divination. I have been an Ovate for five summers. Soon, I will be initiated into Cayri's level and pass this on to the next woman. Each keeper of the staff adds her own carving on the oak. Her wisdom then resides within the staff for the next Ovate to draw upon."

The carving was detailed beyond anything Eric had ever seen. He saw the twisted vine that would come to be associated with the Celtic people, and dragons and peacocks, fish and birds, and a thousand endless knots. He saw dots in the familiar celestial formation that included Orion's belt, Taurus, the Pleiades, and … home.

"How many women have carried your staff?"

She frowned and pursed her lips. "Eric," she said, "it is the other way around. The staff is not mine. I was given to the staff. I belong to the staff for as long as I am deemed worthy. As for the carvings, the staff has allowed the mark of—" She counted, ticking off on her fingers, then said, "An Ovate for each moon, going back three long days."

When she spoke his name, his heart flopped like the landed salmon he spied on the carved oak. Mystified over her measurement of moons and days, he looked over his shoulder towards the henge. Solstice, the longest day of the year—a long day. Her reference to a long day must mean a year, so three long days are three years. Moons must be months, making it three times twelve.

"Thirty-six Ovates," he said. "And how long, I mean, how many long days does the staff spend with each woman?"

Her cool blue eyes sparkled when she smiled. "You learn fast." She held up one hand and waved the fingers. "For this many long days." She repeated the action with her other hand. "Or this many."

"Five," he said, following her. "To ten, maybe twenty," he added as she opened and closed both hands. He did the math and whistled. For statistical measurement he allocated a ten-year increment, times thirty-six equaled—

"Almost four hundred years. Possibly five to six hundred," he said.

"If that is how you call it." She nodded back, miming him. She then changed her nod to a shake and frowned. "But this is not a very long time."

Eric's eyebrows shot up. "Not a long time," he asked, shaking his head, getting into the play, miming her.

"No, because this is not the only staff," she said, her eyes sparkling with laughter.

She played him, he realized, and chuckled. "So, how many staffs are there?" he asked.

"Cayri keeps the pieces," she said. She stood smoothly with the aid of her four-hundred-year-old staff. "After a while, they break."

He shaded his eyes, following her as she rose with the fire at her back. She was a goddess, aflame with an ancient wisdom he couldn't begin to fathom. He thought of his university degrees and how truly pitiful they seemed in the presence of her primitive knowledge.

Rising slowly on legs gone stiff, he was startled when she thrust her staff in his face. For one wild moment he thought she meant to strike him. He looked past the carved wood to her face, and saw a warm smile of encouragement. In his chest, the salmon flopped.

Take it, his heart said.

He reached out and grasped the small end, rising with difficulty.

"Thank you," he said, rubbing at his glutes.

"Come with me. There is something we can do for ye." She turned and moved in the soundless way of the Druae that he had come to expect.

He struggled to keep up with her fluid, long-legged strides. He hitched along on stiff legs and grimaced, berating himself for not spending more days in the gym. "Where are we going?" he asked, catching up with her.

"You will stay with Finn," she said, shooting him a glance. "But you will spend your days with me. I will teach you the Druae way."

His steps slowed to a halt as her words sank in. This was an archaeologist's dream, to study a lost civilization in real time.

And to spend my days with her.

He glanced up. She moved like a woman on a mission, straight ahead with nothing in this universe to stop her. She was dynamic beyond anyone he had ever encountered.

She released her hair and it fell in a cascade to whisper across her shoulders, calling him. He followed the silken strands and placed his lips just above her skin, hovering with perverse delight before allowing himself—

"Are ye coming?" she called.

He blinked and the vision was gone. Before him, she peered into his face, her brow wrinkled. "Are you all right?" she asked, concern pulling at the copper teardrops.

A shudder ripped through him and he gulped, stepping back, trying to shake the sensual image from his nerves.

She is the vision.

She grabbed him and shook gently, but he pulled loose from her grip and stepped away. Where she held him, his flesh burned. "I'm fine," he blurted, rubbing his arms. "You were saying?"

She crossed her arms and stared at him with intelligent, challenging, piercing eyes. He fought the urge to fidget and stood his full six foot, three inches, just managing to tower above her.

Her tattooed eyebrow cocked and a half grin teased one side of her mouth. Without a word she turned and motioned him to follow.

They stopped before a large wooden building. There were windows with panes made of colored chips of glass held together with a concrete-like mud. Eric craned his head back and saw a vent shaft in the roof releasing steam. His eyebrows shot up and he asked, "A bathhouse?"

She wrinkled her brow and the copper teardrop on her forehead pulled to a slant. "Bathhouse?" she repeated. She smiled and the lower teardrop crinkled. She swept aside a fabric curtain and he followed her into a semi-dark room.

Waving her arm, she said, "Here we honor the gift of water." She indicated at least a dozen cubicles separated by walls of timber and thatch. "And so we honor our bodies with the gift of cleansing."

She sniffed lightly and he cringed, knowing he was in bad need of such a cleansing.

"You will find the water able to heal and soothe you," she said, pointing to one of the cubicles.

Peering over the half-door, he saw wooden floor planks covered with soft rugs woven of strips of linen. In the corner, a round tub was carved from a solid tree trunk. Above, copper tubing descended from the rafters to about six feet above the tub. Towels sat on a bench. An iron hook jutted out from a vertical beam. By the tub, a clay container held a pink glob. He sniffed and detected—roses? Something floral?

He scrubbed his face with his hands, suddenly weary and feeling very small. A bathhouse, he thought, shaking his head, on Salisbury Plain, four thousand years ago. "And the water?" he asked, pointing to the hammered copper tubing.

She nodded and grinned. "The metal was Finn's idea, of course. He designed this to bring in the hot water. We tried using wood, but it swelled and we could not carve a single piece long enough, then the joints always leaked."

"How do you heat the water?" he asked, his admiration for these people expanding exponentially. During the years he developed his theory about a lost tribe, he had created an image of them in his mind. It seemed he knew nothing, for the reality of them eclipsed his educated vision at every turn.

"The water comes from an underground stream," she said, "that runs beneath the stone circle. Cayri says the river is connected to the heart of Mother. We heat the water with the crystals because we know they provide a healing power."

He followed her as she passed by other cubicles. All had the same rugs, the iron hook, another pot with its fragrant glob. In some rooms the tubs were larger, in others, the bather had room to stand. On the wall in each room a polished metal piece was hung for a mirror.

She leaned against the entryway of the final cubicle with its half-door open. "In here you can rest your ... sore parts. The water will be very warm at first, then you can cleanse with the mixture in the pot. This one is herbal, so you will not smell like a flower." She smiled and he smiled with her, feeling a sudden giddiness coil in his stomach.

"When you are ready to rinse, the small lever will make the water flow out. Then you can stand and the other lever will bring water from above."

Noting the levers and the simple technology, he marveled at the brilliant simplicity of the setup. When he turned to ask her where the drainage emptied, she was gone.

These people move like the wind.

He sat on a short stool, too tired to be astonished any further. The towels next to him were fluffy and smelled of sunshine. The little pot held something spicy—a manly scent, fresh and wild. The big wooden tub beckoned. He was exhausted beyond belief, and yet his brain was in overdrive.

How did they have such advances? Who were these Star Children? What sort of crystals heated the water? Why was there no trace of the Druae's existence? What happened to them?

He reached over the tub and moved a sliding cover to plug the drain hole. When he wiggled the other lever, hot water began filling the tub from a small hole. He sniffed the water and noted a slight mineral smell, nothing else, and it was hot and inviting.

"When in Rome..." He saw Aydyn had closed the lower half-door when she left. He shrugged and quickly shucked out of his dirty clothes, climbing over the edge of the tub. The water steamed and was heated to the perfect hot tub temperature. He eased in with a hiss of pleasure.

"Oh," he groaned, settling into the healing water. His back pressed into the tub and his legs stretched out against wood worn as smooth as marble. He scooped up some of the herbal mixture from the pot and slathered it on. His pores opened and tingled, surprising him.

"We have a special recipe, known only to Druae women," Aydyn said from the half-door.

Eric flinched. "I thought you left." A blush rose from his neck to his cheeks. His heart began its tattletale pounding and he stammered. "I ... You ... There was no—"

He glanced up, but she kept her gaze downcast, covering the turquoise of her eyes. He wished she would look up at him; the thought of her seeing him nude made his breath stall. The erotic vision that stopped him in his tracks outside flashed through his mind, opening up a floodgate of wanting.

What in the hell, he thought, looking down, *is in this water?*

"I brought you garments," she said. Her voice was tight. "They should fit you and are yours to keep while you are here." Finally, she glanced up at him. The beautiful cool blue of her eyes was now a molten inferno.

She pushed the door open and strode in.

He refused to cringe, and sat tall in the tub, standing his ground, such as it was. He watched her movements—sharp, abrupt, powerful—and he wanted her. Her nearness caused a quick heat to spread through his veins and he hardened in the warm water. He locked eyes with her and the heat in his loins matched the fire in her Druae blue.

She glanced down at the water and her eyes bulged. "Here," she said, stepping aside to set his new clothes on the bench. She bent over and snatched up his soiled garments from the floor. When she rose, they came eye to eye over the edge of the tub.

In her blistering gaze he could see she hated him being here. But her eyes held something else, a primeval fire unlike anything he had ever seen before. He was drawn into that inferno, mesmerized.

She dropped her gaze, hiding her eyes from him, and backed out of the room, moving so silently it was as though she had never been there.

He blinked, and she was gone.

Later, Eric collapsed into Finn's abandoned bed. The water had indeed healed him, and he was now ready for some much needed sleep.

He closed his eyes and saw Aydyn's blazing Druae blue. He smiled and rolled over, just as the tethers of unconsciousness began to reach for him. His brain was bursting with questions for the gods who brought him here. But he was gone before he could whisper the words. Gone before he could ask again.

What happened to the Druae?

∞

In a sheltered valley beyond the western shore of Europe, a tribe of Tarans prospered. Jarech was their chieftain, and Balock, his oldest son.

Outside in the warm night, many sought their day's end before a snapping fire. Stars sparkled in a crystal clear sky, and on the horizon a near full moon rose against the last flush of sunset.

Outside his hut, Balock stared into the flames, his mind as much ablaze as his campfire. He thought again and again of the Druae woman and he clenched his jaws. When she refused his offer, a tiny fear had been born within him, a fear that had wiggled its way from his heart to his gut, and now lived dark and insidious within him. He repressed this weakness, for the son of Jarech had no fear he could not overcome.

But this time—

He growled low in his throat. In his hands he held a Druae short sword made of the new metal, iron. He lusted for the secret of its construction, another Druae beauty that eluded him.

"Their smith, the man Finn, he knows his way with metal," Balock said. He turned the blade into the light of the fire and admired its strength.

His friend, Rannor, cast him a slanted glance. "Who do you fool, Balock? The Druae iron is not all you would take from them." He pointed to the forbidden blade. "Your father is not going to like this."

Balock growled, but held his tongue. He slipped the Druae blade into the sheath and wrapped it in a skin, then wrapped that in another skin. No one but Rannor knew of it, for Druae ironwork was not for sale. Balock had stolen the blade while he was at their spring festival, when the woman rejected him.

"I want the woman," he said, "because she will get me strong sons. I want the iron because it is a powerful weapon."

"And what about the stone circle?" Rannor asked. "Would you give up your free life here on the plains—" He gestured to the wild beauty that surrounded them. "—to supplicate yourself in that circle of cold stone?"

Balock stared into the fire, needing to divert his gaze from his friend's piercing look. "You have seen what they do there," he said. "You have seen the power they wield. Do you not desire to know such a power?"

"Ha," Rannor spit. "Now I know," he hissed. "You fool yourself. The power of the stone circle is Druae, and Druae alone. No plainsman can wield that force." He reached out and grabbed Balock's arm, giving him a rough shake. "The closest you will ever get to Druae is contracting for another of their women. After the scene you caused this year, I doubt any of them will have you."

Balock jerked his arm loose and leaned back. "I will not have to contract another," he said. "I will have her."

Chapter Four

Eric woke refreshed, invigorated and hungry. He dressed in the garments Aydyn brought him and stood by the door, wondering what would happen today. From what she told him yesterday, he would spend the day with her. He didn't know what to think after last night. Their bathhouse encounter made his cheeks flame like he was some kid.

I am insane to have such thoughts about this woman.

"But she is the reason I'm here," he argued.

He liked to believe each man created his own existence by how he thought, what he did, where he went. If so, and Cedric was right about him looking for the remains of a long lost love, then he had created this day by his actions. From the moment he first saw that little hill and the dream began haunting him, he had willingly, if not subconsciously, set himself on the path to find her.

Was I born in the future with memories of what I did in this past?

He shook his head. Whatever the reason, he was here, and she was waiting for him. He set the door aside, thinking it awkward having to move the unattached piece back and forth.

"Welcome to the day."

He stopped mid-step. An older woman he remembered meeting yesterday after saving Maisy stood at the threshold, bearing his clean and folded clothing. His briefs were on top, and she fingered the elastic waistband back and forth. He eyed her keen interest in his garment and prayed to the gods he hadn't skidded his shorts when he went through time.

"This is fascinating," she said. "How wonderful to have the material give and then return." She smiled at him and her Druae blue was the deep glittering aqua of Caribbean water. She extended her hand for the familiar greeting. "Eric, I am Cayri, Aydyn's mother. We met yesterday. Forgive me for not welcoming you earlier, but I have been quite busy since your arrival."

Her smile was warm and engaging, her face alive and sparkling with her welcome. He returned the handshake and felt his own smile broaden in response to her greeting. "I'm sorry to have caused such a stir, Cayri. You know, I'm not sure how it is that I'm here." He craned his neck to look past her, searching for Aydyn.

"She is preparing for tonight's ceremony," Cayri said. She stepped around him and placed the clothing on the bed. When she turned around, she eyed him with a piercing look he knew missed precious little. He resisted the urge to squirm and wondered if all of the Druae were prescient.

If his theory were correct—that the Druae were the ancestors to the Celtic/Druid society—it would seem the reports of Celtic divination and foretelling had some basis. "You knew I was coming," he said. "Do you know why I'm here?"

"There are many reasons for your presence here," she said. "Even I do not know all of them."

She extended her hand and he reached to take what she offered. The tangled loops of gold slid into his palm.

"You will want these," she said. "They are quite beautiful and Aydyn will adore them. They are like nothing else she will ever have, and she will cherish them every day of her life."

He gulped and clenched the earrings in a fist, strangely unsettled by Cayri's words. A crushing foreboding exploded in his chest and his legs wobbled.

Cayri placed her hand on his arm, her eyes creased with pleading. "Do not grieve, Eric, all will be well. I have seen this. You must have faith in the infinite power that brought you here."

A sensation of horrific loss washed over him, then left as quickly as it came. He felt the carousel shift, preparing to toss him off again, and he gasped. "No. I will chose my own—" He looked at the ageless wisdom in Cayri's eyes, eyes that had seen the future and his coming here.

What else has she seen?

He jerked upright, needing to fight the forces that propelled him inexorably toward his fate. He wanted to control his destiny in this time and place. He needed to make his own decisions.

Cayri gave a knowing smile as her eyelids dropped. She nodded in silent agreement, yet denied him further disclosure of what she knew. A shiver tumbled down his spine.

Like Finn, she reads my thoughts.

Eric shook his shoulders to throw off the chill. He was glad he didn't possess such a gift, for he didn't think he was strong enough to view another's thoughts or the future. Life was damned difficult enough without such foreknowledge.

"Knowledge," she said, her words mocking him, "is a tremendous power. In many ways it can defeat the sword." One of her delicate eyebrows arched, and the movement was as eloquent as a thousand words. "With the right knowledge, even death can be defeated. That is why I am here, to guarantee life and the continuity of my people."

Hope shone in her eyes, blinding and contagious. He felt the corners of his mouth twitch to a smile, willing to agree with anything she said.

"How can I help," he asked. "Please, tell me about this prophecy and my part."

From another hidden pocket she pulled a small, carved wood box. It had a clever sliding lid and she placed the earrings inside. "This is my seal," she said, pointing to the surface. An intricate carving in fantastic detail covered the lid. He saw vines and leaves and tiny creatures of the forest. Nestled in the center was an all-seeing eye.

He glanced at her and she blinked. The Druae blue was deep and guileless, innocent. She blinked again and her pupils expanded like an owl at night.

He pulled back.

She blinked once more and her eyes returned to normal. With a sublime smile, she said, "Mother sees all." She tapped the box with her finger. "Your gold will be safe in here. No Druae would disturb the box."

She placed the box and his clothing in a small woven basket beside the bed. He eyed the basket and considered putting on his modern clothes, but his new garments were comfortable. To wear authentic clothing was another part of the archaeologist's dream.

"Save them," she said, pointing to the basket. "You will need them another day." He shook his head, already spinning from talking with someone who knew not only the future, but his thoughts as well. Whatever hidden meaning those words were meant to have, he didn't want to know today. He made the sign of the cross behind his back.

"Walk with me," she said.

She offered her arm and he stepped to her side. He didn't know how much time he had, just knew he couldn't waste a minute while he was here. He refused the habitual desire to glance at his watch, which he still wore, and placed his arm through hers. She nodded yes and he exhaled deeply. As much as he wanted to spend his day with Aydyn, this was another dream come true. He felt his face go soft with wonder. "Can we go see the stones?" he asked.

Cayri laughed. "That is exactly where we are going. See," she said, nodding. "You are here only one day and you are picking up the gift already."

∞

Eric stood on top of the bank circling Stonehenge.

I must thank the gods for bringing me here.

Thank the Goddess, came a silent reproach.

He admired the view from this height. In modern times the bank was so eroded it was hardly noticeable. But today, he stood on a berm of packed earth two meters high. Behind him, the ditch carved in the chalky soil gleamed white against the deep green of the grassy plain.

He lifted his face to the sun and the breeze, and vibrated with exhilaration all the way to his bones. The earth was his mother and he was a child come home.

Above, the sky was a clear blue like he had never seen before. The absolute silence that rode beneath the wind was at first unnerving, and he wondered when man became used to the cacophony of humanity.

From his vantage point he could see there was no horizon, for it was swallowed by the great mass of trees extending as far as he could see and beyond. The hardwood forest was as thick as the rain forest canopy of South America—thick enough for a squirrel to hop across England from the Atlantic to the North Sea.

Before him, the complete and intact Stonehenge stood, as majestic as anything modern man would build. It was even more imposing and impressive within this pristine setting. And there was the power—he felt an energy akin to what he detected at the small hill he excavated, as soon as he topped the bank. He knew there were prominent ley lines in the area, but this tug against his atoms was beyond anything he had ever experienced.

Geomagnetic forces?

The Goddess, came the whisper once again.

He was not a religious or spiritual man; he was man of science and data. He understood that which he could hold in his hands. A voltmeter, he thought, so he could take some readings.

"Mother is inspiring, is she not?" Cayri said, appearing soundlessly at his side.

His knees and organs flinched at her words and silent appearance. "You people move with the wind," he said, clutching his chest. He pulled a comical, injured face and she laughed.

"And like the wind, we will leave no trace," she responded. She made a sad face—the mime of tragedy, and around her eyes the teardrops darkened to a glowing bronze. In a flash, she reversed, smiling like a sprite.

"Why must you disappear?" he pleaded. He thought of his scant collection of evidence for this entire society. "There is so much for you to give to those who follow you. You must want to save this." He swept his hand to encompass the magical place before them. "How can you let go of this wonder?"

"What once was—" she said.

"—will be again," he finished. The Druae's stoic ability to face such destruction was beyond his thinking. He knew what was next, and finished the sentence without conviction. "And what is now, will pass."

"There, you are learning so fast," she answered.

He knew the words, but he didn't have the faith to support such dedication. He shook his head in denial. "I can't."

"And that is why you are here, to learn our way. Then you will know how to help us. That is not so much to ask—knowledge for knowledge?"

Her beautiful face pleaded, reminding him of Aydyn. There was so much he wanted to know about Aydyn and why she so important to him. He felt the yawning precipice open again, and this time he wanted to search deeper.

But his heart called him back, *not yet, not yet.*

"Will you tell me about the stones and the Star Children?" he asked. He heard the childish voice in his words and grimaced. *If I ever return*, he thought, *I will build a fire with my degrees.* "Please?"

"What would you like to know first?"

He resisted the urge to clap his hands and jump up and down. But he turned to the henge and let the wonder of his desire beam from his face, as he had seen Finn do.

"Tell me about the Star Children, Cayri."

∞

Aydyn spent the day in ceremony, resting between cleansing rituals in her hut. She had bathed in the sacred crystallized water, then she was massaged until she was boneless and as fluid as a heavy water skin.

Next, her sister Ovates-in-training blessed her and covered her from her scalp to her toes with the symbols of the Star Children—symbols from the heavens, symbols of eternity.

Tonight she would give herself to the Goddess. Just as a woman gives her body as the vessel for creating a child, so she would give herself as a vessel to the will of the Goddess. She refused to think about where this was taking her, what this was doing to her life. Her only focus was upon completing her duty.

She shivered, even though small warm stones were placed all across her body. To be a vessel of the Goddess was the highest privilege for a Druae woman. Tonight's ceremony in the stone circle will be a ritual for creating a contract between minds—hers and Eric's. She would open her mind to give him all she knew of the Druae. In return, he would give them a way to silence the stones.

He would be their destruction. She would be the salvation.

The prophecy said the key to their future would be discovered through destroying the stones. Everything depended on her success in this contract with Eric. Should she fail and the stones be left to stand …

What will happen to all of us?

She closed her eyes and scrunched them tight, banishing the visions that threatened her strength. A prayer designed to calm the thoughts sprang to her lips and she whispered in soft repetition, "Cara wyn mor, cara wyn mor, cara wyn mor—"

She felt the life of the Goddess beating deep within Mother's body, just as her own heart beat within her chest. Indeed, as she focused on the beat, the two came together. She relaxed her mind and let the power fill her, pushing out any thoughts that would hinder her success.

All her life she had done what they asked of her.

She would not fail now.

∞

Eric walked the great stone circle with Cayri all morning. She spoke to him of the ancient Druae history, about the Star Children and the origins of mankind prior to coming to earth.

"They descended from the sky in great ships, sailing the heavens as we sail upon water."

Soon after that, he recalled becoming incapable of any speech. What little intelligence he claimed slipped away, as insignificant as grains of sand against the sweeping tide of her history. When she stated the entire prophecy again, he stopped asking questions and became brooding and silent, no longer wanting to know about his part in this. As she spoke, all he could think about was the heavens.

How far do we come from? In how many galaxies are we …

He couldn't even finish his thoughts. Every time he opened his mouth to speak, he clapped it shut before uttering a sound. His mind wobbled back and forth between confusion and wonder until he was dizzy.

They returned to the village and he ate something, but he couldn't recall what, such was his dazed state of mind. He refused to look or speak with anyone. He was simply unable to process any more information.

After lunch, Cayri took him to his excavation site. He followed, silent, yet deep within, some of his senses were trickling back.

Who are these people from the stars?

You are, came the silent answer.

At his excavation site, the little hill did not exist. He saw the flat ground and shook his head. He and Cayri entered the chamber by the stone stairs that cut straight down into the earth. He noticed how the stone steps and walls of the stairwell were precisely cut and set, reminding him of stonework he'd seen in Peru and Guatemala.

The ceiling to the chamber was made of sarsen stone slabs; one of those great stones had moved and dropped him into the chamber. He examined the ceiling. The place where he sat and found his initials did not exist.

When do I carve my initials in the rock above?

His curiosity had carried him this far. The knowledge-for-knowledge exchange Cayri proposed seemed at first like another dream come true. But the fact was, knowledge couldn't be unlearned. Once you were exposed to something, you couldn't go back in time and unlearn it. You were, from that moment on, forever changed.

What would he do with this knowledge, he thought, either now, or in his time? A snaking fear crept into his psyche. Was he learning things best not known?

The rest of the chamber seemed as he remembered. The bluestone floor was stunning, polished brightly to a fine smooth finish. The mosaic swept into a cosmic spiral that centered at the pedestal. A blue crystal rested on the pedestal.

"This is one of the crystals from the Star Children?" he asked. "Is this the same crystal that brought me here?"

"Yes, the Star Children gave us these powerful stones, along with instructions on using the forces within them," she answered. She halted and gazed at him with a hooded stare before moving to the wall behind him. "Come here," she called. "You should see this." She pointed to an etching in the stone.

He examined the ancient carving, turning his head from side to side, wanting to refute what his eyes told him. But there was no denying it. A man in a bio-space suit held one hand across his heart, and the other hand pointed towards the sky and the familiar pattern from Orion's Belt to the stars of the Pleiades—pointing home.

"The circle of stones marks a place of power. That is what drew us here," Cayri said. "And them, as well. They came, at first appearing out of the air just as you did. They were like the children of gods and they helped us in our desire to mark the power of the Goddess with the great stones.

"But they went away one day, and we were left to carry on the work alone. We brought the bluestones in, but we were uncertain what to do with them. Then, one day, the great ships appeared in the sky."

Eric propped one palm against his face in his pondering posture and stared at the etching. Cayri had told him the story several times, but each rendition revealed something new.

"So it was the elders in these ships," he said, "who wanted to dismantle the site?"

"Yes, but Arydwyn, a Great Mother of the Druae, told them they did not have the right to take the circle from us, for the power is ours. 'You cannot be responsible for such a force' they said to her."

Cayri gave him a look of pride. "Arydwyn was a powerful woman, gifted with the sight—" She lifted her brow and nodded, warming to the story. "Arydwyn spoke of the Druae commitment to the circle over a vast time span, the many men and hours dedicated to the labor of construction. It was the Druae who brought in the bluestones, because we knew they were a part of the power."

"So they let you have the stone circle?"

"We made a contract," she said.

He nodded. Finn told him that when the Druae commit to do something, they call it a contract, creating an issue of honor.

"How long did the Star Children stay with you?" he asked.

"I keep the pieces of two Staffs of Divination from the time of the Star Children," she said.

He recalled the math from a conversation with Aydyn. Cayri's words would indicate somewhere between seven and eight hundred, possibly a thousand years.

The Star Children were here for a long time. What else did they do on earth while they were here?

He rubbed the bridge of his nose. With so many questions screaming to get out at once, he was getting a headache.

"You have learned much, today," Cayri said, coming to his side. "We will take a rest for now. I would like you to go see Finn. He will help you with tonight's ceremony."

"Will I see Aydyn tonight?" he asked. He hadn't seen her all day and his eyes were hungry for her face.

"Go," Cayri said. "Find Finn."

∞

They stood outside the circle, a crowd of men painted blue.

"You look verra well now," Finn said, grinning.

Eric had found Finn as Cayri instructed, and was promptly subjected to an intense cleansing, complete with a hot oil massage and meditation. Afterwards, he was given a light repast of dried deer meat and flat bread, but he refused the offer of beer and drank only water. Concerned about being given drugs, he had carefully watched all he consumed.

Now, his curious anticipation was a crawling line of ants up his legs. "What will happen?" he asked. He saw no clue from the appearance and demeanor of the other men.

"Just stay with me," Finn said.

Where would I go, Eric thought? He was so relaxed after the bath and massage that he didn't care what happened next. If he died tonight, he'd go a happy man—with a face painted a lovely shade of blue.

"You canna bring any metal into the circle for this ceremony," Finn had warned. "So make sure you leave off your watch."

Eric recalled the powerful pull he felt within the stone circle. Geomagnetic forces?

The Goddess.

He squirmed at the thought and hunched his shoulders. If he had a voltmeter—

"Dinna fidget so, ye smear the woad and get it on yer fine new leggings," Finn admonished. He poked Eric in the ribs with a well-aimed jab. "And ye better get used to that because I learned it from her. Now, when the procession begins, just follow me. Ye are an honored guest and of great importance. Ye will enter last, opposite Aydyn, but you will follow me."

He pointed to the sky. "The sun will set there, and when the long stone shadow strikes the altar stone, the moon—" He swept his arm to a point beyond what Eric knew as the fallen Station Stone 91. "The moon, she will rise … there."

Eric closed his eyes and whispered his thanks—to the Goddess. For him to be here was beyond an archaeologist's wildest thrill. He didn't know what he did to deserve this. He didn't know what would happen tomorrow. But tonight, he would be a part of this primitive society.

Ahead, he could see the first of the Druae men moving to line up at the entrance beyond the heel stone. Opposite them, the women lined up to enter at the same time. He searched for Aydyn, but couldn't see her.

The line ahead was moving. "Keep up wi me," Finn whispered as he took off. Eric followed and soon they reached the point of entry. Finn turned again and hissed, "Keep yer eyes on me now."

Eric gulped, but the hammering in his chest was a familiar alarm. He looked opposite, and there Aydyn was: the only woman completely painted blue with woad, because she was the only woman completely naked.

He slammed his eyes on Finn's trotting figure ahead. His breath stuttered in his throat and he gasped for air as he struggled to keep up. He focused on lifting his feet, even as he was painfully aware of Aydyn pacing next to him, stride for stride. Afraid he would stumble and fall in front of these beautiful people, he dared not look at her again.

No need, for what he saw would burn in his memory for all eternity.

They reached the circle of stones and the line of men turned right, the women turned left. They skirted along the inside of the outer ring of stones until they met behind the altar stone. There, the two lines crossed each other. Eric passed through just in front of Aydyn, and then he lost her as he followed Finn.

The men kept to the inner circle until they reached their point of entry. There, when the lines crossed again, they went deeper, stepping in front of the inner circle of bluestones.

He felt the tug of the power increase when they entered the stones. The scientist in his mind screamed for a seismograph and spectroscope, but his heart cried the loudest—for the Goddess.

When they circled around and reached the altar stone a second time, the lines crossed and then poured down the horseshoe-shaped line of bluestones. He kept Finn in front of him as the lines circled, crossed, and realigned like an intricate line dance.

They came to a sudden stop and all went still. The Druae were layered along the bluestones from the inner circle to the horseshoe. Eric was at the top of the horseshoe, with Finn on one side and Cayri on his other. The tallest trilithon stood behind them, and the altar stone gleamed bright in the fading sunlight.

The absolute silence was deafening. Not a bird, a bug, or a leaf moved in the still air. His molecules hummed with the power of the stones—and then the vibration stopped. The top of the sun dipped below the tree line on the horizon, spiking a shadow from the heel stone to run like molten iron all the way to the altar stone.

Finn's elbow gigged Eric in the ribs. He turned to the right and watched as the moon rose from the sea of trees—a full, brilliant disk whose glow fell upon them just as the last of the sun's light slipped from the western sky.

His eyes locked onto the moon and the whispering Goddess sang through his atoms. His feet hummed and attached themselves to the earth while his soul whistled through the heavens. Between the two, his heart thrummed with a message.

Aydyn!

She stood on the altar stone, appearing with the moon. Her long hair fell loose, floating to the small of her back. Another vision of her opened, not in his eyes, but in his heart, and he rocked back on his heels.

Her skin was like nothing he had ever known before, smooth and wild and sweet. He inhaled, drawing each note of her scent deep into his very fiber, seeking to drown within it. She released her hair, and it cascaded to whisper across her shoulders, calling him closer to the treasure of her heart. He followed the silken strands and placed his lips just above her skin, hovering with perverse delight before allowing himself the joy of tasting her—

The thrill of knowing this woman and her people filled him suddenly with a joy he couldn't describe. He swayed again on his feet and opened his eyes. Aydyn was still on the altar stone, her arms thrust to the heavens—a cosmic Venus. He hungered for her Druae blue and, just as he wished it, she delivered her gaze to him.

Her eyes glowed with an unearthly light, as blue as the sky, brighter than the stars. He stared all around. The moon filled the sky, pregnant and glorious before the deepening night. The dim twilight of sunset was gone, leaving only moonlight and the glowing preternatural eyes of the Druae women.

He noted that all the women's eyes glowed with the same light. His scientific mind cried for a microscope and DNA testing equipment.

Listen to the Goddess, his body whispered.

The vibration increased from his feet all the way up his spine and into his sinuses. He felt pulled and pushed at the same time, as though the power wanted to disperse his atoms across the universe.

Aydyn danced across the altar stone, as graceful and as silent as the breeze. Her arms reached up to the heavens and the tips of her breasts pushed through the mantle of her hair.

Eric felt himself grow hard and ground his teeth, quickly elevating his gaze to her long muscular arms. He followed her stare upward to the heavens, where the constellation Taurus glittered.

Home.

The tempo within him increased as Aydyn tapped one foot. She leaped across the great stone and flung both arms out parallel to the ground, pointing to the north and south station stones. Her back arched, dipping her hair below her buttocks. Eric cringed, wondering that her spine didn't snap.

She called up the power. He felt it rise from the earth, increasing in intensity through his legs and into his chest so that he thought he could surely fly as one of the immortal gods. When the power reached his chest, his heart joined the collective heartbeat.

Aydyn pointed her hands at the station stones with a snap of her forearm, and the crystal on top of each great stone flickered to glowing life.

The Druae hummed, whether through their minds or through their lips, he couldn't say. The sound came from everywhere and everything—the stones, the earth, the people.

Aydyn turned in a pirouette and flicked her hands at the other two stones. Two more crystals came to life and the Druae hummed even louder.

The power was all consuming, making his atoms quiver. He was reminded of his travel through time, but this time the power felt modulated, controlled.

Aydyn!

He looked around. Everyone's eyes glowed just as the crystals did. Those crystals, now fully lit like giant spotlights, beamed into the night sky with an intensity that made him squint. He threw his head back, and the four rays of blue light cut through the heavens to disappear into the Taurus constellation.

The Druae began to cry, a soft low note that rang with primitive mystery. He watched Finn and Cayri, saw the power of the Goddess fueling their cries. Finn's face was rapt, his eyes closed with ecstasy. Cayri held out her arms and threw her head back in a state of obvious rapture.

The cry escalated, growing into a declaration of power. The energy rippled through him and he looked at the ground to see if he was floating on a skin of energy. Aydyn held her arms up and her head thrown back like Cayri, giving her heart to the heavens. With a scream of ecstasy, she jerked upright.

When she opened her eyes, Eric felt her silent command, just as the little hill called to him before his transport through time. He stepped to the altar stone, filled with the power of the Goddess, a primitive and primal force that modern mankind had never known.

He was a child of the earth. She was a child of the heavens, a star from another galaxy. Her eyes questioned him and his heart answered. In one slip of a moment, he knew the relentless search he had been on for his entire life had completed a circle and come home.

At last, I have found you.

She offered him her hand, and he took it.

∞

Balock grunted and stared into the flickering flames. His disbelief continued to simmer, scalding him time and time again.

She made me look like a fool.

Why would she refuse his offer for a marriage contract? His family was wealthy. He was well formed and considered desirable. Her rejection had caught him unaware.

The late night moon broke through the clouds and brilliant white moonlight beamed down upon him. He shivered and glanced around, feeling the stare of unknown eyes upon him. A low growl rumbled in his throat and he slid his bronze knife free. It shone dull in the moonlight and he cursed, wishing he had the secret of iron.

"Who dares to watch me?" he snarled under his breath. He stood and spun around, baring the knife to challenge the spy.

The village was silent. He stood alone in the quiet night.

He squinted into the darkness beyond the firelight, but nothing moved—no gleaming feral eyes stared back at him. He glanced at the sleeping dogs spread around the village and shrugged.

No one stirred. He was the only one who felt the alarm.

Someone watches me.

He slid to the ground and hunkered down before his fire. Keeping a quick eye on the pervading darkness, he rubbed the back of his neck, trying to smooth the hairs that refused to lie down.

Again, he stood and looked all around, but there was no one but him. Finally satisfied, he sat and pulled out the bundle of skins that hid the Druae sword. He licked his lips and slowly unwrapped it, thinking of her. Soon, he felt himself harden and he smiled.

It will be like this with her.

The last skin dropped away from the stolen weapon and the

Druae metal gleamed in the firelight. He stroked the long blade, remembering her blue eyes, and he throbbed with desire.

He stroked himself and reached to set the Druae knife down. When the knife touched the ground, the moon eased out from behind a cloud and cold white moonlight washed over the silver, turning the metal blood red. He pulled back with a gasp and looked at the moon.

She stared down upon him—seeing him, knowing him.

Cool moonlight bathed him and he withered, as soft as old fruit. He hissed, trying to rub himself back to life. With his eyes closed he called for the vision to return, but she was gone, taking the power in his loins. He cringed and threw a skin over the Druae blade.

With a feral squint, he glared at the moon, now sliding back to the shelter of clouds. The light was white and pure and he snarled, shaking his fist.

"We shall see," he spit. He hurried to snatch up his weapons, grabbing the Druae blade and kicking the dog before he ducked inside.

CHAPTER FIVE

Aydyn rose from her bed after a night of troubled dreams. Last night's moon ceremony had left her drained and exhausted. Afterwards, she bathed privately in her hut and then fell into a deep sleep filled with dreams about his—

—hands. And those long fingers, bringing sweet …

"Stop," she commanded. A shiver raced from her scalp to her toes and she stomped her foot. "Stop this. I have my duty to fulfill. There is no room for—"

But the visions swam through her mind until she squeezed her eyes shut. "Please, stop," she begged.

A Druae warrior and Ovate knows only a life of duty.

And the dreams were not about duty. They were all sweetness—laughter and joy, longing and desire, heat and ecstasy.

She was an Ovate. She knew the taste of destiny, and these dreams were filled with its flavor. She sat on the stool by her bed and let her forehead rest against the staff. "Please," she said softly, praying for the wisdom of the ancients to fill her with peace.

This madness cannot be—not now, not in this life.

"There are other things I must do," she whispered. Her lips trembled with fear and wanting. *If such sweetness is not for this life, then where does this desire belong?*

That such desire existed in her dreams dared to give her hope. With a shake of her shoulders, she stood, releasing the troubling thoughts that held her. Her duty began today—by showing the stranger the Druae way. Then he would show them how to silence the stones.

"But how?" she asked, doubting his ability to save them. He was a landed fish, so unsure of everything around him. She knew he could not even start a fire. How do they live in the future without this skill?

As an Ovate, she was learning to control her power to move through the realms of time and see future events. But there were restrictions. Not every moment was theirs for the seeing.

She snorted and stamped the heavy staff against the floor. The dream was real. And so, if it once was, then it will be again. She smiled and whispered her thanks to the staff, placing a loving kiss against the carved surface. She was fortunate to have so much wisdom to draw on. She glanced outside and for once, her duty seemed less onerous. It was a fine summer day, and a very special man waited for her.

On the short walk to Finn's hut, she passed a basket of fruit and grabbed apples. When she backed up to grab extras, she noticed her people were staring at her. A murmur spread through the village as others came rushing out of their huts. Soon, they all came to see her.

She stood tall and returned their gaze until one by one, each gave her the nod. They acknowledged and honored her for giving herself to the Goddess for them. Her spine lifted and her shoulders edged back for she was proud to be Druae, proud to bear the power and the duty of the Goddess for her people.

She nodded once in return to all.

Sweeping her gaze across the compound, she found Eric standing with her brother before the stone house, each holding a piece of fresh morning bread. Eric's green eyes met hers and across the distance, the heat fired instantly in her chest.

How does he do that?

She lifted her chin and marched towards him. The people cleared as she approached, and a wake of watchful faces spread out behind her. She stopped beside Finn. He grinned from ear to ear and mischief sparked in his gray eyes. "Eric is just telling me about—"

"The future, I know," she said, smiling. She resisted the urge to fan at her flaming chest and eyed Eric's hand holding the flat bread. His beautiful fingers fascinated her. The way they knew how to touch her …

She jerked her head up and the flame in her cheeks grew hotter, spreading to the roots of her hair. She shifted foot to foot, wishing she could dive into a cool spring.

"Sis, are ye all right?" Finn asked. He peered at her with a teasing remark ready at his lips.

She gave him a steady look. In one quick step, she moved into position to deliver an elbow to his ribs. He saw her intent and danced away, laughing and shaking a finger. His face was so comical, she laughed with him. She glanced at Eric and he, too, chuckled. His green eyes flashed the color of early morning forest and he laughed with ease, showing her very good teeth.

"He wants to know about the crystals," Finn said.

"I can show them to you," she answered, smiling at Eric. She handed him one of her apples and he gave her part of his bread.

"Good morning, Aydyn," he said.

His words filled her ears, but his voice went all the way to her marrow. A blanket of warmth settled around her heart and she cocked her head, wondering at this new sensation within. A fine vibration came from the warmth, and she thought of a cat purring beneath loving hands.

He says my name and I want to roll over and give him my belly.

All command of her body suddenly failed her in a cascading riot. She fumbled with the bread just as one of her apples jumped from her fingers. She snatched at the apple and managed to capture it against her body with her elbow, but her fingers forgot about the bread. She watched, astonished as it slipped free of her grasp. She lunged for it, and lost both the apple and her staff. The oak's heavy gold cap struck Finn in the hand, knocking the bread from his fingers.

"Oww," he yelped, glaring at her. "Sis, have ye lost yer—"

She snatched back the staff and ducked after the apples and the bread. An unrelenting fire burned under her skin and she kept her head tucked while she wiped dirt from the fruit.

What just happened? I have not dropped anything since I finished my warrior's training.

"Aydyn, yer dangerous wi that thing," Finn whined. He rubbed his knuckles and she felt his eyes boring into her back.

Collecting her food, she stood, avoiding his eye. "Aye, I am dangerous," she spit back. "As a warrior, I am allowed."

With her staff, the bread and apple again in control, she affected an innocent face, as though nothing was amiss. But her heart hammered wildly and she held the apple and her wayward staff with trembling fingers.

Remember your duty.

My duty, she argued, *is the will of the Goddess.*

She looked at Eric and prayed horns had not also sprouted from her head. From the corner of her vision she saw Finn eye her as though she had done just that.

She turned her back on her brother, looking Eric in the face for the first time since he spoke. His eyes so clearly reflected his thoughts. He reminded her of the innocent, unknowing lambs. Such ignorance must foster great freedom, she thought.

She dropped her eyelids, shielding her Druae blue, grateful that she was not such a lamb. "Uncle Talie would like to see you," she said.

"Who is Uncle Talie?" he asked.

His voice rolled over her again, only this time she was ready. She clenched her muscles and braced herself. "He is the Druae bard," she answered. "He keeps our history in his head."

She tapped her head against her staff and crossed her eyes. He laughed and she liked the sound of his humor. "He wants to meet you," she said, "so he can make a song about you."

The laughter faded from his face and he shifted from foot to foot, as if to run. "I'm not so sure I want a song written about me," he said. "That would leave evidence of my presence. I've done so much already."

He stuttered, looking around with that lost look in his eyes. "Uncle Talie is the one to decide what is best to tell," she said. "You are a person of great importance. It is our way to honor you with a song." She coaxed him like a child, wondering again at his innocence.

"Oh, ye want to have a song, brother," Finn said. He clapped Eric on the back and his face beamed with his eternal good humor. "Having a song about ye, now that is immortality."

Aydyn saw the dispute hovering on Eric's face and drew him away from her brother. "Do you have work to do, brother?" she said pointedly. She pushed Finn gently in the direction of the smith. "There will be no song for you the way you are going."

"Aye, I will have a song," Finn said, waving his hips in suggestion of his 'other' reputation. He struck a pose with a wicked grin, clutching his fist to his chest in a Druae declaration. "I have my duty. And you—" He waved his heavy eyebrows, again lewdly suggestive. "You have yours." He turned on his heel and left, his shoulders shaking with unknown glee.

Eric stepped to her side and they watched Finn's retreating figure.

"He's awfully cheery, isn't he?" he said.

"Aye, he is way too cheery," she agreed quickly. "And he has no … no proper—"

"Sense of duty?" he finished.

"Exactly," she said.

"And does he …?" He waved one finger in a circle at his forehead.

She laughed. "Yes, he can read your thoughts. Try turning your back on him—I find that helps."

"And your mother? She's like Finn. Plus, she sees the future?"

His eyes were big, innocent again, and Aydyn sympathized. The gift of sight generated many different reactions. She was thankful he was not frightened of the power as some people were.

"Many of the Druae are blessed with these gifts," she said. "Like our blue eyes, the gift is a much sought after trait in marriage contracts."

"I'm not sure I would want a mate that could read my thoughts," he said. "That could lead to trouble."

His eyes sparkled and she saw a grin teasing at the corner of his mouth. She tore her eyes away. His lips were full and they laughed with ease. She liked that. "Trouble?" she asked, hiding her eyes.

She turned and started walking across the village. "Aye, ask Finn about trouble. His gifts," she said with a telling nod, "get him into all sorts of trouble. But Uncle Talie does not have the gift of sight or mind."

They reached a stone and wood hut, a mansion by Druae standards. Taliesin's location in the center of the compound was a coveted position just behind the stone bake house. He always got warm bread.

She stopped at the edge of the fire pit. "Uncle Talie is interested in the past," she said. "You will like him. Uncle Talie," she called. The door to the hut lifted away and Taliesin stepped out. She glanced at Eric. "Not what you expected?"

He nodded. "No. I was thinking short and round. He's like a tall version of Finn."

"Exactly. And if you get the two of them together, they will make you laugh and cry in turns," she said under her breath.

Taliesin stepped forward and reared to his full height. Towering over Eric by at least a hand span, his long gray hair and beard streamed to his waist, both interspersed with braids and dotted with beads. The gray eyes were bright with the same cheery light that plagued Finn. He carried a staff much like Aydyn's, but without the gold.

"Uncle Talie, he is here—but he does not want a song."

"Not have a song?" Taliesin asked. "Now who would not want a song?"

Eric cringed.

Aydyn giggled. She nudged Eric into the space between the fire pit and the front door. "Uncle, you will need to bring him a stool to sit on."

∞

Later that afternoon, Aydyn collected Eric from her uncle's hut. She chuckled, knowing well that her Uncle was a man of many words.

"Please," Eric said, "no more relatives." He wiped at his forehead and whistled, "Whew."

They entered the meat house where fresh cooked food was available for anyone with hunger. The large hut had thatch windows that lifted out, opening the room to cross drafts. An adjacent stone hut held all the cooking fires.

They sat at a table, each with a bowl of stew. She watched as he scooped the thick gravy and vegetables with his bread. "I will get you a spoon," she said. "Usually, everyone makes their own and carries it with them."

He stopped eating and put his bread down, a slow blush creeping up his neck. He glanced around, seeming to need something. "A lack of utensils doesn't seem to have slowed me down," he said.

He glanced around once again and she wondered what he wanted. Finally, she asked, "What are you looking for?"

"A napkin. I need a napkin," he answered, waving his fingers. "Something to wipe my mouth and hands on, you know—when you eat." He gave her a lopsided smile and that soft look crept into his eyes. She wondered how it was to live without the burden of duty, in a future where your life did not depend on your skill to light a fire, yet you must be concerned about wiping your mouth when you ate.

"Your uncle," he said.

She watched him wipe at his mouth with his fingers. Then he didn't seem to know what to do with the grease on his fingers.

"That man knows how to talk," he said. "He fairly well wore me out." Surreptitiously, he wiped his fingers on the table leg.

"Now you know why he is our Bard," she said. "He has more stories in his head than you can imagine—stories going back to the time of Arydwyn."

A group of four young men entered and began collecting a supply of provisions from baskets of dried meat.

"Where are they off to?" Eric asked.

"They will take the message of the prophecy to the four corners," she answered.

Each man carried two small packs looped across their shoulders and hanging to their hips.

"If they put their packs on their backs," Eric said, "they can carry more." He pointed to his back and Aydyn wrinkled her brow. "Call them over and I will show you," he said.

She saw he was trying to give them something from the future. "Are you not fearful of telling us some secret of your world." She waved her hands at the invisible, threatening specter.

"You would be learning this soon, anyway," he said.

She ignored his smug look and called out, "Doyle, bring me those bags."

The young man came and Eric stood. "Place them like this," he said, laying them side-by-side on the table. "But change the straps so they come from the center to go over the shoulders and attach at the bottom. The weight rides on your back and stays behind you. With a little lightweight support, you can enlarge the bags to carry quite a bit." He showed her how large a pack the design would accommodate.

She gave him a slow smile.

Brilliant.

"Go to Moiré," she said to Doyle. "She has spare linen. And add leather here at the corners." She looked at Eric, and he gave a quick nod. "Go," she said, "get Neil and Ryan to help. Make the four of you such a rig."

"And you want to put a loop of some kind here to attach your water … skins," Eric said. "Here, one on each side for balance, at hip level." He showed them and the men's eyes lit with understanding. They left in an excited flurry, thanking Eric with profuse slaps on the back.

"Tell me where they go," he asked. "And what happens after they deliver the message?"

"When you believe as we do," she said, "you must make plans. These four men will go the four closest villages with Druae contracts. Those villages will send new messengers to the next, releasing these men. Doyle and his men will be back in a few days, but by the next full moon, all the Druae will have heard the news. They will know the day of their duty comes near."

He eyed her, his amazement clear in his eyes. "Go on."

"In the spring, at Beltane," she continued, "we have a ceremony, and all the Druae come home. They are here for many days to celebrate. We light fires, and the crystals, of course." He nodded, and she could see he recalled her lighting the crystals last night.

"This is also a time for arranging marriages," she said. "Men from many tribes and villages come to offer contracts for Druae women, for we are prized as mates."

She took their bowls to a side table, rinsed them in water and turned. "When we learned long ago that the passing of the Druae was meant to come, we knew we would some day need a new home, so this is how we cast the Druae seeds far and wide."

"But, what if—what if … ?" He grimaced, clearly distressed over the prophecy.

She reached out and placed her hand on his shoulder. "We have time, Eric. We know something happens soon, we just do not know by what hand, or how."

"I wish I had never come," he said. The grief flowed across his face and his voice was thick with pain. "If I had not come, the Druae would—" He looked up and his eyes were filled with scorching self-reproach.

She shook her head. "The Druae would still be planning for the prophecy and the end would still happen. This is a waste to grieve over this. What is now, shall pass."

Slowly he nodded with her. "Yeah, yeah," he said weakly. "And what once was, will be again."

"You have trouble with this concept, why?" she asked. She was born with this comprehension and could not fathom living without knowing what she knew about life, the stars and where they all came from, about the future and how—

"What once was," she repeated, "will be again." She shrugged, unable to put her faith into different words.

"How are you able to believe?" he asked. "How can you believe so completely that you plan your lives and your future around a prophecy left eons ago?" He ran his hand through his hair and the pain in his eyes tore at her heart.

"You have great freedom in your time, am I right?" she asked. When he nodded, she said, "You are given the freedom to believe or not believe?"

"In my time, we are given many choices of what to believe in, and each man makes his own decision. Each man is responsible for himself," he said.

She reared back. "You are not part of a tribe with a connection to your past and your future? Is there not something in your life that is so great you have no choice but to believe?"

He shook his head and her insides shivered for the solitary picture he painted. "You do not feel connected to the earth, to the stars, to the power that is beyond us? There is no Goddess in your time?" she asked. She shook her head. The thought was so alien and dire, it was beyond her ken.

No duty, but at the cost of knowledge.

She shuddered from her shoulders to her hip. The oblivion he lived within terrified her.

I will keep my duty.

They walked to the livestock pens in a clearing on the northeast side of the village. "Do you hunt? In your time?" she asked. They came to a small hut with a low roof and short thatched walls.

She ducked into the cool darkness of the falcon hutch. Several birds of prey rested in individual cages. Each wore a delicate linen hood and small bells were tied to their feet. She opened a door and removed her favorite, a small, but swift red falcon.

"This is Rowan." She handed him one of the leather gloves and he slipped it on. She lifted the hood and Rowan's black eyes blinked in the dim light. He took the bird and his face lit with wonder. She recalled how he wore the same look the night she took him to the bathhouse.

He stroked Rowan's russet feathers and the bird trilled with pleasure, wiggling her tail feathers. She pranced and preened, lifting one leg and coiling the foot into tight ball. "She is beautiful," he said. He held her close to his face and examined her.

"She likes you," Aydyn said. She watched him entice the falcon, stroking her wings and petting her chest. The bird pranced, happy to be in his hands. Aydyn watched. She too, wanted to be in his hands.

"We do not have this species in my time. She is extinct," he said. He cooed at the bird and she stroked his face with her beak. "I cannot believe I am holding an extinct species."

"It would seem you do have some connection to the Goddess after all, or Rowan would not have taken to you so thoroughly," she said. She stepped back and crossed her arms, watching her fierce hunting falcon coo and prance down Eric's shoulder. He laughed and tickled the bird's chest feathers with his long fingers—and she remembered the touch of those hands from her dream.

His fingers delved deep within her, reaching where no one had ever touched her before. He ignited a fire that burned too hot, yet cried for more. She needed to feel him, deeper—

She gasped and stepped back, startling the bird. Rowan batted her wings and squawked, her shrill calls disturbing the other birds. Eric calmed Rowan with soft whispers while Aydyn slipped the hood over the bird's head with trembling fingers.

He eased the falcon back into her cage. "Are you all right?" he asked as he gently latched the cage door.

Aydyn eyed him critically as forest green met Druae blue. *Perhaps he is not such a fish after all*, she thought. There was much to learn about this man.

Remember your duty.

She thought of the future he came from, where everyone had the freedom to decide not to believe. She clenched her hands. She did not have that choice. The bitter ash of duty peppered her tongue and she blurted out, "You have studied the stones. Do you have had any ideas about how we can … ?" Her question was thoughtless and she glanced up, suddenly embarrassed.

He shook his head and stepped back, throwing his hands out at her, as though to push her back. "No," he stammered, "I—I have not. I mean, I never said I would ..." He shook his head. "I cannot believe you are asking me to destroy something so magnificent."

She did not want to be here talking to this man about the end of the Druae. And she did not want him to push her away. But she had a duty she believed was crucial to the survival of her people, who did not have the luxury of his ignorance. She drew back and turned the full heat of her Druae blue upon him.

"If you cannot believe for yourself," she cried, "then believe for us. Believe for little Maisy, whose life you have already saved."

She gasped and fought for control, horrified that tears pricked at her eyes. "If we do not fulfill our part of the prophecy, the Druae will see no future, just as you say of Rowan." She jerked her head towards the bird, and hissed, "We will be just another ... extinct species."

She looked down and squeezed her eyes tight. The pain of knowing and yet not knowing their future tore at her.

I must not fail.

She needed him to believe. She looked up and poured all the power of her faith into her flooded eyes, offering him the hope of the Goddess.

Please believe.

His green eyes crinkled with pain and he shook his head. He stepped back and clamped his hands to his sides. "I can't," he whispered. "I'm sorry."

She turned and left without a word.

∞

Aydyn paused at the fire pit boundary before her mother's hut. Her heart trembled in her chest and she wanted to scream and shout at the heavens.

How do you make the ignorant believe?

"Come in daughter," Cayri called from the doorway. Aydyn looked up and saw her mother waited in the open door with her arm extended in welcome.

"You knew I was coming?" she asked.

"No daughter, I heard you huffing and puffing out here. Please come in, before you light something on fire." She waved her arm and Aydyn slipped inside.

"Mother, this is hopeless. We will never get him to—" She strode into her mother's hut, stamping her staff with each step. She folded her legs beneath her and sank to the wood floor with her back propped against the wall, exhaling a loud snort of derision. "He does not believe, Mother. How do you make someone understand, when there is no faith or belief?"

Cayri eased to the floor opposite her. "Give him time. He has only been here a few days and there is much for him to learn. We have all the time we need."

Aydyn squirmed. "But will there be time for—"

"Just see your duty," Cayri said softly. She reached to grasp Aydyn's hand. "Remember, there is all of infinity to work with. Look outside of this time and place for your answers."

Aydyn sat back and closed her eyes. She hated when her mother gave her answers to questions not yet asked. "Have you seen? Do you know what is the threat?"

Cayri hooded her eyes and Aydyn knew she withheld something; her powers of divination were more advanced than Aydyn's. She also knew her mother would never divulge anything out of place.

Aydyn exhaled her grief. "He claims he has no connection to the earth. He feels no connection to the Goddess, not even to the stars," she said. "I am not sure he believes everything about the Star Children and the prophecy."

"Oh, he is connected, believe me, or he would not be here," Cayri said. "Did he not rise to the call of the power during the ceremony last night? Do not worry about Eric, my daughter. He will travel the path, for that is why he is here."

She leaned forward and moonlight streamed in the doorway, reaching to grace her face with a glow. Conspiracy snapped in her eyes. Aydyn leaned in, coiled with expectation.

"Tomorrow you go to hunt, am I right?" Cayri asked, smiling with wisdom as ancient as the stars. "Then you must take him into the woods, where he may experience that which he denies."

Aydyn seized the thought and sat back, allowing herself a glimmer of hope. Nowhere else was the power of the Goddess stronger. "Yes," she said, "I will take him into the forest."

∞

Eric lay exhausted in the bed.

Please, no more.

His head was filled with thoughts that spun first one way, then went full circle in the opposite direction. He sighed, sick with the certainty that he had, at last, taken on too much. The human mind cannot slip from one paradigm to another in a matter of hours—the discontinuity was devastating.

"Breathe," he whispered. He filled his lungs with a great desperate lungful and exhaled, counting slowly through a full expiration. "One, two, three …"

The Star Children. The prophecy. Him helping the Druae destroy Stonehenge. The end of these beautiful people.

How was he supposed to help them survive? Did this all have to happen as they said? He rubbed his temples and groaned.

What else can I do?

By the Druae's philosophy, whatever he was going to do, he had already done. "No," he wailed in silent protest.

It cannot be like this. I can't do what they ask.

He shifted deeper into the covers, and whispered in a feverish mantra. "Please don't—please don't ask me to do this."

Chapter Six

Eric exited Finn's hut. His night had been filled with dreams of the Druae, and him running after an elusive destination. After tossing and turning for hours, he rose with the dawn, driven from the warm bed by the relentless circle of thoughts.

Eyeing the fire pit, he picked up the stone and flint kept stored beside each hut with a stack of kindling. After several minutes of effort, he surprised himself by striking a spark into the base of his kindling. He placed his fingers together and blew, as he had seen Taliesin do. A small blaze erupted, growing to a brisk fire as he added larger pieces of wood.

He notched his calendar stick, marking the passage of another day. He was learning to listen to his body as a clock for the day, but needing to know the date was a compulsion he could not relinquish.

The peace and quiet in the early morning mist soothed his psyche. When he first came here the silence was unsettling; it was too quiet for his modern mind. But now his ears had shifted to reach beyond the deafening silence, discovering the sounds of wind and water, fire and forest.

He leaned back against the log beside his robust fire and gazed out at the treetops just visible above a rise in the terrain. The forest was an eighty-foot-high entity that exuded an aura and a sense of consciousness he had never noticed in modern times. He was in love with the vibrant quality of the forest.

"It is the Goddess," Finn said.

The words were soft, yet Finn's sudden appearance from behind caused Eric to flinch. He grinned up at his new friend, astounded by the mental abilities of these people. Their heightened psychic sense impressed him at every turn and he struggled with thinking of them as primitive. "I thought you couldn't do that from the back," he said.

"Aye, well, let her continue to think that, then," Finn answered. He wore his perpetual grin of good spirits as he settled next to Eric.

Eric laughed, the sudden noise spitting from his lips. Finn clapped him on the back, his own laughter twinkling in his eyes.

"She thinks—" Eric sputtered. He chuckled and laughed, eyeing Finn with newfound admiration.

"I know what she thinks, brother," Finn answered, "most of the time, that is." He motioned to the fire pit. "Did ye do that yerself?"

Eric nodded. "I did, after watching Talie light his—and it was not so hard as I thought. In the future, I have had less success with such things."

"Well, tis good for you to learn these valuable skills from us," Finn said. He sipped his mug of beer and Eric saw him cast a slanted glance his way.

What does he know?

"What I know is not important," Finn said.

Eric looked up, feeling the familiar beat rattling his heart. Aydyn walked towards them, carrying Rowan on her leather-gloved wrist, with a five-foot long bow and a quiver of arrows on her back.

He felt his eyes bug and his eyebrows shoot up. She wore a brief leather outfit that bared her midriff, and a loincloth left little to the imagination. Her well-muscled legs—

—wrapped around him and entwined with his until he couldn't tell which legs belonged to who. She rubbed against him, and his swelling hardness dragged against her thigh, reaching higher.

He gulped and fumbled with his mug, neatly pitching it into the fire. He jumped up and snatched the mug from the edge of the flames just as she arrived.

Finn chuckled and gave an innocent shrug. When Eric shot him a questioning glance, he held his hand up in front of his eyes to say he saw nothing.

Eric turned to face her. His heart hammered wildly at her presence, joining with the heat of his recent vision. The startling sight of her legs scalded him, even as it offered what felt like a beloved memory. He stared at her face, afraid to glance any lower, especially with Finn right beside him.

He was having a damned difficult enough time understanding

his thoughts without having half the village peeking into his mind.

"Good morning, Aydyn," he said.

The tattoos on her face glowed in the morning mist. Her energy was a palpable tug, and he braced himself against the urge to rub against her. He looked down to get a grip on his wildly swinging biology when he noticed the hairs on his arm lifting.

She carries the power of the Goddess.

She bowed her head to him in silent greeting. He remembered his rejection of her plea from last night and ground his teeth, his mind shouting, *I am still an archaeologist.*

Stupid, his heart responded.

She took off without a word, moving swiftly towards the forest with the bird now bobbing along on top of her bow tip. He watched them, two species on the verge of extinction, and a flood of mixed emotions filled him. His admiration for Aydyn grew with each interaction, as did his trepidation over his ability to help her.

The bird he couldn't save, but the people—

Can I stand by and let these people vanish, as lost as the wind? What have I done that brings me here to them?

"She has already done the ceremony." Finn stepped to Eric's side, now sporting his own enormous bow. Several young men had gathered behind them without Eric hearing a sound; each carried a bow and quivers filled with deadly iron-tipped arrows.

"She has given her thanks to the Goddess for what we will bring home," Finn said. His eyes shifted to gaze over Eric's shoulder into the forest, sparking an icy shiver to flash down his arms.

"The Goddess is heartless," Finn said, "but she cannot be denied. We must always honor her for her gifts, even though we may not understand them." His eyes came back to the present, and he nodded towards Aydyn's shrinking figure. "She is one with the Goddess, now."

Eric watched as Aydyn's head disappeared below the rise in the hill. A fierce pride raced through him for knowing her and her people, and yet he cringed, knowing he was a coward. He witnessed their faith and expression of their power, and still he denied them the only thing they asked of him.

"This all comes in the spring, a single leaf at a time," Finn said. He waved at the endless expanse of forest, his voice and demeanor unusually solemn.

No question rose in Eric's mind to enlighten the cryptic remark, so he stashed it in his ever-growing file marked riddles. "What do we do next?" he asked.

"We follow the Goddess," Finn said, nodding to the forest. His normal jovial expression returned and Eric breathed a sigh of relief. He didn't want any more answers just yet. He stared at the place where Aydyn had disappeared below the rise. His eyes had returned to that spot a dozen times and he didn't need to be asked if he wanted to follow.

"Does she hunt with the bird?"

Finn started off at a slow trot. "Aye, they are quite a team, those two," he said. Something in his tone alerted Eric and he tried to see Finn's expression. He caught a brief glimpse of smothered laughter before Finn took off at a lope.

∞

Eric crouched with Finn and the other men on a hillside. Twenty yards up slope, Aydyn stood in a small clearing with Rowan. Both were bathed in early morning light as the sun burned the mist from the air. A silence pressed down upon them, and he squirmed, feeling as if the forest was holding its breath.

Aydyn removed Rowan's hood and brought the bird to her face, eye-to-eye. She whispered soft words and the two rested their heads together. At last, Rowan stirred her wings and Aydyn removed the small, weighted bells.

"Go swiftly," she said in a final, soft command before throwing the bird into the air.

The men craned their necks, following the bird's ascent. Rowan caught the rising swell of warm air from the clearing and drifted above the trees, where she moved into a large circling pattern. Farther and farther she flew, until they lost sight of her beyond the tops of the trees.

Eric frowned. "I thought the bird was used to do the hunting—generally small game." He nodded to the large bows they carried, and asked, "What do you hunt?"

"Aye, there are times when Aydyn hunts with Rowan for small game," Finn said. "But today, we ask for boar and deer. Rowan will return soon."

As they watched Aydyn from their shelter in the ferns, Eric began to fidget with anticipation. He had actually started a fire with a flint today, and now he was hunting with an ancient culture.

Finn jabbed him in the ribs. "Watch," he hissed.

Aydyn stood with her back to them, her arm upraised. They heard Rowan before they saw her and looked up as her wings whooshed above them. She sailed out of the silent forest, came back around, tucked her wings, and dive-bombed into the clearing.

Eric held his breath, certain the bird dove for Aydyn with questionable intent. He tensed, and just as he was ready to jump up, Finn grabbed his arm. Rowan screeched and Eric flinched, but the bird pulled up at the last possible second with stunning precision. He watched as Rowan landed gently on Aydyn's upraised hand.

The mist drifted and a blade of light stabbed through the trees, landing on Aydyn and Rowan like a spotlight. Aydyn turned to the men. Her eyes were black as night—and Rowan's eyes were as blue as the sky.

Eric gasped and shrank back.

The Goddess.

"She sees what Rowan sees while the bird is in flight," Finn whispered. "That is how Aydyn knows where the deer and the boar are. Rowan scouts for us."

Aydyn replaced Rowan's hood, then looked up—her eyes had returned to normal. She pointed to the east, lifting two fingers. Two of the men slipped off in that direction.

She turned and pointed to the north, this time with three fingers raised. The two remaining men slipped off that way. Finn said, "I don't think ye can keep up with us, so stay behind us and travel as quietly as ye can." He pulled a bright blue cloth from a pouch at his side and gave the cloth to Eric. "Tie this around yer neck, so no one shoots ye. There is probably no chance of that, for ye make too much noise." He grinned and gave Eric another jab before slipping away.

Eric watched them move into the forest, disappearing without a sound. Aydyn was already gone. He never saw her move before she vanished. He tied the bright blue cloth around his neck, not wanting to invite one of those vicious arrows.

He followed behind the men, but they soon left him far behind. Moving alone through the silent, yet sentient trees, the air felt heavy with expectation. Nature, just as Finn had said, was heartless. In this vast ecosystem, every hour, every moment, something was born—and something died.

Only the Goddess knows who travels which path.

He paused in a small vale. Ancient oaks surrounded him on higher ground, but down below, young elms and beech cast dappled shade. The sun rode high in the sky and he realized he was hot and thirsty. He leaned against a tree and wiped his face with the blue cloth. The silence of the forest pressed down upon him until his ears rang. He shook his head, and when he looked up, he heard a bubbling spring. He turned towards the sound, his mouth watering in anticipation.

"Would ye drink from the spring, young man?"

"Aah," he shouted, jumping back.

An old woman stood at his side. "Would ye drink from the spring?" she asked again.

The hair on the back of his neck came to full attention. While she looked harmless and bore no weapons, he still backed up a step. He reached for the water skin he carried at his waist and eyed her carefully while he drank.

She wore a neat ensemble of linen, leather and fur. Her gray hair fell in a tidy braid down the length of her back, and she stood tall in spite of her apparent age. She exuded an aura of mystery and wisdom, and yet the light of youth sparkled in her clear blue eyes. He peered closer, and for a second he thought he recognized something of Aydyn in the lined face.

Even though she had no tattoos, he thought she might be one of the great mothers. He glanced around and saw nothing in the way of a hut. He sniffed and smelled no hint of a nearby fire.

"Who are you?" he asked.

"When ye find yourself thirsty again, remember to seek the spring."

She offered him no answer to his question, only the mysterious command. Again the hairs on the back of his neck stood up. The yawning precipice that had plagued him since the night before he crossed time appeared again in his mind. This time it came with a new whisper from the leaves in the trees.

Believe.

Icy tendrils laced down his back in a primal reaction. He glanced around and stamped his foot on the soft ground, needing contact with the solid earth in this ancient world of visions, mind readers, and cryptic messages.

His gaze swept back to the old woman, but she had already slipped back into the trees. He watched the tail of her bobbing braid until she disappeared.

Perplexed, he looked up, then flinched, startled. Before him, Rowan sat on the lowest branch of a tree, staring with Aydyn's blue eyes. She peered at him, cocking her head side-to-side in that curious bird fashion before rising gracefully into the air.

He looked again for the old woman, but there was no trace of her, even the undergrowth bore no evidence of her passing. He strained to hear the bubbling spring, but it, too, was gone.

He hissed and backed away from the clearing, making Cedric's sign of the cross. He turned to follow the bird without looking back.

∞

Eric could hear that something was not right.

What's wrong with this picture?

He broke from the trees about a quarter mile east of where he had entered with the hunting party. Time was obviously well after midday because his stomach grumbled. He made his way to the clearing that kept the livestock and peeked inside the falcon hutch. Rowan rested in her perch, hooded, with one leg drawn up.

Unsure what to do, he stared at the village. His rapid heartbeat left a sour taste in his tacky mouth, but the hairs on the back of his neck were calm. He did not feel threatened, just sick with foreboding.

He walked slowly to the rear of the first hut. There was not a sign or sound of anyone. As he walked further, the abandoned village fanned his trepidation with each step. Sweat chilled on the back of his neck. He spit to clear the fear from his mouth.

Where is Aydyn?

He walked a little faster, rushing now past hut after hut. He hunkered down and skirted the inside perimeter of the village, turning his head from side to side, searching for her.

The chill on his neck rolled down his back and he came to a stop. "Breathe," he whispered as he cocked his head. Then he heard a murmur of voices. He followed the sound to the largest hut in the center of the village.

He tiptoed to the corner and peered around just as a stream of villagers exited. They wore expressions of pain and grief, and he knew with sick certainty someone had died. He went to the door and scanned the crowd pouring out, but he did not see her anywhere. His panic grew and he wanted to shout out her name, when a hand lay upon his shoulder from behind.

"Aghh," he cried. He fell back against the hut and clutched his chest. Glaring at Finn, he hissed, "I'm gonna put a bell around your neck."

"She is not hurt, but she is disturbed and resting in her hut," Finn said. "We have lost young Denan. A boar knocked him out of a tree, he fell and broke his neck." He nodded to the last of the villagers to exit. "Denan's mother and sire, Cat and Desmond."

Eric watched them leave, with Cat's shoulders shaking amid the soft muffle of her sobs. He was stunned.

"The Goddess gives," Finn said, watching the parents cluster their remaining children close. "But then she takes—with a plan that is known only to her."

"And no one knew of this?" Eric cried. "Not one of you held some understanding of what was about to happen? What is the good of this knowledge if you can't save lives?" he cried.

I could loose Aydyn just as easily. She could be gone like that, and I would have lost her again.

A tight fist swelled in his chest and there was no room for air. He fell back against the hut and dug his fingers into the rough wooden wall, a single thought shredding his heart.

What if I lost her again?

Finn shook his shoulder. "Breathe," he commanded.

Eric sucked in air, forcing the fist from his chest. He looked at Finn's clear eyes and tears of relief sprang from his lids. He blinked, exhaling a deep breath. "I can't lose her, not when I have just found her," he whispered.

"Aye, well now, such is not a worry for today," Finn said.

"Do you know—" Eric blurted, lunging at him.

Finn pressed one hand against Eric's chest and shook his head. "If I knew and could tell ye—I would. But I canna, so dinna ask me." He gazed around the village. "We all die, many times, just as we are reborn many times. Death is merely another door opening to another adventure." He flashed a grin, a child's glee lighting his eyes. "Tis not the passing what is important, but the adventure that is so grand."

He walked and Eric fell in step. "This afternoon will be a time of meditation for those who seek the spirit of Denan. Once we have his fire ceremony tonight, he will be gone."

"I know you do not bury your dead," Eric said, "because I have not found them—and believe me, I have looked for ..."

"Aye, brother, and that is what brought ye to us," Finn said. "Tonight we will light Denan's fire in the stone circle, releasing his spirit to return—" He pointed to the sky, at Taurus. "Home."

Eric shifted on his feet, still unable to wrap his mind around the idea of the human species populating the stars. He looked up at Orion's belt and remembered his childhood fantasy of wanting to meet those who populated the cosmos. Academia had taken that dream from him. He smiled, longing to be free enough to wish for that dream again.

They stood before Finn's hut. A childish urge came over Eric to do something wild, something not allowed. He grinned and jabbed Finn in the ribs. "Can I show you another way to do this?" he asked. He picked up the unattached door and tossed it aside.

Finn's gray eyes brightened. "Aye, and more things from the future, if ye have a mind. I was wanting to ask ye—"

∞

Just before sunset, the Druae once again stood on the plain outside the causeway entrance to the stone circle. Every one was there dressed in their finest, down to the smallest baby. And this time, each man, woman and child able to hold a weapon carried a Druae blade of some length.

If this is several hundred years before the Iron Age, how could Finn produce such fine workmanship before its time? Unless the knowledge was attained through the Star Children? And with all this iron, how did I not find any?

The Druae filled the henge in a stately procession. Eric followed Finn, Cayri and Aydyn, and behind him, Cat and Desmond walked with their small brood. Cat's eyes were red, but she held her head high. Desmond gripped her hand and they smiled at one another with tremulous lip and chin.

Eric watched them, saw Desmond tighten his grip on Cat's hand as the two nodded in sync. He looked away and his eyes watered. The grace and courage of these people stunned him. They made him proud to be a human. He frowned, unable to remember if he had ever felt so in his time.

They filed in until Eric stood by the largest trilithon. An eight-foot high wood and thatch platform was erected perpendicular to the altar stone and faced the direction they entered. He knew that Denan's body lay at rest on top, yet he did not see a supply of combustible material. He looked over at Aydyn, but her face was closed to him.

The sun was gone, only a glimmer of light lingered on the horizon. The moon watched from just above the outer ring of capped stones.

Taliesin stepped out from the inner row of bluestones. "Death with oil," he called out. "Death with joy, death with light, death with gladness." He walked, weaving around the Druae as they stood by their bluestones. "Death without pain, death without fear, death that is not death."

The Druae began to sway and hum. They waved like sea grass on the ocean floor, and the vibration of their humming was as pervasive as a tuning fork. Eric's eardrums tickled.

"From whence we began," Talie cried, "we will travel, to start anew, to live again. The endless cycle begins in the heavens—and returns to the heavens."

He waved his arm to the fading light in the western sky as the last vestige of the sun passed the crest of the world. To his right, the moon glowed in its last night of full glory, rising to cast shadows among the great stones.

Eric swayed from side to side, flowing with Finn's movements on his left. He peeked at Aydyn and she stood with her eyes closed, her arms at her side, palms up. He had not had time to speak with her since returning this afternoon.

He closed his eyes and gave himself to the vibration, this power somehow different from the force he experienced the night Aydyn lit the crystals. The energy poured into his body from the earth, from the air, from his bone marrow, filling him with a thrumming energy. He thought again of the voltmeter, but let go of his desire to measure this phenomenon. He didn't need a machine to explain what he felt.

Talie stopped before Denan's platform. He pulled his hand from a pocket and thrust his arm out. In his palm, a small blue crystal sparkled in the moonlight.

"We release Denan from his duty with the Druae," Talie cried.

"We release Denan," the Druae repeated.

The small crystal in Talie's hand came to life. "We send Denan with our love," he cried, and the crystal glowed bright.

The Druae crossed their right hands over their hearts and pointed to the sky with their left. Eric remembered the carving of the man in the space suit etched in the rock wall of the chamber.

Going home.

"Until we see him again," Talie cried.

"Until we see him again."

Talie tossed the crystal up to Denan's body.

Eric held his breath. The bluestones picked up the glow of the crystal, lighting not from within, but with an outer skin of light that radiated from about a half-inch above the surface. Finn grabbed Eric's hand, then jabbed him in the ribs and nodded until Eric took Cayri's hand on the other side.

Eric's hands sizzled as a connection was made in the Druae grasp. The power tugged at him until his molecules swirled and spun and opened. He felt like his atoms were evaporating and he would drift to the heavens if he were not anchored on either side.

The energy circled through his body, starting with his genitals, then his belly, his heart, and lastly up through the crown of his head. He opened his eyes and saw he glowed with blue light, as did the Druae, the bluestones, and the crystal atop Denan's body. The tingling coalesced and lifted from his head. As he stared in wonder, the light rose from everyone's head and shot in a bright blue arc to Denan's body.

The platform flared with the light of a star in a brilliant blue burst, causing Eric to turn his head.

"Og arawyn bot wyn!" the Druae shouted. "Og arawyn bot wyn! Og arawyn bot wyn!"

The lights went out.

The bluestones no longer glowed. The vibration tingled away to nothing. Eric gasped and flexed his fingers, feeling the last sizzle fade from his bones. The ceremony was over and the Druae mingled. A great sigh passed through them—and then everyone smiled.

Finn grabbed him in a fierce bear hug, "Denan's gone home, the lucky beggar," he said, laughing.

All around him, the Druae hugged each other and danced. Eric stuttered, "What—what happened? Why do you laugh?"

"Be happy for Denan," Cayri said. "He is gone home, see." She pointed to the top of the platform and Eric saw the body was gone. He gasped and squinted, but there nothing there. No ash, no debris—no body.

He turned to Finn, who beamed with his usual good spirits. "What has happened here, Finn? Where is Denan's body?" He rubbernecked, looking for Aydyn, but she was lost in the press of celebrating Druae.

"Denan's gone through the door. Ye know, the door to another adventure," Finn said.

Eric's knees wobbled. This morning he lit a fire. Then the hunt. And Aydyn's eyes. The mystery of the woman in the woods. His fear of losing Aydyn when he returned. It had been one hell of a day.

"Aye, brother, ye had a busy day," Finn said, "but there is still much to come." He clapped Eric on the back and gave him a shake. "There will be a celebration, with food and stories to tell." He wagged his big brows and Eric felt a half chuckle stir. "We shall drink and trade stories, the past for the future. Do we have a contract?"

Eric nodded, trying to emotionally catch up with these wild, exuberant people. Most of the Druae had gone back to the village and only a few lingered in the circle. Talie and Aydyn were tossing lively banter as they took down the platform that had held Denan's body.

As he watched them, the hairs lifted on the back of his neck. Aydyn separated the top piece of the platform from its supports and set it on the ground. She reached down and plucked the small blue crystal from the thatch and tossed it to Talie.

Eric examined the platform, touching the thatch and sniffing it. But there was no evidence of combustion, not even a singe mark. Yet the body was gone. He stared up at the sky and Taurus winked from across the galaxy.

Where did he go?

He threw his head back and stared at Taurus until a roar of questions swept through his head, but still he had no answers. From beyond the circle of stones, Aydyn called, "Eric, we are leaving."

The Druae were all gone, and he was the last, trailing behind Aydyn and Talie as they packed the platform out on a small cart. Every few steps he stopped to look up at the night sky, yet all he could do was shake his head and continue walking. Aydyn and

Talie's soft laughter reached his ears and he gave the sky one last chance, but no epiphany waited for him in the stars.

He shrugged and ran to catch up.

∞

A circle of fires bloomed in the village, flaring from every fire pit, reaching for the heavens.

The Druae party well.

Eric lounged before the fire outside Finn's hut with an empty mug in his hand. Finally, he had a buzz sufficient enough to dim the roar of his questions.

He had danced and sang with them—and laughed until his face hurt. After eating, the flutes and drums came out, and the Salisbury plain rocked with the haunting sound of their music. Their lives were so rich, so full with doing and being one with each other. They held a thread of continuity between themselves and their environment that modern man had lost.

And is too stupid to realize what is gone.

He held the small blue crystal Talie gave him for the evening. He thought of Aydyn drawing up the power of the Goddess and lighting the big crystals two nights ago—and it seemed modern man had certainly accepted a lesser life.

In the henge, when the Druae began humming tonight, the power stirred, as if in answer to their call. He remembered how his fingers sizzled when he joined hands with Finn and Cayri—when he became part of the circuit. And the energy that flowed through that circuit is what consumed Denan's body.

Or transported him across time and space.

"Why not," he laughed. "If I can travel across time and space in a snap, why not Denan?"

The crystal burned warm in his hand.

It must be accessing a wormhole.

Every galaxy has at least one—according to the most recent scientific research of his day. "Huh," he grunted. "Stephen Hawking just needs to spend the day with Talie if he wants to know the secrets of the universe."

"Who is Stephen Hawking?"

Eric glared up at Aydyn, who stood grinning at him from the end of the log. "All of you need bells around your necks." Clutching his chest, he pulled a face of fright, earning him the sound of her bright laughter.

"May I sit with you?" she asked.

The familiar hammering started up in his chest, and he set his cup down lest he perform a juggling act. *Please, no visions* he prayed, *not now*. He nodded, and she neatly slid down beside him.

Her eyes were bright and her tattoos glowed in the firelight. His desire to touch the luxurious braid over her shoulder was so strong he edged his hand under his rump, trapping his compulsion.

She sighed and eased back against the log with her long legs bent before her. She wore linen leggings and a long tunic decorated with blue and amber beads. She seemed to have no purpose but to sit with him, so he relaxed.

He stared at the fire and palmed the crystal. Did the crystals come from—home? And where exactly was home? Did the Druae know where the body went?

"Do you have any questions you would like to ask?" she said.

"This afternoon," he said, "people were sad." He waved at the still lively remnants of Denan's party. "Yet, now, you have laughter. How do make that—change?"

"This morning when we woke," she answered, "Denan was a part of us. When he ceased to live among us, we grieved because his spirit had no home. That is why we had his fire ceremony as soon as possible, so that he can find his next adventure, his next home. Until then, he is caught in our world, unable to travel on."

She smiled and he felt like a simple child that had to have everything explained.

"What is the custom in your time?" she asked.

"The most common practice is to put the body in a pretty box and bury it," he said.

She pulled back, her face an expression of abject horror. She covered her mouth with both hands. "You do not—"

He shrugged. "It's not my idea. I like what you do better. Why does it disturb you so much, the way we—"

"To be buried in the ground," she said, "prevents you from going home—to the heavens. You would be trapped, cut off from your next adventure." She shook her head, and he could see she was unable to grasp such a fate. "To be so would be … unthinkable."

She leaned over and plucked the crystal from his hand. "In the old days we used fire, before the Star Children instructed us in the use of the crystals." As she rolled the crystal in her palm, it began to glow. "After we are gone from the great circle, we will go back to the old ways. But I would never want to be buried in the ground." She frowned and shook her head. "Mother says we must return to the stars. That is how we gain—"

"Your next adventure," he said.

"You are learning well, Eric Beck."

When she said his name, a hum of pleasure lit his core. Her Druae blue sparkled at him with wisdom, and a well of faith and strength that was beyond his understanding. He wanted so badly to believe as she did—to be able to fall into that well.

He picked up her hand. The heart of a man, or a woman, is in the hand. Her hands were not delicate or dainty. The fingers were long and strong, powerful and tanned, the nails trimmed short. He rubbed the calluses from her bow practice that ran along her thumb and forefinger.

On the back of her hand, he saw evidence of a life filled with knives, arrowheads and swords. He traced the scars with his finger, wondering at a spirit that embraced such a difficult life with so much verve and certainty.

He turned her hand palm up. Her skin was warm and dry, and he had a sudden wild desire to lick the salt from her wrist. The need to taste her rolled through him. He released her hand and sat back.

"You do not fear death, do you?" he asked.

"We all face death," she said. She seemed surprised at his question, but shrugged with elegance and power. "Life is often the more difficult event."

In her eyes he saw conviction at a depth unknown to him. But then, he had never before witnessed a body disappearing right in front of him—to travel the cosmos and return home. "What is 'og arawyn bot wyn'?"

"That is from the old language," she said. "It means 'I wish I were you.'"

"I wish I were you," he whispered.

She stood and he rose with her. "I noticed you looking at our blades tonight," she said. "Would you like to see how Finn works with the metal?"

She is going to leave and I don't know how to stop her.

"The iron," he said, "Yes, I would like that."

She took a step and he grabbed her hand. He floundered in a spinning morass of marvel peppered with questions and doubts—and she was the one constant that sustained him. She was warm and solid and smelled wonderful of flowers. He needed her, needed her unwavering strength and impossible conviction.

"Tomorrow," he said. He squeezed her fingers, wanting to hear her say the words. When she squeezed back, his heart stuttered against his ribs.

"Yes," she said, "tomorrow."

∞

Aydyn walked away from Eric, striding on legs that threatened to collapse.

I did not know I possessed such strength.

When he picked up her hand and began stroking, she never flinched. She did not jerk loose. She did not stand and run. She did not shrink. Instead, she had braced herself against the power of his touch—and discovered how strong she really was.

She cradled the hand he touched as though the Goddess had transformed her common flesh, for when he touched her, the heavens sang. From her heart to her woman's core, she felt a key enter a lock, releasing within her a magical torrent of sensation.

And desire.

The fire within her simmered, then flared when they touched. She sucked in her breath, remembering the sweet, hot, swollen feeling that filled her legs and hips, making her want to—

"Sheeew," she whistled through her teeth.

She had never felt that, not with any who had proposed a contract. Every year at Beltane they came with sweet talk, or horses and gold to buy her. But she had turned them all away, for they left her cold.

Not so with this one.

His scent remained on her hand. She inhaled deeply and the familiar warmth spread through her, making her knees weak. She surged with a longing to open her legs ...

She stopped before her hut. Her heart and soul rang with a need that mystified her, even as her body cried for a succor she hesitated to identify. She gazed back across the clearing to Finn's hut.

Eric sat before his fire, a man searching for answers to the many questions filling his mind.

She rubbed her precious hand against her legging and a shiver curled her toes. She, too, had questions.

Chapter Seven

Eric held the door in place while Finn put the finishing touches on his version of a door hinge. Two wooden pegs—one coming out of the ground, one exiting the wood frame from above—now held the door firmly in place.

"Aye, brother," Finn said, "ye have done a mighty thing here." He swung the thatch panel back and forth, clearly delighted with its free movement on the new hinges.

Eric grinned, pleased with himself. He wanted to give the Druae something after all they have given him. He had described a modern door, and Finn created this peg-and-disc design to fit the Druae's needs.

"Now that I see how this one works," Finn said, "they are easy to make. We can all have one by nightfall." He turned and flashed a great smile at Eric. "We owe ye, for this and more," he said. He crossed his right hand over his chest and tapped his heart in the Druae salutation for respect and affection. "I will tell the boys what to carve, and then meet ye at the smith hut."

"Wait," Eric blurted in a late thought, but Finn was already gone. "Oh well," he muttered.

Damn, so much for ordering a spoon carved.

"No need," Aydyn said.

He didn't flinch this time, finally learning how his hammering heart forewarned her presence. She stepped within the fire pit boundary and held out a linen wrapped package.

"Go ahead, it will not bite you," she chided.

Her voice was warm, making his heart rev like a big Chrysler engine. His fingers shook and the knot defied him. Finally, the string gave way to reveal a wooden spoon, neatly carved and stained blue. A small hole on the handle sported a leather string.

"Wow," he said. He rubbed at the smooth, hard wood and marveled at the effort that had produced such work. He looked at the linen wrapping. There were ten eight-inch squares, each with a tight, hand-stitched border.

"For your mouth," she said, gesturing with her hand.

Her eyes fell on his face, and Eric's lips tingled beneath her gaze. Her touch, even in his mind, was nuclear. "Thank you. Did you make them?" He examined the detail in the stitching, hoping the fine work was hers.

"Yes, I did them last night," she said.

His heart faltered, squeezed by the welling emotion flowing through his chest. That she had made the napkins for him made him grin with delight. He knew he must look a fool, but he didn't care. He gazed into the inviting bright blue of her eyes and her sparkling tattoos, and suddenly his heart opened and his mind begged to know—

Who are you? Why do you make me feel like this?

She blinked and slanted him a hooded look. Her lips twitched, and she whispered, "I would ask you the same."

He grabbed her and pulled her close. A heat and a desire to know her, to touch her, to taste her raged within him. He was the first man, the last man, the only man—who had found his mate.

Her arms were warm beneath his hands and he stroked her skin with his fingers, reveling in the touch of her flesh. He knew now that she was the one he searched for all those years in the field as an archaeologist. Somehow, he was born with memories of his need for her, memories of his connection to her.

"Eric," she breathed, her face just inches from his.

The scent of her hair, her skin, her breath, flowed through him and his heart finally slowed, now languished and complete.

"Eric," she repeated.

He delved into the turquoise of her eyes and could not get enough. The bottom fell out from beneath his feet, and he flew on the wings of the Goddess.

"Eric."

He let her go and stepped away. His hands, his heart, his loins, all burned with a need and a fire to be one with this woman. He took another step back, afraid of what he might do. With a long ragged exhale, he stood and pressed his hands against his thighs.

Aydyn stood still as a statue, pitched slightly forward on her toes. Her eyes were like stars and a flush brightened her cheeks. She panted and her arms were stiff, her hands fisted at her sides.

When she didn't speak, he feared he had offended her and stepped back again. "Please forgive me. I …" He stuttered and hunched his shoulders.

She shook her head and moved away, leaving him cringing inside. He wanted her to blast him for loosing his cool, as he deserved. Instead, she pushed the hair from her face with trembling fingers—but no condemnation followed.

"No, I …" She fussed with the front of her short tunic, then coughed and flung her braid over her shoulder in an obvious struggle to appear as if nothing had happened.

"You will want to put that in yer pack," she said, motioning to the blue spoon and linen pieces. He heard the quiver in her voice as he tucked the items away.

They stood apart and eyed each other. A twitch came to her lips. The spreading grin blossomed and she looked down to hide her smile, but he saw it. His own lips twitched and he felt a chuckle hitch in his belly. He looked her square in the eye and prayed he wouldn't burst out laughing.

"Shall we go see Finn?" he asked.

∞

In the short walk to the smith hut, Eric worked himself into a state of juvenile excitement. He had long admired Finn's workmanship—to see its creation was a thrill he would have never imagined.

The smith hut was actually a round stone house on the northwest side of the village, as far from the forest as possible. Massive stacks of wood equaling hundreds of cords waited to be consumed in Finn's fires, and a team of boys worked the bellows, pumping air into the forge.

Eric and Aydyn watched from the door, standing back from the waves of intense heat that rolled out the door. Finn worked with a short sword blade, using large tongs to hold the metal deep in the red coals until it glowed.

"Aye, there ye are now," Finn shouted over the roar of the fire. He pulled the blade out of the coals and held it up for inspection, turning the red hot metal several times before thrusting the piece into a clay pot of water. He released the blade from the tongs, leaving it to steam and hiss in the water. Wiping the sweat from his bare chest with a cloth, he walked towards them.

He nodded to Eric and eyed Aydyn, saying, "A fine morning, Sis." He stared at her for long seconds, but she ignored him, presenting her back to him as she moved to a row of chests by the wall.

Eric raised his hands, making a T to ward off any attempts by Finn to probe his thoughts. Finn grinned, and asked, "So what would ye like to see?"

Eric followed Aydyn as she examined a row of storage chests. She opened one, and his mouth dropped open in a silent "oh." Weapons with copper accents, silver beading, carved amber inlays—and more—filled the chest. "Oh my—" He reached out to hug her. Pulling her close, he whispered, "Thank you," into her ear.

She turned to him and their eyes caught. Their faces were close enough for him to breathe her exhalation. Her breath and her entire scent was wild and clean, and so familiar.

A sensation of contentment, of fulfillment, of completing the circle he had chased after for so long settled around his heart. An expanded awareness of her was born in his molecules—for her scent, her aura, her state of mind and all of her. She filled him to bursting. All he could do was stare at her lips.

"Umhuh," Finn said. He stood watching them with his arms crossed on his mighty chest.

Aydyn walked to a stack of completed blades. She picked up an eighteen-inch short sword from the top of the pile. The hand guard was silver and the hilt wrapped in leather. Carved amber decorated the base of the blade. She held it out to him.

"This, this is—" Eric stuttered. He took the blade, noticing her trembling fingers before his focus shifted to the weapon. The sword was iron, not bronze, with a razor sharp edge. "It's perfect, Finn," he said. "Your workmanship with the metal is amazing." He jabbed the air, testing the weapon's weight.

Finn came to Eric's side and lifted the blade from him. "Here, give me that before ye get hurt." He stepped out into a fighting stance and parried and lunged. The fierce blade sang in his hand, slicing through the air. Eric shivered. What Finn did with the blade was warfare, what he did was play.

Finn lunged and sidestepped, turned on his heel and delivered a killing strike across his front. He paused with the blade extended before him and his eyes fired with the primitive power to kill.

"Finn's blades are like no other," Aydyn said. "When the Star Children lived among us, they taught us the secret of working the metal. The techniques are Druae, perfected over countless long days. Combined with Finn's expertise, the result is a weapon worth more than gold, horses—or women."

Finn waved the blade and the air molecules hissed as the razor sharp edge sliced through. "A Druae blade can draw blood from the air," Finn said. He cocked an eye to Aydyn. "Has he seen ye shoot, Sis?"

Eric eyed Aydyn. "No, I haven't. Is she any good?"

She sidestepped and cocked her elbow, but Eric was ready. He twisted and shot his fingers out, tickling her ribs until she doubled over. "No," she squealed, trying to twist away, but he gave her no mercy, tickling her until they both fell to the ground laughing.

Aydyn panted and wiped at her streaming eyes, pushing the hair from her face. Laughter sparkled in her Druae blue, even as she wagged her finger at him with a promise of retribution.

"Uh, hmm. Ahh," Finn mumbled, standing over them.

Aydyn scrambled up off the ground, brushing at her leggings and tunic. She gave her back to her brother and offered Eric her hand. She held back a grin, and Eric squelched his laughter as he rose.

"You were saying, uh—something," Eric said. He ran his hand over his face, laying down a solemn and steady expression. "You say she can shoot?" he asked.

Aydyn stood subdued at Eric's side, her expression as obvious as a cartoon wolf sporting a fleece skin.

Finn grinned openly. "If the Druae blade can draw blood from the air, then a Druae arrow can do no less. Show him the horse, Sis." He turned and walked back to his forge, removing the cooled blade from the clay pot. "Now go, before ye fool around and knock something over," he called over his shoulder.

They walked outside the smith house. "So tell me about the horse," Eric said.

She smiled, and he knew he had never seen anyone so lovely. The color of her eyes against the copper tattoos enchanted him. There was nothing about her that disappointed him, and he hoped she would be able to say the same of him. She turned, taking them back towards the village.

"The horse," she said, "I won from a boastful plainsman."

Her face was so blatantly smug, he chuckled and asked, "And what did you do to this plainsman?"

They reached her hut and she ducked inside. She came out with her five-foot bow slung across her back and a quiver of arrows attached to her waist.

She looked up, her face full of feminine innocence, yet her warrior's stance spoke with all the confidence in the world. "I showed him how to shoot," she said, and winked with her tattooed eye. "Come, we will get the horse so I can show ye."

Beyond the falcon hutch were pens and corrals holding all the Druae livestock. They passed chickens, sheep, goats and pigs, then horses. A small herd of brown and red rugged mountain ponies grazed beyond in a small field, but in the corral, a grand stallion paced, strawberry roan with long, silver-blonde mane and tail. When Aydyn whistled, his ears flicked her way.

"Donnye," she called softly, and the stallion came prancing to the rail. He nosed her hand and snuffled, then sniffed Eric's outstretched hand. The horse butted Eric's shoulder and Aydyn laughed.

"Good, he likes you," she said.

Eric rubbed Donnye's broad head above his eyes. "So what does Donnye do if he doesn't like you?"

Aydyn pulled a dried apple from her pouch and shook her head, drawing her brows together in an ominous frown. "You do not want to know." She acted as though they discussed the end of the world, then smiled brightly and handed him the apple.

Aydyn ducked between the rails of the corral while Eric palmed the fruit to the horse. Donnye snatched up the apple in a single bite, chewing with pleasure while Aydyn slipped a length of braided leather over his head. Another braided rope went around his girth at the withers, where she tied down her bow. With a spring-loaded bound, she straddled the horse.

Eric unlatched the gate and stepped back as she brought the stallion out. She rode to his side and offered him her hand. He gulped, seeing a problem with the seating arrangement.

At this range, you won't need a mind reader to figure out what I'm thinking.

He took her hand. Her grip was strong, almost crushing and he held on, leaping up onto the horse's rump. The stallion's coat was glossy and slick, and he immediately began to slide off the other side. She caught him with her other hand and steadied him until he got his seat. He settled in, wiggling his butt into position and pulling his heels out of the horse's flanks.

"Do you ride horses, in your time?" she asked over her shoulder.

"Yes," he replied. He sat with his hands at his sides, even though his inclination was to grip her hips for balance. But he didn't want to—

"We will ride easy, no jumping," she said, teasing.

He cringed, that she could read him so easily. He put his hands on her hips, barely touching her, just as the horse shifted. He began to slide, and by reflex, sank his fingers into her muscled hips for an anchor. His groin slammed into her buttocks and his chest filled her back. When his chin hit her shoulder, his breath froze in his throat. The horse was warm beneath him, but a different heat came from her, burning far more than his skin. He locked his jaws and fought the urge to grind his hips into her bottom.

"Ready?" she asked.

He gulped. Behind them, Stonehenge stood majestic, mysterious and commanding—glorious beyond anything modern man suspected. Before him sat a woman who called upon what he believed were planetary and cosmic forces to tap into other dimensions.

Am I ready to follow her?

His heart pounded just inches from hers—so close he felt his heartbeat adjust to move in sync with her. His logical mind screamed that he was nowhere near brave enough to follow this woman bareback on a wild horse through a primitive countryside.

And yet, he hated to disappoint her.

"Sure," he said, rubbing his chin against her shoulder.

∞

They rode Donnye west, beyond the chamber he discovered just days ago. At the edge of the woods, they stopped and dismounted. Eric took the time to examine her bow. It was a composite of wood with a sinew wrap, but unlike a regular English longbow, hers had a re-curve at each tip.

"This design was given us by the Star Children," Aydyn said. She pulled on the string and the tension released with a solid twang. He tried it, and gave a low whistle, guessing the pull to be about forty-five pounds.

Several large bales of tightly packed thatch were stacked for target shooting. She pulled a piece of blue linen about twelve inches square from her quiver and secured it with leather ties to the thatch. He could see she was setting a stage, and he watched with giddy anticipation, wondering what new miraculous feat she would perform today.

"It was two Beltane fires back," she said.

Her smile was pure and innocent, and he could envision her baffled opponents.

How could you suspect such a sweet face to be devious?

He smiled, encouraging her. She collected her bow and the horse, and walked. "Beltane draws many tribes. They come from across the water, from strange lands where there are no trees, and beyond," she said. "We have seen the yellow people with slanted eyes, and the white haired giants from the north come in their long boats."

They stopped a hundred and fifty yards from the target and she gave him the horse's reins. She pulled out a slim leather arm guard and wrapped it around her wrist. "The dark men come from the plains with their long moustaches. They are proud, as they should be, for their skill is legend."

She fit a small wooden pick over her thumb and notched an arrow. When she looked up, a fierce smile of gleaming teeth split her face. "They declared a winner from this point with a center shot—like this." She pulled the string back with the pick, pointing the arrow straight up. The smile disappeared as she compressed her lips in concentration. The tattooed eye came down to the string as she pulled back and brought the weapon down, leveled onto the target, and released.

"Go look," she said.

He ran as far as he could, but a stitch in his side brought him to a walk before he completed a hundred yards. He reached the target, and a perfect center shot nailed the linen. He waved a thumbs-up and she waved him back.

He walked the last fifty yards, not wanting to arrive gasping. "So what did you do?" he asked. He gazed back at the blue target, which he could just see at this distance. A shiver of expectation filled his arms with goose flesh.

"I asked them if I could shoot from somewhere else," she said.

Her voice was soft, sweet and inviting, drawing him towards her.

She was dynamic and mysterious, alluring and frightening, beautiful and compelling. Her blue eyes sparkled with suppressed mirth and her smile would have opened the gates of heaven.

"Where did you shoot from?" he asked, fully expecting to hear her say, "The moon."

She jumped up on Donnye and offered him her hand. He drew back. "No," he chided her. "You did not?"

"Aye," she said, nodding with mischief. She pulled him up and he nestled in behind her. Wrapping his fingers around her waist, he whispered into her ear, "Show me what you did."

She tapped the horse in the flanks and they rode to a position over one hundred yards back. He couldn't even see the blue patch.

How in the hell did she make a qualified shot from here?

"Like this," she said.

She eyed her target and he knew she tapped into some vision beyond normal human capability. She notched the arrow and pulled back on the string, again straight up at first and then lowering towards the target. Muscles bulged in her arms and across her back. The bow looked ready to explode. She gazed down the length of the arrow for the span of an eye blink, and he shivered.

What would it be like, he wondered, *to know the receiving end of her arrows?*

She released, and the arrow shot from the string like a missile. An eerie *thwwp* noise followed, and his eyes bulged as she pulled another arrow, notched and sent it flying. Another followed, and another in rapid succession.

His breath stalled in his throat. He had never seen anyone move so fast. In a feral burst of pride, her teeth burned white against the tan of her cheeks, her copper tattoos, and the brilliant blue of her eyes.

The crazy emotions she fired in him swarmed to engulf his heart. He stepped close enough to smell her, and his arm slipped around her waist. His hand splayed out against the back of her tunic and his fingers begged for the feel of her bare skin. The smell of wild flowers and clean sweat filled his nostrils. He inhaled deeply, wanting more.

He pulled her close and she dropped the bow. He looked down into her face, and her eyes called to him—blue lights and blue depths, deep enough to hold the cosmos—or a man's heart. He felt her heart thudding against his chest, right below his own heart, and a sense of rightness filled him.

Her lips parted and he could have shouted with joy. He wanted her to want him, for he had so much to give—if she would let him. He lowered his head slowly, savoring the closeness of her, the live scent of her breath, the heat of their sweat mingling through her tunic as his fingers massaged her back.

He paused, his lips so close, yet not quite touching.

Please, please, he begged. He held himself back and the heat of her burned him at every touch. She shifted her weight, opening her legs, and he stepped in. She moved towards him, straddling his leg. He closed his eyes. She clutched his arms as if to prevent them both from falling, but it was too late.

He tasted her lips, moist and inviting against his. Her lips moved lightly against his, hesitant, and desire burst within, consuming him from his heart all the way to his loins. The need for her flowed into him.

He breathed against her mouth, and then her lips were his and he was lost. Her sweetness filled his mouth as she opened even further, and he knew a joy he never imagined possible.

She was the Goddess, and he was her mate—for she had called him across time.

The fire of his need became an inferno he offered to her. He took her tongue in his mouth, taking no less than he gave. He stroked and laved her mouth; her tongue was his to cherish, sweet and wild. She rode his thigh as they stood, belly to belly. Her damp heat pressed against him and his hardness jutted between them, begging for attention.

He growled deep in his throat and pulled her even closer. A rumble of response came from her chest, and he plunged his tongue deep in her mouth. She parried and stroked him, suckling him in return with small whimpering noises as she rubbed insistently against his leg. Her wetness blazed against his flesh, driving him further.

One more touch, and I will explode.

He tore himself from her mouth, gasping for air. Her eyes fluttered open, warm and heavy, as lost as he. She licked her lips and he groaned. He stepped back with stiff arms, panting to contain what was about to burst from him.

Dancing away, he pulled at his leggings. He looked at Aydyn and she blinked, an owl in sudden daylight.

"I'm sorry," he sputtered. He took a couple steps away and bent over with his hands on his knees. "Breathe," he commanded. He stared at the ground and took several deep breaths, willing the volcano between his legs to cool down.

He eyed Aydyn over his shoulder. She fussed with her clothing and smoothed her hair, her flaming cheeks clear evidence he was not alone. "Whew," he chuckled. He blew a hard breath out and rose, fanning his aroused groin. Sweat ran down his back and he whistled through pursed lips.

She turned to him, displaying the vivid splashes across her cheeks. She picked up her bow, her face carefully composed, and acted as if nothing was amiss.

"Okay, then," he said with a last tug at his clothing.

Without a word, she jumped to Donnye's back and held out her hand. He took her trembling fingers for a long moment before he jumped, feeling the frantic pulse at her wrist. He gave up wondering why and how he came to be here. She was here, and that was all he needed to know. She was the answer to all his questions.

"Let's take a look at your target," he said.

As they rode back, she said, "When I asked them to shoot from another spot, they laughed and joked about letting the little girl shoot. But when they discovered I wanted a longer shot, they slapped each other on the backs like fools. Only the tall men with white hair understood."

They reached the target and he slid from Donnye's back. When he saw the linen square, his mouth dropped open. Four arrows perfectly surrounded the center shot so close that the iron arrowheads shredded the first arrow. The five arrows had to be pulled out as one.

She slid down and stood beside him, arms crossed, one hip cocked. "When they saw this, they quit laughing."

Her tone was smug, and rightly so. He could hear the plainsmen guffawing laughter, until they faced the illumination of her target.

"And the horse," he asked, "was he a wager?"

"The northmen knew what I could do with the bow," she said. Her eyes sparkled with memory and she gazed at the linen. "Before I shot, they wanted the plainsmen to wager the horse. But the plainsmen said I had nothing of equal value, except for a Druae blade, and those are not for sale or trade. So we made the challenge just for honor."

She shrugged, nonchalant in her superiority, and he was instantly sorry for the stupid men who had underestimated a Goddess warrior. Donnye nickered and nudged her, urging her on, so Eric smiled, adding his encouragement.

"If they had not laughed so hard," she said, "Donnye would not be here." She scrubbed the horse's broad forehead and he bobbed his head in pleasure.

"The next morning, Donnye was tied before my hut, complete with all his gear, in a very public statement honoring my skill." She stroked Donnye's soft ruddy nose and he sighed and snuffled her hand. "He is a fine animal, and we have already contracted him for breeding." Her voice faded and she added in a whisper, "I wonder now if he will get to breed those foals."

They stood shoulder to shoulder. She sighed and dropped her forehead to Donnye's, resting head-to-head. Eric's heart seized in a crushing pain. She and the horse, both so spectacular, would pass, and he knew his world would be a smaller, darker place without them.

My world, he thought, *what is my world? Do I belong here, or in the future? Wherever she is—that is where I belong.*

His belly clenched when he thought about going back. Staying here terrified him, and yet going back saddened him beyond belief. He frowned and shook his head, unable to bear the thought. "Aydyn, will they send me home?" he asked. The grief in his heart poured into his eyes as he turned towards her.

She stared at him, her face stricken with horror. He frowned and glanced around, thinking she saw some threat he hadn't noticed.

"What?" he asked. A prickling foreboding crept along his scalp and he reached for her.

She pushed him back with a hard shove, squinting at him like he was a bug. "Ye want to go back?" she asked, spitting the venomous words.

He shook his head and sputtered, "No. I mean, that's not what I was asking. I—" He stopped. The outraged look on her face clearly told him he had screwed up somehow. He ran a hand through his hair and started again. "Please, you don't understand." He reached for her again, but she slapped at his hands and stepped back, her pain filled eyes glittering.

"No," he shouted.

She dashed her hand across her eyes and snatched up Donnye's reins. "I wish you had never come," she said, cool and hard, her words brittle. She brushed by him, knocking him out of the way, and leaped up on the horse.

"Your journey home—" she said, wheeling the horse around.

"Wait, please," he pleaded.

"—begins now." She dug her heels in Donnye's flanks, and they were gone in a burst of heaving horseflesh.

As they disappeared, he felt the weight of the world fall upon his shoulders. "What happened, dammit?"

Growling, he kicked at the earth and lunged at the sky, swinging his fists, pummeling the unseen. Spying a plum-sized rock, he launched it as hard as he could at nothing in particular. "There," he spit, somewhat mollified. He jerked his clothing straight with a strut and a nod.

He stood with his hands on his hips, panting until his senses and his breath returned. He stared at her last location, remembering their searing kiss—and his lips twitched to a smile. He put his hand to his face and pondered the morning's events. The kiss, the heat, her touch …

His thigh tingled where her scent branded him, and his smile grew until he threw his head back and roared with laughter.

She kissed me.

He jacked his fist into the air and jumped, skipping about in a circle of joy, laughing and hooting. "Thank you!" he shouted. Tears streamed from his eyes and he stopped to wipe his face. "Thank you," he whispered. "Thank you, Goddess."

He threw a kiss to the sky and turned back towards the village.

∞

"Stupid, stupid, fool" Aydyn sobbed.

Duty is all I will know in this life.

Scalding tears poured down her face and streamed down her throat, threatening to drown her heart. She turned Donnye away from the village, needing the comfort and solitude of the forest. She lashed the horse and he flew, scattering her tears to the four winds.

Chapter Eight

Balock strode into his father's hut. "Greetings, Father," he said with a bow.

"You are about early this morning," Jarech said. He sat working a piece of harness and gave Balock a piercing look. "What do you want?"

Balock forced himself not to cringe under his father's intense scrutiny. "I have something to show you," he said.

Kneeling beside his father, he glanced around, careful that no one else should see or hear. He opened the package of skins that hid the Druae blade; the razor edge gleamed with deadly beauty as he turned it in the light. He held the sword out to his father.

Jarech reared back, staring at the blade, but did not take the offering. "If that is Druae, then you are more foolish than I thought." He leaned close and examined the blade. "Ssss, what a shame, for it is a beauty." He glared at Balock. "You stole this, and yet you dare to touch it. That girl—she has spelled you—and your madness will be the end of us all." He reached over and struck Balock in the head. "You are worse than a fool," he snarled, "you are an idiot." He pulled back for another blow.

"Oww," Balock cried. He rubbed his head and held a hand out to stop what he saw was coming. "Father, hear me out," he pleaded.

He snatched up the harness his father held and sliced through the leather with the iron. The hide fell away from the Druae blade without a fight. He turned and raised the iron blade with clear intent on his father.

Jarech cried and grabbed his closest weapon, a bronze short sword. He brought the weapon up in a block as Balock struck. The iron cleaved neatly into the bronze. Balock then flipped his blade and snapped the bronze in two.

"Aghh," Jarech shouted. He lunged to his feet and smashed his fist into Balock's face, splitting one lip. He pulled back for another strike, but stopped when Balock bowed and presented the iron blade.

Jarech stepped back with his fist in the air, refusing to touch the iron. "The metal is filled with their magic, that is how the blade can be so strong," he said. "To touch a Druae blade is death." He eyed Balock, clearly waiting for his son to drop dead.

"No, Father," Balock said. He held the Druae blade to the light with both hands. "Yes, there is magic, but not with spells. The magic is in the making of the metal. I have been handling the iron—"

"Since you stole the piece at Beltane," Jarech said. "We are lucky they have not come to kill us all." He hunched his shoulders and peeked out the door. "They will know you for the thief, Balock," he hissed. "After what you did, they will know to look for you." He turned and growled, "Your madness and your theft will be the end of us all."

Balock extended the knife and Jarech leaned close, admiring the silver decorating the hilt. "Go ahead," Balock said. "It fairly sings with power."

Jarech stretched out a tentative finger, eyeing his son.

Balock nodded, saying, "Since Beltane, and I am still alive."

Jarech touched the blade, but nothing happened.

Balock offered, and this time Jarech took the weapon. He hefted the sword and pursed his lips in a silent salutation as he thrust, parried, and swung a killing strike.

Balock's grin was sure. To hold a Druae blade was to know power.

Jarech turned and slashed at a bronze lamp, cleaving it in two. His eyes shone with the thrill, the balance, and the power of the weapon. Balock saw the lust in his father's face. He smiled, knowing fertile ground existed for him to sow the seeds of his plan.

"Think, Father," Balock said. "Think of the power we would hold with more of these. I saw chests full with their excess weapons—"

Jarech stroked the fine silver on the hilt and flicked his thumb across the blade. A thin line of blood welled and he snatched his hand back. "I do not deny the value," he said, eyeing Balock.

Balock spread his hands and stepped back. "The blade is yours, if you desire, Father."

Jarech rummaged through a stack of weapons in the corner and pulled out a sheath that would fit the Druae blade. He discarded the old bronze piece and slipped the iron inside. "We will keep this to ourselves," he said. He carefully tucked the new iron blade under the skins on his bed.

Balock stepped to the door. "You will think on what I said, Father?" he asked.

"Aye," Jarech said. He pulled at his long moustache and stared at the bed. "Give me time, and I will do just that."

∞

Eric watched while Finn worked. First the plunge into the forge, then the glowing hot metal was beat with the hammer. The tortured iron cried, its pain ringing across the village.

"How long will she be gone?" Eric asked when the hammering ceased.

Four days had passed, and still Aydyn did not return. In her absence, he spent his time with Finn, learning the Star Children secrets of working iron.

"You are not worried that she is gone this long?" he asked. He opened another of the dozen chests lining the walls of Finn's smith house. Knife blades of every length, shape and thickness filled the chests. The handles were all unadorned, waiting to be decorated during the long winter months spent indoors.

Finn fitted another piece into the tongs and thrust the iron into the furnace coals. "Gilye," he shouted, "pump that bellows, man." The coals flared with the influx of oxygen and Finn pushed the metal deeper. He wiped the sweat from his face and walked to where Eric sat.

"If she was hurt," Finn said, "we would know, so stop fashing yer poor self with worry. She knows those woods like the back of her hand, and she will come out when she is ready." He dried his chest and gave Eric a steady look. "And, no, I do not know where she is or what she is doing."

Finn reached for a mug of beer, kept cool in a recess in the rock wall. He took several long gulps, smacked his lips and wiped his mouth on a linen napkin. "Ye know, the women, they love ye for this," he said. He held the cloth out and chuckled. "I have seen a stack of these in every home. And, brother, the new door," he said, flashing his teeth in a great smile. "I tell ye, we are heroes."

Finn sipped again. "Did ye see all the variety of decorations the women are putting up now, making each door unique." He slapped Eric on the back. "I think ye have come a long way since ye arrived. I can remember when ye refused to go outside. Now ye have left yer mark on us."

Eric hunched his shoulders, not wanting to think about the newly decorated doors. Who knew that the wooden hinges he and Finn devised would transform a utilitarian piece of thatch into an opportunity for artistic expression? He rubbed the back of his neck.

What have I done?

Finn tapped his elbow into Eric's ribs. "Woo ho, brother, do ye regret what ye gave us? There is a look of trouble about yer face."

"No," Eric said, waving his hand at the new doors—evidence of his presence. "It's not that. These will all be gone long before—"

He sighed and leaned back against a chest. "It's not this—it's her. I've been looking for her since the day I was born. And now that I have found her, everything is upsidedown. I don't know what's right, or wrong. I don't know how or why I'm here, or for how long."

He stopped and pierced Finn with his gaze. "How am I supposed to live my life," he sputtered, "not knowing when or if I will return? Hell, for all I know, I might meet my demise here."

Finn gave up nothing. Eric was learning that the Druae could be very open with their emotions through their facial expressions, or they could wear the best poker face in the world.

Eric gazed out the door. Every day he was here, his actions held the potential for untold ramifications in the future. Beyond that, each day within itself was an endless parade of fatal opportunities. He recalled Aydyn's bow, and was forced to remember he was in a dangerous prehistoric time, and not on an exotic camping trip. He gazed at the tree line on the horizon. She was out there somewhere. The need for her burned within him, regardless of what time he was in.

What we will do—we have already done. He shook his head, refusing to comply. *I will choose my fate and my tomorrows, beginning today.*

"Teach me how to fight," he said.

"With a sword?" Finn asked. He pulled his brows together and glared at Eric like he had asked to fly to the moon.

Eric picked up a finished short sword with a twenty-four-inch iron blade and a simple, hide-wrapped handle. He hefted the weapon and it felt good. He thrust and parried, the perfect balance making the weapon flow from his hand. "Your workmanship, Finn, will become a legend," he said.

Finn chuckled. "Brother, such an honest compliment might get ye my cooperation, ye know that."

The beauty of the sword as an instrument of destruction was unsurpassed. Eric turned the blade against the light. The edge gleamed, daring all to touch it without bleeding. He waved the blade and the fine edge sang, slicing the air. He looked down, fully expecting to see droplets of blood on the ground.

"I would like to learn, Finn. Will you teach me?" Eric eyed the blade with admiration. "What if I find myself in a situation where I need to protect myself?" He gave his best hopeful look, knowing the Druae respected that emotion.

Finn stood with his arms crossed and a hooded look guarding his eyes. He took the blade from Eric and returned it to the chest. "Aye, brother, tis a fair request, but ye wilna be starting with this."

A thrill shimmied from Eric's scalp to his toes. When Finn gave him a sharp look, he coughed and pulled a stern expression. "I am prepared to work," he said. "I know this won't be easy." He eyed the chests filled with weapons, and a brief image of him swinging a sword in the heat of battle danced through his mind.

Finn burst out in laughter and smacked Eric soundly on the back, knocking him off balance. As Eric staggered, Finn snatched his arm and pulled him outside. They walked to the back, where a ten-foot high stack of cut logs waited to be split for the forge.

"First, ye swing this iron," Finn said. He reached down and grasped an axe from the chopping block.

Eric took the axe and guessed the weight at about fifteen pounds. He looked at the massive stack of wood and bared his teeth in a grimace of hapless expectation.

What have I done?

"Good Lord," he mumbled with hunched shoulders. "Those words have become my motto." He shot his eyes to the heavens and prayed for compassion.

Finn reached through the open window, snatched up a pair of

leather gloves and tossed them to Eric. "These should fit," he said.

Eric pulled the gloves on and picked up the axe, reminding himself of how many ways he wanted this. "How long do I—" he said, glancing up, but Finn was gone. He set a log on the block. A couple of practice swings and he whistled with growing respect for the woodsmen.

He recalled how his mother always wanted him to be a lawyer. When he declared his heart set on archaeology, she admonished him with, "You'll get your hands dirty." If he had become a lawyer, would he have then found Aydyn in a courtroom? He tried to imagine her wearing pumps and a suit, and decided archaeology was the right choice.

He split several logs in two and tossed the pieces into a nearby pile. His shoulders cried at the unaccustomed activity, but he swung the heavy axe again. "Come on, baby," he said. "Tomorrow starts today."

He lifted the axe and rolled his shoulders, knowing the pain would come. "Every surviving life form," he grunted, "has had to realize this one inevitability." He wiped his face on one of Aydyn's linen squares and waved his hand before an imaginary class.

"Evolution and survival are based on any species' ability to adapt to its environment."

Another log split cleanly.

"I will adapt—and I will survive," he said.

Just let me kiss that blue-eyed woman again.

∞

Aydyn walked Donnye to his corral. Before releasing him, she scratched his silky forelock, and whispered, "You will have your mares, do not worry." She gazed towards the village and looked for Eric, praying she would not run into him.

Please, Goddess, show me the way to my desire.

She slipped through the gate and walked straight to her mother's hut. Cayri was busily attaching a bouquet of dry flowers and herbs to a new wooden crosspiece in the thatch door. Aydyn watched her mother operate the door, swinging it smoothly from open to closed, and back.

Cayri clapped her hands with joy and stepped back, admiring her new door and decoration. "How easy this is. I wonder we did not think of this ourselves." She eyed Aydyn and one brow lifted as she asked, "Did you enjoy the forest?"

"Aye, Mother, it was good for me to go." Aydyn tilted her head, examining the new door design. She pulled on the wooden handle and the door opened with ease. "Why does he do this?" she asked. "Does he not worry about changing his precious future?"

Cayri gave Aydyn a sharp look, but continued to adjust her flowers. "Have you seen him?"

Aydyn shuffled her feet. "No, and I am leaving again. I just wanted to return Donnye."

Cayri glanced at Aydyn over her shoulder. "What do you seek, daughter, that you do not already know?"

"The future," Aydyn blurted. "I wish to know my future, his future—our future." She leveled a gaze at Cayri. "I go to sleep on the hill."

Cayri's brows arched, and she placed a hand on Aydyn's arm. "You have such questions you cannot answer on your own? What are you thinking?"

"I would create my own fate, Mother, away from this life of duty. Is that not what you told me to do?"

"Is your duty really so difficult to see?" Cayri asked. She turned back to admiring her door. "Eric fights his destiny because he has trouble accepting that what will be has already happened." She looked back to pierce her daughter with a searching look, but said nothing further.

Aydyn dropped her shoulders. Her heart hammered in time with her racing thoughts, and she shielded herself from her mother's probing. "I seek a destiny for us—together, that is all." She lifted her gaze. "Tell me, does the prophecy say if he goes back?"

Cayri opened her door and Aydyn stepped inside. A small flame danced in a bronze lamp suspended from the ceiling, dispelling the gloom of dusk. She settled into a pile of furs on the hardwood floor and waited for her mother to speak. Cayri passed her a water skin and Aydyn wanted to scream at her mother to just answer the question. She accepted the bag and nodded her thanks with a carefully composed face.

"This detail you speak of," Cayri said, at last, "is not mentioned."

Aydyn exhaled with relief. "I thought as much, but I wanted to hear you say it." She closed her eyes and sent a silent prayer of thanks to the Goddess and the spring of wisdom.

Cayri reared back and gave Aydyn an astonished look. "You have seen the woman and the spring!"

Aydyn busied herself with the water skin, excitement making her heart and fingers tremble. She took small, slow sips, savoring the cool water—and the memory of her discovery. "The day we hunted," she said, "I followed Eric through Rowan's eyes. The crone appeared and offered him the spring, but he refused. I do not think he understood what she was offering."

She stared past her mother's searching look, into the distance of memory. "It was easy to find her again," she whispered, "once I decided, I had to know." She came back to her mother. "I have one more question. On the day Eric arrived, you said we could send him back, but you protested, saying he must stay to fulfill the prophecy. Tell me—will we have the power to send him back after the prophecy is complete and the stones are silenced?" She held her breath.

Cayri sat back with hooded eyes for long moments before answering. "Yes. A simple reversal is possible with the crystals alone."

Aydyn's heart opened and her thanks flowed to the Goddess and her mother. "You gave me the answer when you told me to look outside of this time and place."

Cayri grasped Aydyn's hand. "I love you, my daughter. I know this duty lies heavily across your shoulders, and I would do what I can to ease this transition for you." She cupped Aydyn's head and stroked the sleek hair. "Child, we are never called upon to serve beyond our ability. For you to find the woman and the spring is an omen of great strength. What drives you to seek the knowledge from the hill?" Cayri asked.

"To know if desire has a place in my life," Aydyn said. She glanced up, but her mother was suddenly busy rearranging the furs. "But what about my duty, Mother? I cannot shirk—"

"Of course not, but is it not possible they are one in the same— your duty and your desire?" Cayri asked.

The words made Aydyn sag with fatigue, weary as she was from trying to work out all the possibilities. She blinked and rubbed her palms against her eyes, moaning, "No."

Cayri rose and pulled Aydyn to her feet. "You are tired and in need of rest and hot water," she said. She sniffed and drew back with a wrinkled nose. "A great deal of hot water."

"I will bathe and stay the night," Aydyn said, "but I intend to leave before the sun rises." She stood and stretched, ready for that hot water. Her mother's words had opened a door for her. Now all she had to do was sleep upon the hill.

"You do not have to do this," Cayri chided. "All you need is here, right now. I would bid you to seek out Eric. Speak with him before you—"

"No, Mother, I will not speak with Eric. My head is clear for the first time since he arrived. I cannot think straight when he—" Heat flared deep in her hips and she felt the burn rise and flush her face. She dropped her gaze, "Eric confuses me. I do not need that right now."

"But he has—" Cayri started.

Aydyn held her hand up against her mother's protest. She shook her head, pleading, "Give me your blessing and I will be back in time for the next full moon."

Cayri looked ready to object, but Aydyn stood her ground. She bowed her head and remained with her fist over her heart, waiting.

"Then go with the Goddess," Cayri whispered. She hugged Aydyn and kissed her forehead.

Aydyn pushed the new door open and disappeared in the deepening twilight.

∞

Eric worked with the axe in the cool morning breeze. After three days of dedication to the mountain of logs, the axe was lighter and Eric made it hiss through the air. His biceps bulged, tight within his skin, and he wondered if it were possible to build muscle in so short a time.

What is happening to me?

He felt like a dynamo, something far beyond what he was when he arrived. Had the crystal-treated water he bathed in affected him? Or were there subatomic changes created by the high energy levels in the stones?

Or maybe—

A chill scooted across his neck and he turned to see Cayri watching him from the shade of a big oak tree. He planted the axe in the block and waved, calling, "Cayri." Walking towards her, he struggled to pull his tunic on over his sweated body.

"You are growing," Cayri said. She pointed to his shoulders

and Eric tugged the tunic into place. He grinned and waved at the log pile. "Finn keeps me busy earning my keep," he said. "Thank goodness you feed me well."

Cayri laughed and he relaxed, his brief sense of foreboding evaporating. "What can I do for you, Cayri?"

She turned and smiled. "Walk with me."

He fell into step, following her towards Stonehenge. "I spoke with Aydyn last night," she said casually.

His heart accelerated, but he maintained his cool. "Is she back now?"

"No, she has come and gone, but she will return by the next full moon."

Three weeks! Where has she gone?

His disappointment was a crushing expansion in his chest. He focused on the towering stones ahead, willing his heart to calm down.

They entered Stonehenge. The day promised to be warm, and the sun was stirring the mists through the giant stones. The energy pulled at him, and he watched the hairs rise up on his arm. The tingle flowed into his feet, then his fingers, and on up to the crown of his head.

It must be a battery for planetary energy.

They stepped through the massive trilithons, passing from sun to shadow. Rabbits scampered through the lush grass and bees followed in pursuit of flowers. Cayri reached the horizontal altar stone and sat. He joined her, surprised to feel heat in the stone so early in the day.

"Mother," Cayri said, waving to the earth before them. "She is filled with the promise of life. The sun is her lover, and his fire brings her the power to create the promise."

Eric felt a force emanate from the stone. "What I feel—this is Goddess energy, and these stones store her power, am I right?" He splayed his hand out against the stone and his flesh thrummed. "In my time, we have a device called a computer. The power symbol on this device is the same symbol you have here."

He traced it on the altar stone: a circle pierced by a short straight line. "When I realized the symbol pierced circle was also an ancient power symbol, I knew Stonehenge was an energy port in some way."

Cayri cocked her head and smiled. "The stones are part of what connects us to our home—our first Mother, just like the opening we all have here." She pointed to her abdomen.

"Our umbilical connection to the stars," he said.

A wormhole powered by Mother's terrestrial energy.

Cayri nodded in agreement. "The Druae have lived with the power of the Goddess, this energy as you call it, since a time considered old, even for us. The power, as were the Star Children, has long been both protector and benefactor. And yet the life of every Druae who walks these stones is pledged to their ultimate destruction. Only when we have fulfilled our contract with the Star Children by silencing the stones and disabling this energy are we then free to claim a new future. We will not fail in this, our destiny."

"Mankind of the future," he said, "does not have this blind faith and driving conviction to define and sustain his path, as you do. Instead, we have the freedom to choose—" He shrugged in weak defense. "This luxury—the acceptance of the lesser conviction in trade for the freedom to worship at the idol of choice, I think, has cost us more than we know."

"Then you can appreciate the difficulty Aydyn is facing," Cayri said. "She is inherently bound to duty that does not offer her a choice, and yet she yearns for—"

Eric's ears strained in the pause, knowing Cayri's words pulsed with hidden meaning.

"Aydyn seeks this freedom you speak of. She is enticed," Cayri said. She leaned back and watched him with a guarded gaze.

He had no idea what Cayri's words meant, but some response was required. The yawning precipice that came with the gold earrings suddenly appeared, challenging him anew as he teetered on a fine edge as sharp as any of Finn's blades.

A heart-sucking flare of alarm seized him. "Where has she gone?" he asked, afraid for Aydyn's wild heart. "What is she doing?"

"She has gone deep in the forest to a small hill of special oak trees. Ancient lore says one who sleeps within this sacred grove dreams of the future."

She eyed him with cool Druae blue. Gooseflesh raced along his arms, pressing him on toward comprehension—

"To dream on the hill requires a powerful will and a strong heart," Cayri said. "The dreamer sees a glimpse of the inevitable—a vision of that which we cannot alter. Only the strongest can bear the truth learned from their dreams."

Eric gazed through the great stones. Knowing the inevitable future was beyond his means, he didn't have the strength to witness what came beyond tomorrow. All the labor he was doing in Finn's woodpile was falsely noble, driven more by fear than courage.

Believe, cried his heart. *Believe in Aydyn. Believe in the power of the Goddess.*

He had seen a non-stop parade of fantastic events since he came here, events he would clearly define as miracles. But modern academia would sponge off these incredible episodes as phenomena of the senses and therefore suspect.

"Well, academia had never seen the heavens lit by a naked woman dipped in blue," he mumbled under his breath. "Miracles must have become the province of divinity when we forgot how to perform our own."

Aydyn, his beautiful, wild woman dared a great deal. He smiled and leaned back on the stone.

I hope I am a part of her dreams.

Chapter Nine

Aydyn stood before the sacred hill.

The ancient oaks were in a perfect circle, guarding the top of a small hill. Golden, late afternoon sunlight flowed over the crest, lighting the grove in warm invitation.

She was no fool; the most dangerous adventures often began with such an innocent disguise. Anticipation with a thread of fear raced down her spine and settled in her belly. "Why am I here?" she asked the wind. She spoke the words, knowing she could not deny this pursuit any more than she could stop breathing.

To know what will be.

She made her camp at the base of the hill and cleared a space to work. She prepared a small fire with cherry wood kindling, part of her private store of wood carefully harvested and blessed with enchanting spells. Water came from a nearby stream and filled two clay pots on the fire.

While the water heated, she arranged the items she would need on top of the hill: a fan of broom, herbs, flowers, a linen cover, and a giant bearskin.

The light in the oak grove faded to violet and she returned to the fire. She tied her hair back in a long braid before removing her clothes. Shivers skittered across her arms as she kneeled, reaching for a pot of slippery root cleansing paste blessed to protect travelers.

She brought the pot to her chest and bowed her head. "Be with me, Goddess. Guide and protect me across the barrier, and through the mists of time. Grant me the power to see that which will be, what can be, what has always been. I seek this knowledge in service to you."

She rubbed the rose-scented paste all over her body, straining to cover her back. The paste dried quickly and she rubbed it off with a dry cloth. "Purify this skin in your infinite fire," she chanted, "just as my heart is purified in the mists of infinite time." She dropped the cloth into the fire and a wave of rainbow sparks burst into the air.

Her skin took on a glow, tingling with the protection spell that now encased her. Next, she sprinkled herbs into her two boiling pots. One received eyebright, the other mugwort for a divination tea. Stirring the tea, she repeated her prayer. "Give me strength, lift my wings, bear me unto my dreams."

By now, the Goddess had arrived. Moonlight graced the hill crest with a white glow. Aydyn sat nude before the remnants of her sacred fire, sipping the tea, letting the liquid warm her naked body. The power of the drug flowed through her limbs, making her feel insubstantial, as though her flesh were nothing more than a mist.

Setting the tea aside, she took a deep, steadying breath, then dipped a cloth into the eyebright and dabbed the solution onto her eyelids. An explosion of light and color tore across her closed eyes. "Goddess," she gasped, as shivers snaked down her thighs. She exhaled slowly, then dipped the cloth and touched her eyes again, and again. The colors behind her eyes gave way to patterns spiraling into the infinite.

I am ready.

She poured the tea on her fire, dousing the flames. Slowly, she walked up the hill, whispering the ancient names. "Aradwyn, Gilean, Syraman, Paradyn." At the top of the hill, she bowed to each of the four directions. "Of fire, of earth, of water, of air, I ask to travel with your blessing."

She picked up the broom and swept the ground where she would sleep, purifying and protecting the area. She placed three Iris: one on the east boundary of her space, one on the north, and west. The flowers brought faith, wisdom, and valor. On the south boundary she placed a dried lily. She found this first lily of the season just prior to Eric's arrival; it added strength.

Next, she scattered swine snout, summer's bride, and goat weed on the ground before spreading out the great bearskin. She sat naked on the large pelt and crushed a handful of woodbine in her hand, rubbing this final flower of divination on her forehead. She kneeled, placing her forehead to the ground, drawing the power of Mother through her crown into her heart.

The connection began with a simple beat, deep below the

bearskin.

"Mother," she whispered. The power swelled up through her feet, knees and hands, joining in the center—until Mother's tone rang through her. Her heart moved as one with the Goddess.

Rising to her knees, she saw Taurus wink far above. She spread her arms open to her ancestral home, and cried, "Mother!"

To receive specific guidance, she must seed the mists of time with the emotions that drove her heart and defined her need. She let her head drop back and pictured Eric. A thrill for their unknown future whistled through her and filled her with hope.

She envisioned them together, surrounded by love and passion, then released this vision with her need to know their true path. A tiny, blue sparkle of light jumped from her chest, dancing free as a firefly to rise higher and higher, disappearing into the field of stars littering the sky.

Aydyn drew her hands back to her chest and bowed her head. "Thank you," she whispered, "for showing me what will be."

She lay down on the bearskin and drew the light cloth over her nakedness. The evening was warm and yet she shivered, digging deep into the fur. She would sleep with no fire or weapons, for the Goddess protected her in her journey. Strength alone must sustain her across the barrier and into the otherworld.

The night sky was brilliant with stars and a milky light pulsed deep in the farthest reaches of the heavens. The pulse grew, whispering her name, causing the hairs along her arms to lift. She resisted the urge to rub her prickled flesh, instead, opening her mind and her heart to the answers she sought.

The pulsing light sped across the mists of time in answer to her call. She sensed it rushing towards her, felt the familiar sensation of floating outside of time.

Her spirit swelled with an ancient power. Her faith, will and desire coalesced, feeding a point within her with a force that grew stronger and stronger until she exploded into a cloud of light. Her newly liberated particles reached for a joyous, heavenly reunion. She was vapor among the stars, and her soul ran free.

Light joined with light, and the mists of time and potential swirled around the bearskin. The cosmos receded into infinity, leaving only Aydyn's particles of emotion-fed light to fill the black, empty void. Time waited, without certainty, a sea of possibility.

She was light—and heat and passion. Her unquenchable longing searched the unknown, for the future that is cast in the stars.

She floated in another world, where dreams were more real than life. Eric's face appeared and instantly she knew he was her destiny, just as she was his. But only they could make their union as infinite as time.

Light pulsed with heat, and heat swelled with desire. The mist and the light danced and sparkled as Aydyn felt her essence reclaim her body. She smiled, her lips trembling with the intense pulses of her power. Warmth moved into her bones, making them liquid; her core throbbed with the unfulfilled need to be with him.

She called, "Eric." The vibration of his name sang from her lips in the siren's heart song.

The sparkling mist moved in a mad, pulsing dance. Tension gathered in her fingertips, her woman's core, and all along her spine as she waited. "Eric," she repeated, sending her power with the call, commanding. She closed her dream eyes and envisioned him close to her, felt his heat warming her.

She opened her eyes and he was there. The thrill of calling him surged through her as his energy joined hers. Brilliant lights showered them, igniting the mists of time in a rainbow of colors.

"Follow me," she whispered. She drew one finger to his lips. His energy thrummed in her heart and the warmth spread from her bones to her loins. Where they touched, tiny stars were born.

Anticipation flooded her belly with fireflies. She felt a weight at her earlobes, something heavy, like gold. She reached for him, lacing their hands together, and the power flowed between them in a delicious arc. Her contentment was a fierce new sensation.

He slid his hands down her arms, leaving a wake of gooseflesh. She shivered, lost between what was real and what was not. He rubbed the bumps away, pulling her closer until his breath fanned against her neck.

Her hair spilled loose and he inhaled, following the scent to her shoulder. Hovering, he held just himself close enough for her to feel his breath lightly caressing her, yet without actually touching her. She squirmed, whimpering with need. When he finally touched her, tears burst against her tightly scrunched eyelids, so great was her relief, so intense her joy.

Amongst the infinite stars, I have finally found you.

"I will be yours forever," she whispered.

"Aydyn," he murmured against her neck, sending a fresh wave of bumps along her arms. His hands slipped to her waist, pulling her against him.

She preened, giving him her neck. His breath was heavy against her skin as his lips claimed the sensitive junction of her neck and shoulder. She pressed back, liquid to her bones, pulled into a vortex of spinning oblivion. Her center was molten, swirling out to her fingertips in searching waves. Her hips moved against him, the message beyond words.

She needed to taste him, needed him to taste her. She moaned, a small sound of angst deep in her throat, but he was there with what she needed. He kissed her mouth, plunging deeply, branding her with his heat.

Slowly he scorched a trail with his lips, beginning with her neck and moving down. She undulated her hips with a primal beat, pressing, pulling, pressing— and her breath was a mad animal caught in her chest, fighting to escape.

Dear Goddess, *she prayed,* thank you.

Suddenly, his lovely torture stopped. She lifted her head, dragging her eyes to his face. He thrummed with a power that excited her with possibility, potential and—promise.

We will burn alive.

He held her gaze, the promise in his eyes foretelling heights of ecstasy until she trembled with expectation.

Come to me, my love, that we may be one.

The power kept building, going further, reaching deeper as she rode the vortex. The coiling tension tore through her core as the piercing sweetness caught and tossed her beyond the night sky to explode across the heavens.

∞

Wispy gray dawn slowly invaded the ancient oaks. Pale gold sunlight came quickly after, as if eager to bring the small hilltop into the light of day.

Aydyn lay on the bearskin, stroking the heavy fur. She remembered the day she brought the beast down with her bow, embedding three arrows in the bear's massive chest.

The clarity of that moment would live in her memory forever. The bear wanted to live. She could see that in his black eyes, along with his desire to tear her to pieces if he could only get his paws on her before he died.

But her arrows had proved stronger, her courage and will the mightier of the two. She faced him boldly, firing from the ground. When he finally gave his last breath, one great paw extended an arrow's length from her feet.

She pulled the fur into her face, inhaling the wild, earthy smell. "I will need all of my strength—and yours," she whispered. Tears of uncertainty, an unknown in her life until Eric arrived, stabbed at her eyelids. She pressed her palms to her eyes.

I am not strong enough …

She hugged the bearskin close, listening to the trees stir in the early morning breeze. A voice called her name from far away, an echo from her time between worlds, crying out—

Remember, Aydyn, remember.

"The power to call him to me," she whispered. She sat up and the skin fell away. Gold light spilled across her breasts, warming her heart, filling her mind with the vision of her and Eric melded together. Her body sang with the memory of a new force within her—a power born in the heavens and forged between two souls in their ultimate reunion.

"Together," she whispered.

The blessing of the Goddess encouraged her heart and mind, giving her strength. Suddenly, the future beckoned.

∞

Aydyn stood with her brother, watching Eric shoot his new bow.

Dear Goddess, this cannot be.

"He is not bad, ye know," Finn said. "He has been quite busy in yer absence. He has his own sword now—a bronze one—and he handles himself verra well for someone just starting."

Aydyn felt the heat of her brother's inquisitive eye upon her. She shrugged, nonchalant, even though her heart ran where her feet could not take her.

"What does he think he is doing?" she asked. "When I last saw him he said—"

A small coal of anger fired in her belly and she stamped the ground with her staff. Turning on her brother, she impaled him with a look of escalating disbelief. "You let him do this? You have been encouraging him to train for battle? You would let him think—?"

Her voice was rising, growing shrill even to her own ears, yet she could not stop. She was filled with dread, seeing in her mind, Eric with a sword thrust through his—

"You will stop right now, I will not allow this to go any further," she said, panting through straining nostrils. Her belly quivered and her mouth was so dry she could not lick her lips. She grabbed her brother's arm with fingers like talons. "He will get himself killed."

Finn drew his head back and brought his bushy brows together. "Aye, and so we all die, but—" He paused, staring at her as though she had gone mad. "Sis, what did ye see on the hill?" he asked. He glanced from her to Eric.

She fought to control her raging anger and grief. "Aye," she spit, avoiding his question. "But he will not die here, not while I am alive."

"He is a grown man with a mind of his own," Finn argued. "We made a contract. He tries hard and wants to learn—"

"I cannot allow—" she insisted.

Finn pulled his arm from her grip and shrugged. "Ye cannot stop him, I fear. He wants to stay."

Aydyn squeezed her eyes shut. *No*, her heart cried, *dear Goddess, you cannot ask this of me.* She placed her head against the staff and begged the wisdom to flood her heart. Her insides quaked, and she realized the final truth: she was not strong enough.

She watched Eric shoot; his powerful arm pulled the tight string back and she pursed her lips with ridiculous hope. The shot was decent, but he did not have the eye for accuracy at a distance. "How is his sword arm?" she asked, not wanting to know. She frowned as Eric reached for another arrow. "Is he?"

"Aye, he has put on a little meat," Finn said, his lips twitching with a grin he failed to suppress.

"And what do you know?" she asked. Her elbow found his ribs before he could move out of the way.

"Oww, Sis." He stepped back and rubbed at his side, even as his grin spread further.

Eric spotted them and waved on his way back from gathering his arrows. Aydyn could see he was coming their way. She turned to leave, not wanting to face him with Finn's enquiring mind so close at hand. As she slipped away, the sound of Finn's laughter chased her.

"He is not so big as the bear!" he shouted.

∞

Eric reached Finn just in time to see Aydyn disappear over the rise of a hill. He stopped to untie his wristband, counting long seconds while he gained control of his pounding heart. He didn't realize it was possible to miss someone so much.

He saw Finn give him a slanted look, and grunted in return. They stood side by side, gazing at the space Aydyn had just vacated.

"She's going to be difficult, I can see." Eric stated.

Finn snorted. "Ye can count on that, brother," he said. He gave Eric a grim nod and a sympathetic eye. "I think ye have some work before ye."

Eric brought his hand to his chin and nodded. "Yes, and I think it is time for a new contract," he said. He grinned with determination until Finn caught his tone and joined him.

"Exactly," Finn said.

"How would you go about this," Eric questioned, "if you were in my situation?"

"Well, ye need something to strengthen yer hold before beginning any new negotiation." He stared over the distant hill and asked, "Do ye have anything she wants?"

The answer drummed in Eric's heart, and he silently sent his thanks to the Goddess. He touched his leg where she had rubbed her scent on him the day they kissed. "I believe I do," he said.

∞

Eric woke, eager for the day. He had developed a plan last night, with Finn's advice, and was ready to begin Project Wild Woman. He rubbed his hands together with anticipation.

After collecting his morning bread, he walked across the village compound to Anna's. Out front, little Maisy played. "Good morning, Maisy," he called.

Maisy ran to him and raised her arms. When he picked her up, she gave him a juicy smack on the cheek.

"Is it time, Eric?" she asked.

He lifted his brows and made big eyes of surprise. Anna stepped out the door, and Maisy turned to her mother. "Mama, can I go with Eric? He needs my help." She giggled and stuck her thumb in her mouth.

"She has been staying by the door for two days, waiting for you,"

Anna said. She pulled gently on the hand Maisy held clamped in her mouth; the thumb emerged with a pop. Before Anna could scold her, Maisy buried the hand in her tunic and turned her face into Eric's neck.

Eric smiled, seeing mothers, children and thumbs had changed little in almost four thousand years. Drawing Maisy's chin up, he asked, "You know why I am here?" When she nodded solemnly, he glanced at Anna.

"She has something to show you," Anna said with a shrug. "That is all I know. Have her back before mid-meal, and see if you can keep that," she said, pulling on the thumb, "out of her mouth."

He set Maisy down and she grabbed his hand. "This way, Eric, this way."

They walked beyond the stone circle and the land dipped to the river Avon. Large oaks gave way to elm and ash, with undergrowth of hazel and holly. Maisy soon was off chasing butterflies and Eric was content to follow along and see what developed. They reached the top of a hill; the river glistened in the summer sun. Willow, poplar and rhododendron crowded the riverbank.

"Why are we here, Maisy?" he asked.

"Flowers, see the pretty flowers," she said around her thumb. She popped the wrinkled digit from her mouth and pointed.

Bluebells, purple cornflowers, and red clover bloomed in a riot of color and scent. Tiny white blossoms shaped like stars nestled between large, red, heart-shaped flowers. Maisy disappeared behind a huge bank of honeysuckle, calling, "Here, come see, come see."

He came around the fragrant honeysuckle. There was Maisy in the midst of a garden of wild roses; pale pink, vivid red, golden yellow, purest white. She pointed to a white bloom, crying, "Give her this one, this one."

He pulled out the small knife he had earned from Finn and cut the white rose free, trimming off the thorns. Kneeling before Maisy, he said, "This one is for you, because you are so pretty."

She took the flower and her face split with a smile. "I love these flowers," she said.

Eric gazed at the little girl and remembered the woman selling roses in the pub. He considered his simple plans to woo Aydyn juxtaposed against the manipulations of unknown forces commanding the universe. He shook his head.

Who am I to think I can play in this arena?

"Don't tell me what I can't do," he muttered, recalling his determination to drive his own destiny. His plan this morning was to ask Anna where she got the small flowers for her door, intending to create a posy of dried flowers for Aydyn.

Maisy's roses would be stunning.

She tugged at his hand. Pointing to her ears, she asked, "Do you still have the pretty gold?"

Before he could answer, her child's face pulled a solemn look and she crooked her finger, calling him closer. He kneeled down. She blinked, a wise old owl within a little girl's face. "You remember what the lady told us?" She nodded her head up and down, prompting him until he nodded with her.

"She said we should not be afraid, right?" he answered.

She nodded, and tugged on his tunic, drawing him closer. "Tell Aydyn, too," she whispered. "Even she gets scared sometimes."

He hugged her and whispered, "We all get scared sometimes." She pursed her lips and nodded, her eyes alive with childish wisdom. In his mind, her sweet face filled his page for "precious."

"I am not afraid," she boasted. "The Goddess showed me everything. She told me you would save us."

Eric was bereft of any wisdom that would match this child's. He had been so caught up with Aydyn, he forgot the part he was yet to play. The future loomed heavy and impossible before him. "What did the Goddess show you?" he asked.

Maisy sealed her lips around her thumb and shook her head. She pulled the thumb out long enough to blurt, "She told me not tell you," before reclaiming the thumb.

"Of course," he muttered. He eyed Little Miss Precious and considered an alternate page for her. She wiggled from his arms and took off after a low flying butterfly.

He watched her dance away with the certainty of youth. Such faith was beyond him, in spite of all he had learned. His heart clogged with trepidation and his shoulders sagged. He was doomed, just as Cedric said.

How do I change these events? I can't lose Aydyn, now that I have found her.

He paused, unmoving in the cool morning forest. He cocked his head and waited for a whispering voice to enlighten him, but there was no Goddess with him today. He gathered up his bouquet of roses and trailed after Maisy's skipping figure.

∞

Eric left the roses for Aydyn in a clay vase. The next day, there was a dried arrangement for her new door. On day three, he left a fork he had carved and polished to a perfect smooth finish.

Every day he glanced at her hut. While his presents disappeared daily, she studiously avoided him. Project Wild Woman, he thought, was proving to be even more difficult than he imagined. Without a store to shop in, he was fast running out of ideas for gifts.

When he saw Cayri trimming Aydyn's hair with a sharp knife, he smacked his forehead. He ran to Finn with his idea for the scissors. Their creation ended up costing him a dozen tales from the future, his only currency of barter with the smith.

They sat outside Finn's hut in the late afternoon heat. Eric examined the finished scissors. Finn had crafted bone and silver handles onto razor sharp iron blades decorated with a dancing vine.

"Finn, your work would command the highest price in the future," he said. "It is a shame you cannot—"

"Brother, I would love to see yer time," Finn said, rolling his eyes in ecstasy. "I would verra much like to see these men of music ye call Standing Stones—"

"Rolling Stones," Eric said, grinning.

"—and to travel to the heavens to walk upon distant worlds," Finn finished.

Eric pictured Finn at both events. From what he had seen so far, neither seemed implausible for the talented smith. He picked up a scrap of tanned hide and cut with the scissors. The blades slid together with a *sss* reminiscent of swordplay in a martial arts movie. "I will find these in the future," he said. "The handles are gone, but the iron and your distinctive workmanship survive."

"Do ye miss the future? All the wondrous things ye been telling me about?" Finn asked. "We must seem a verra simple people."

Eric shook his head. "No, I do not miss the future at all," he said.

He didn't bother boring Finn with his babblings of how beautiful the Druae people were, and how privileged and honored he was to know them. No, he thought, the only thing missing was the other half of his soul, and she wasn't talking.

"Ye have been a patient man," Finn said. He gave a sympathetic grin and rolled his eyes.

Eric nodded, used to these half spoken conversations with Finn. He stared at Aydyn's hut and the silent longing for her gnawed at him like a small animal.

To have come so far, to be so close, and yet—

"She is verra hard headed," Finn said. "Ye cannot force her. The man, from across the water—" He jutted his chin to the east. "He asked for her at Beltane and she said she did not want him. When he tried to force himself on her—"

He gazed off into memory before finishing, "She tossed him on his backside and nearly broke his sword arm in the doing. The poor man yelped like a kicked pup."

They continued to gaze silently at her door, two men pondering the mysteries of women. "I must talk to her," Eric said.

Finn eyed him like he had volunteered to eat fire, then his face brightened. "I have a cover of fox skins that Aydyn has always wanted. Because I respect ye for the hard work ye have to do, I will give ye the fox—"

Eric burst in knowing laughter. He waved his finger at Finn. "You just want—"

Finn's bright eyes filled his face. "Aye, brother, ye know me well. Tell me again about the boats and the people they pull behind on a rope." He stood and held his hand out, bent his legs and waved, duplicating Eric's illustration of water skiing.

Eric rubbed his face and begged the Goddess to forgive him these transgressions from the future. Finn had pestered him night and day for stories until he finally relented. At first he had difficulty deciding where to start, but once Finn developed a picture of Eric's time, his appetite to hear more became insatiable. He wanted to know everything.

Finn held his fist out in the Druae way of confirming a brief agreement. Eric returned the tap.

"Ye take the scissors and the fox cover to her tonight, after the full moon ceremony, and I bet she will talk to ye," Finn said. He pulled his bushy eyebrows together in skepticism, adding, "I just hope ye know what yer doing."

CHAPTER TEN

Aydyn waited in line with her people outside the stone circle, preparing to enter for the full moon ceremony. She was alone, unable to hide from Eric any longer. She watched as he chatted with Anna and Maisy, then stopped to share some joke with Neil and Ryan.

He has become one of us with ease.

Taliesin joined the small crowd of men and a spurt of raucous laughter erupted. He pulled Eric away and they chatted briefly before he clapped Eric on the back and walked off.

Eric turned abruptly, and looked straight into her gaze. He came towards her, confidence, strength and purpose filling his stride. The muscles of his shoulders bulged.

"Aydyn," he said.

She had nowhere to run. He was within arm's reach, and if she just raised her hand she could touch him. But she did not, because her heart was a coward.

"Eric," she answered, glancing down to hide her face. She calmed her breath and twined her fingers together to keep them from doing something foolish. Slowly, she brought her gaze up his body to his face. Forest green met Druae blue, and the connection slipped within her instantly, releasing a shock wave of need. She called on her warrior's skill and commanded her body to relax, when what she really wanted—

"I have missed you," he said, reaching out to her.

She could not avoid his touch. When he grabbed one of her hands, the wild animal in her chest stood still, the chaos in her mind fell silent, and all her doubts evaporated. With his warm touch, all her late night longings came rushing forth.

"I know," she breathed in a rush, afraid to say more. She closed her eyes and told the dream *no, not now*, but the memory of their passion flooded her limbs, drawn by his presence, his smell, his touch. She had avoided him for this very reason. But the Goddess had no mercy for those who served her. She could hide no more.

Your duty and your desire are one.

Her knees quaked and her mind cried, *not fair*. Both duty and desire could not exist together, for she did not have the strength to hold both sacred as each deserved.

He squeezed her hand and the heat from his touch ran up her arms, replacing the chill of fear with fire—

The fire of life, whispered the Goddess.

"Talk to me," he said, "please."

His pleading was too much. She eased her hand from his; there were too many knowing eyes about. She pulled back, saying, "Not now. Later. After the ceremony."

The corners of his eyes crinkled with pain and she looked away. The line of people started moving and she sprinted to Cayri's side. Clasping her mother's hand, she filed past the opening in the bank.

The Druae entered, always in an intricate dance, weaving through the great stones to stand within the bluestone circle. Everyone held hands, creating a continuous circle of power.

Aydyn hummed, calling the energy with every fiber of her being. The Goddess was a part of her. She gave her heart and soul to this power that connected her people to the stars—a connection that would soon be destroyed.

She weaved on her feet and opened her heart, deepening the call, needing to feel the power consume her. The hair along her arms lifted and her fingers tingled. Tiny sparks flared and jumped from person to person as the power came to all.

She saw Eric caught between Finn and Taliesin. His eyes glowed, alive with the power of the Goddess. The bluestones hummed as the Goddess embraced her children. Blue light came from nowhere and everywhere to fill the circle, building until the entire center of the stone circle was brilliant with light spreading up over their heads.

She could hear the power growing, and threw her head back. The vibration linked her heart, her bones, and her organs to everyone within the circle as they joined with the Goddess.

"Druae!" she shouted to the full moon that rose.

"Druae!" cried every voice.

"Druae, Druae, Druae," they shouted, raising their linked hands to the heavens.

The power pulsed through her as she brought her hands down. Still gripping her mother on one side and Delaney on the other, she looked around. Every face held star-lit eyes, and the brilliant light rose into the night sky.

She released her grip with Delany and her mother. This last phase was a moment of simple gratitude for the blessing of the Goddess. She brought clenched fists to her chest, and whispered, "Thank you, Goddess."

Those words rippled around the circle and the light began to fade. In a blink, the glow slipped from them and disappeared into the night sky.

Aydyn remained still, cradling the remnants of the Goddess within her. Her meeting with Eric awaited, and she hoarded the last traces of power, knowing she would need all her strength to face him.

Dear Goddess, help me.

Just as he had been snatched from his time and dropped here, she too, was being propelled along another such inevitable path.

One she desired and feared with equal passion.

One she could not escape.

∞

Fresh from bathing, he arrived at her hut bearing more gifts. Aydyn saw he carried a fox cover and her heart squeezed. She had never had this *attention* before.

Remember your duty, her mind whispered.

When she found the first roses by her door, her heart sang with joy. She saved everything he gave her in a cedar box. The fork was so special she refused to use it, wanting to treasure what he made for her until the end of her days.

"Aydyn?"

"Oh, uh—" she stuttered. She stepped aside and waved him in, inhaling his clean scent when he passed. He turned, presenting her with the fox fur, and her throat was too crowded to allow words. She watched his face. The hope shining in his eyes nearly undid her tight control.

"I have always admired this," she said, stroking the fine fur. "How did you—?"

"I have revealed countless secrets about life in the twenty-first century," he said. "Probably earning myself some fearful repercussions, wherever I end up—"

He shrugged, laughing lights in his eyes, and she noticed how he filled his tunic now. His muscles bulged, pulling at the cloth—and her thoughts. She tore her gaze away.

"I have something else," he said, reaching into the inner folds of the fox.

He pulled out a device she had never seen. She stared, giddy with the wonder of such amazing things he must know. "What does this do?" she asked.

"This is for cutting your hair, instead of using a knife." He pulled on a tuft of fox and sniped through it with ease. "Like this," he said. "And you want to cut only hair with them. We call them scissors."

She took the device and worked the blades, saying, "Scissors." She placed his presents on her bed and recalled the feel of fox fur against her legs in the dream. Her heart cried out with sweet remembrance, but inside she cringed, a coward.

No, not now.

"Why do you do this?" she asked abruptly. "The flowers and—this," she nodded to the fox. She stepped back, putting space between them, but he grabbed her hand. His fingers were warm and clean and she longed to feel them touching her.

"I have been trying to get your attention," he said, peeking into her face, smiling with encouragement.

Troubled laughter rolled painfully from her chest. "You think you need all of this to get my attention?"

"I need your attention," he said, "to do this." He pulled her to him before she could get away. One arm went around her shoulder and the heat of his touch dazed her into immobility. He released her hand and captured her chin, guiding her mouth.

She could have overpowered him, if she had any strength in her arms. She could have cried for help, if she had a voice. She could have run, if she stood on two legs.

But she had no such abilities. All that filled her was the unrelenting need for his touch. She let him tilt her head and moaned with relief when his mouth descended. Her sigh became his breath as she gave into him, unable to fight any longer.

Desire, her heart cried.

Softly, very softly his lips touched hers. Back and forth, he grazed her with the lightest touch as he inhaled and moaned with pleasure.

Her chest swelled with an unbearable sweetness and she pursed her lips, calling more from him in return for what she gave him now. She sighed when she tasted him, clean and fresh with mint. Her tongue teased, drawing him deeper.

His arm tightened around her back and she wrapped him in her embrace, thrusting her hips against his hardness. She moaned into his mouth when he grabbed her from behind and ground against her. Joy rumbled in his throat, and answering triumph sang in her belly. She rose up on her toes and tilted her hips so she could rub her womanhood on the rigid flesh poking from his tunic.

He tore his mouth from hers. "You are killing me," he said, breathing against her cheek.

Tears pricked her eyelids and she turned her face into his neck. "I know," she stammered, "I—"

He kissed the top of her head, whispering, "I have searched for you for so long." He pressed his mouth to her head, warming her scalp with his words. "Stop running from me."

You must decide, commanded the Goddess.

Aydyn squeezed her eyes tight and buried her face against his neck. "You do not know what you ask of me," she whispered. "Forgive me," she pleaded, as hot tears gathered in her eyes. "But I am not so strong after all."

"Shh," he whispered. "You are, my love. How can you not believe so? You are the Goddess."

He tried to peek into her face, but she hid. She could not look him in the eye and speak of her fear. Even after all her brave words on the hill, she, a warrior, was afraid.

"No, I am not strong enough, Eric," she insisted, shaking her head. She needed to make him understand before her grief and fear ate her alive. She saw him again in her mind's eye, impaled on a sword—and the first tear slipped down her cheek.

He stroked her head and asked, "Not strong enough for what, sweetheart?"

She heard the declaration in his words, the concern in his voice—and another tear rolled and dripped between them. A voice bearing impossible pain spoke the tortuous words for her as the drops continued to fall. "I am not strong enough to love you, Eric. I could not bear to love you, for loosing you would kill me," she cried.

Finally the words were out, she no longer carried them alone. She sagged against him as the waves of crippling fear shook her and unintelligible sobs rose from her chest. Tears covered her face and she blubbered like a child.

The pain poured from her heart and mind. She sobbed harder and the tears became a torrent. He sat on the bed and pulled her to him, rocking, and stoked her head, whispering little noises of comfort. He cooed and shushed her until her sobs finally settled into great gasping inhalations.

He continued to stroke her as her breath returned to normal. She wiped her face with a cloth and let him hold her, needing his warmth to fill her emptiness. Never had she cried so hard, not even when her father died. He held her close without any demands.

A malaise of exhaustion overwhelmed her and she wrapped her arms around him, closing her eyes and pushing her nose into his smell. Her eyelids felt gritty and swollen, but the bliss of oblivion moved in, taking her to the world beyond.

She slipped deep into the void. Grief and worry, her constant companions since his arrival, released her heart. The battle between duty and desire retired quietly to the corners of her mind. Life and death decisions bowed into the shadows. She dug into the covers, into his arms and safe, at last.

So deep was her release, so consuming her exhaustion, she never realized danger had come.

∞

"Kurgans," Balock spit. "We have to stop them. They grow bolder every year."

He watched his father survey the damage to their village. Dark smoke curled from a distant field, and livestock ran loose in all directions, hotly pursued by everyone able to run. Behind them, a woman wailed and rocked over a lifeless, bloodied body.

"Turonis," Balock said, "is dead." He grabbed his father's arm and hissed, "Several head of cattle, two horses, a hay field torched, and—" He looked back at Catalana; she held on to Turonis, her grief reduced to keening sobs. "—and one good man dead."

With each item of accounting, corded muscles in Jarech's jaws went tighter and tighter. But he remained silent.

"Each time, they take more, and more," Balock said. He squeezed his father's arm and waved to the scene before them. "Maybe tomorrow they will return to take what they have left tonight. Perhaps we should just give them our gold, the cattle, our women— and save all of this … noise."

Jarech jerked his arm loose and threatened Balock with a fist. Before he could speak, Rannor came running to where they stood. "They took the boy, the slave," he said between breaths.

Balock sneered, disgust clear in his voice. "Add a slave purchased with gold to our losses." He leaned over to whisper in his father's ear. "If we had the iron, we could reclaim what they have taken from us, and even the score."

"Do not press me," Jarech snarled under his breath. "What you propose is risky. We could loose everything."

Balock snorted, pointing. "We are losing everything now!" he shouted. He turned on his heel and left his father to stew. As he strode through the cries, the curses, and the chaos, he kept his smile well concealed.

∞

Deep in the netherworld, Aydyn ran, lost in a swirling gray mist. She couldn't find Eric; panic was wild in her chest. She tried to call out to him, but when her mouth opened, no sound came forth.

Frightened, she grabbed her bow, but the string fell away in pieces. Her staff! She reached for it, and the gold cap tumbled loose. She turned for her sword, but the hilt snapped away in her hand.

She heard him calling and ran towards his voice, but couldn't see him. "Eric!" she cried, and the sound echoed at her from all directions.

Finally, she saw him waving to her, beckoning.

Her relief was overwhelming and she raised her hand, but something moved in the mist behind him. Something she couldn't see, yet she was sick with fright. She lunged, fighting to fly but her legs were bound. She struggled, desperate to break free, when suddenly there was nothing solid beneath her feet. With a great gasp, she was falling, falling—

A hand closed over Aydyn's mouth and her eyes bolted open.

Danger!

Finn lifted a finger to his silent lips. She nodded. He eased his hand from her mouth and she turned her ears to the village. She closed her eyes and filled her mind with a map of the compound. As every sound came to her, she placed it on the map.

Little moved about in the remnants of dark night. Someone snored, another coughed. A dog chased a rabbit in his dreams.

In the distance, Donnye whinnied, soft and low—troubled.

She swung out of bed fully clothed, as Eric had left her. She grabbed her bow and quiver just as Finn stepped through her door. Following, she found Talie, Cayri and several Druae men ready at her door.

Aydyn touched her mother and motioned, moving her arms and pointing to her eyes.

Bring me Rowan.

Cayri nodded and slipped silently towards the falcon hutch.

Aydyn panted silently. Only moments ago she was fighting the dream, and she still reeled from the sickening lurch as she fell through the mist.

Cayri emerged quickly from the gray morning light, carrying Rowan on her wrist. Aydyn took the bird and removed the hood. Rowan trilled and fluttered her wings, rubbing her beak against Aydyn's temple. Aydyn touched her head to Rowan's and made the mind link. She pictured Donnye and the bird squawked and shook her feet, asking for her freedom. Aydyn released the leather ties and threw Rowan into the morning sky.

Without a word, the party moved to the animal pens. As Aydyn expected, Donnye was gone, along with their cattle.

Finn checked the ground surrounding the pens. "It is the Northmen," he said. He held up a short flint knife wrapped with the distinctive leather braid of their distant northern neighbors. "My guess is Wolfgar. He has had his eye on that stallion since you won him."

"They must have a ship on the river," Aydyn said. She turned away and sat with her head in her hands. She focused on Rowan's quick mind and called her to connect. She blinked, and opened with the bird's sight.

For several long moments she viewed the bird's world. She cocked her head, watching as the party of thieves separated. "Follow them," she said, and Rowan turned to give chase. Aydyn saw what she needed. "Find Donnye."

The bird climbed higher until life on the ground was reduced to tiny specks. She cast her head side to side until she found her prey.

"I see," Aydyn whispered. "Come home."

Aydyn blinked and shook her head. She pressed her palms into eyes still swollen from last night's crying. "They have taken the cattle south to a temporary corral. The rest of the party is loading Donnye on a boat at the river." She looked up. "Talie, take the men and go get the livestock, but leave me Neil, Doyle and Gilye."

The three men stepped aside with Aydyn and Finn. "They are in a clearing at the small river bend," she said. "Go silent and be careful. If it is Wolfgar, then this is a lark for him. He thinks everything is fair game—if he can steal it. Find them and watch until we arrive."

Talie nodded and the men turned and took off at a ground eating pace.

"Mother, I would like you to go with us," Aydyn said. "Those Northmen are all frightened of you and they will not expect you to be there. If we need you to put the eye of the Goddess on them, their god Thor will take to the water."

Cayri nodded and they gathered their weapons.

"What is happening?" Eric said. He stepped out from around the falcon hutch. His hair was smoothed back from his face and he rubbed his half wakened eyes. He glanced at their weapons. "Is there some trouble?"

"This is our business," Aydyn said. "We will be back soon." She turned her back on him, but he was in front of her before she took two steps.

"Are you going into danger?" he asked. He stood close and gave her no room. The rest of her party stepped back, leaving her to talk to him.

"Donnye has run off," she said. "You are not needed." She stared at the base of his throat, unwilling to turn her face up to him at this range.

He touched the tip of her bow over her shoulder. "You will not leave me here."

"I will leave you here," she said softly, "for you will be in my way."

"You cannot stop me," he answered.

"You cannot keep up," she challenged.

"Don't tell me what I cannot do," he warned.

She stepped back and smiled sweetly. Unwilling to waste more time arguing with him, she said, "Finn, he is in your care." Without another word, she turned on her heel and left at a brisk pace.

They reached the river before the thieves could push off. Crouching in the underbrush with Finn and the others at her back, she was surprised to see Eric had indeed, kept up. She caught Finn's eye and motioned to Eric. Finn nodded and moved to his side.

A boat big enough to hold Donnye and the cattle rode the shore. On deck, Wolfgar stood with Donnye as if without a care.

Aydyn shook her head. "Cayri, stay back in case I need you to create a diversion. Neil, take Doyle and Gilye. Find a position and cover every man. If you see us in trouble, shoot."

Finn crouched at Eric's side as Aydyn pointed at him. "Keep him safe." Eric opened his mouth, but she turned her back on him and stepped out from the brush.

On the deck of the boat, Wolfgar tied Donnye to a beam. The horse caught her scent and whinnied. He sidestepped and tossed his head, rolling his eyes to find her. She notched an arrow and pulled the bow tight. "That is a nice horse you have there," she called out.

Wolfgar looked up, surprising her with a smile of greeting.

"Took you long enough to get here, Aydyn," he called.

She leveled her arrow at him and walked casually to within an easy shot of his chest. "Wolfgar, what are you doing?" she called down the shaft of her arrow.

"I am stealing your horse. What does it look like?" He motioned to one of his men on the bank who held a rope.

"Your man does not want to let go of that rope," she said calmly. "He will sprout Druae iron if he does."

Wolfgar grinned and walked to the edge of the deck, his hands planted on his hips. For the first time, she felt a shiver of concern.

"A curious situation, Aydyn. You have aim on me," he said. "And I have aim on you." He motioned to men hidden high in the trees, each with arrows drawn against them, including Eric.

She paused less than a heartbeat. Even though Wolfgar's position was not so strong as he thought, she could not risk Eric. He was the prophecy.

She lowered her bow and grinned casually, mimicking Wolfgar. She sauntered to the bank, and called to him, laughing. "You are a funny man, Wolfgar." She stood relaxed with her bow and arrow in one hand, her other hand on her cocked hip. "You saw me shoot that day," she tossed out. "You should worry that I make yours a belly shot."

The words were delivered with absolute certainty while she leveled her bored gaze on him. Her eye pinned him like a rat on a spit until she felt the doubt flicker though his mind. "What do you want, Wolfgar? Do you want to die a long, pain-filled death on this beautiful day, or is there something else you seek?"

He squinted and shifted foot to foot.

She relaxed her stance and lowered her loosely cocked bow.

He pointed to the stallion. "I would like his seed in my herd."

Aydyn held back a sigh of relief. "You raise fine sheep up there in the cold," she countered. "I like the quality of wool I see you wear at Beltane."

He stepped to the rail and leaned out. "I could bring you ewes with lambs in the spring."

She responded with, "I will trade you mares with his seed, ready to deliver."

Wolfgar rubbed his chin. "Well now, that sounds like a nice trade," he said.

Aydyn laughed and shook her head. "If you wanted the stallion's seed, why not ask?"

He shrugged, flashing white teeth. "Loryn told me to go make trouble—somewhere else. She has one of those Druae staffs, you know." He smiled with good nature and rubbed his forehead.

"Yes, I know. I helped her find the seasoned wood. Tell my Druae cousin we miss her," she said. "Now take your men down and give me my horse."

Wolfgar laughed and called for a second shore rope. The boat was pulled parallel to the shore, and Donnye pranced across a loading plank.

"Would you have belly shot me?" he chided.

"Would you have stolen my horse?" she asked. "And what about my cattle?"

"They are down river. Tell Torc I have won the bet, and to give you back the cattle. I will gather my men and go up river for someone else's cattle," he laughed.

She held Donnye as his men shinnied down from the trees. "What bet did you win?"

"Torc said you would kill me first, then take back your horse. I told him, 'Not Aydyn, she is too smart. She will find a way to win, and see a profit.'" He waved as his men pushed the boat off the bank and clambered aboard.

"Go with the Goddess," Aydyn called. "And stay out of my cow pens."

"See you in the spring," he shouted through cupped hands.

Finn, Cayri, and Eric came out from their hiding places and gathered around Aydyn and Donnye.

"Well, Sis, ye did a fine thing there—" Finn said.

"Go find Talie and help them bring back the cattle," Aydyn said, cutting him off. She jumped onto Donnye's back, avoiding Eric, who tried to capture her attention. Without another word, she wheeled the horse around and left them to stare at her back.

She rode towards the village, veered north and turned into the forest. Once Donnye reached the cool interior under the canopy, she let him pick his own way.

She hugged her arms to her body, desperate to hang onto something. Each day, her decisions were getting harder to make.

Unable to bear the thought of all she was about to lose, her shoulders slumped and she let her arms hang lifeless, giving up her fight. Opening her heart, she willed the wisdom of the Goddess to give her relief.

She bobbed on Donnye as he wandered with his nose buried in lush grass. Father Sun warmed the top of her head, and the soft breath of the Goddess stirred the leaves in the trees. The life and vitality of the forest surrounded her, protecting her, nurturing, even as it demanded so much.

The dream, her body cried. She and Eric burning in a blaze of destiny and desire.

The future, her mind warred. Her people and their home. Would Eric be their salvation? What would happen to them?

The desire, her heart sang. What was she willing to do to see the dream come true? Would she let that slip away because she was not strong enough?

Your duty, reminded the Goddess. *Always see your duty, and all will be well.*

Her heart surged with these wild thoughts. She moaned and rolled her head, irresistibly drawn to her most difficult path. And the most thrilling.

She could not face the turmoil any longer, could not deny her heart and keep living. "Argh," she cried, scrubbing her face. Was there truly a way to see both her duty and her desire honored?

If she were not brave enough to try, not strong enough to risk everything—then there would be no reason to live.

So there must be a way. Hope, impossible hope, teased without reason. *Maybe*, she thought, *between the two of them ...*

A smile came slowly to her lips as the giddy thrill curled in her womb and spread through her body. She shifted on Donnye's back, feeling warmth reach between her legs, stirring a more primal heat.

"So be it," she whispered, relinquishing her fight. Intense relief flooded her being in immediate answer.

A new power born of determination surged through her. She cocked her head, taking measure of the force, allowing excitement to sing through her body. Gathering Donnye's reins, she pulled his head up. "Come on, big boy," she said, turning him towards the village. "Our destiny awaits—with or without us."

She laughed and tapped Donnye's flanks, urging him home.

CHAPTER ELEVEN

Aydyn lay back and dug her toes into the warm sand, pleased with her world. Sun reflected off the glittering ocean and warmed her face, arms and legs, matching the warmth that filled her heart.

She sat up and watched as Maisy and the other children ran down the beach, checking the shallow pans set out to collect salt. They darted from pan to pan, squealing when they found one filled with the powdery salt. After four days, their little bare legs were as brown as nuts.

Next to her, Eric lay in the sand. She gazed at him, shading her face with her free hand.

I will hold these golden days with him forever in my mind.

An easy peace had developed between them since her return after the incident with Wolfgar, in spite of the simmering desire that dogged their every moment.

The pain of being so close and yet apart was a luxury she intended to prolong for as long as possible. She knew the dream awaited them in the future, and until then, she would savor every moment, planning to consume him one tiny nibble at a time up to that glorious moment.

For she did not know what would come afterwards.

"This is a very popular activity in my time," he said. He held her hand, captured in the sand between them.

"Collecting salt?" she asked.

His hand snatched at her, jerking her down to lie on top of him. "No, silly woman—*this*. Lying on the beach with a beautiful—"

He tickled her ear with his lips and she wrapped her arms around him. Rolling, she pulled him on top of her, hip to hip. He moved his lips against her neck and she sighed with utter contentment.

"—impossible, stubborn ..." he added.

"I am not stubborn," she defended as she nipped at his neck with her teeth. She could feel him growing hard, probing her belly through her light tunic.

This is my real power.

She pressed her hips against him in return and sucked his neck, licking the salt from his skin. His sun-warmed flesh rippled with a rash of bumps.

"I am not impossible—" she whispered. "In fact," she said as she reached down to grasp his hardness, "I am really quite sweet."

His glittering green eyes captured her. She met his gaze, nose to nose, and their tightly controlled breath fanned each other's face. "Sweet, my ass—" he growled as he brought his lips to hers in a crushing kiss.

She let him plunder her mouth and lay his claim. She brought her hands to his head and held him, aiding him while she undulated her hips into him. Their tongues dueled back and forth, demanding and delivering until they broke for air.

They lay panting, cheek-to-cheek. She chuckled and tried to get her elbow into him. He rolled aside and danced his fingers across her ribs.

"No," she cried, backpedaling through the sand to get away from him. "You are not fair."

"And you," he said, waving a threatening finger in her face, "—are not sweet." He stood up and brushed the sand from his bare legs. "Unlike you, I am not a princess. I cannot lay about all day."

"What is so important—"

He silenced her with a kiss from his finger to her lips. "Nothing is more important than you, my love. And to that end, I have a surprise."

He pulled her to her feet. Plucking a small yellow flower that grew in the brush behind them, he presented it with a bow. "Will you meet me for dinner this evening, beautiful lady?" he asked.

Butterflies filled her belly when he talked like this. She imagined it would be this way if they were in his time. "We are not eating with the others?" she said, waving to their camp just off the sand.

He swept her close, his arm pulling her tight. Their limbs mingled from ankle to shoulder and she sniffed his sun-warmed scent. As his smell always affected her, her knees wobbled. She leaned into him as he nuzzled her neck.

"Meet me here, just before sunset," he whispered, sliding his tongue across her skin. She rubbed her breasts into his chest, needing to feel his warm hands touching her.

"Nuh uh," he chided. He released her, backing away, and shook his head. "Later," he said with a wink.

He waved his finger at her and motioned for her to turn around. "You have done enough to me for now; go tend your duty." He gave her a small push and she pouted at him over her shoulder. She pushed her rear at him and licked her top lip, lowering her eyelids and drawing up her shoulder.

His immediate laughter was easy and bright. He threw his head back, giving her the opportunity to admire the strong brown neck above his expanded shoulders. His vitality seemed to have exploded since he arrived, and she hoped she was a part of that powerful transformation.

He crossed his fingers in the sign he made and backed away from her, laughing and wiping at the tears in his eyes.

"Sunset," he called.

∞

Aydyn bathed and put on a pale green tunic and a short skirt she had decorated with shells gathered since they arrived at the shore. Her skin was brown from the sun and her hair glistened from a fresh water wash and a squeeze of lemon.

She walked out to the sand where he said to meet him, but the shore was deserted. She frowned and looked around. A small pile of rose petals began a trail leading over the dune. She scooped up a handful of the fragrant leaves and followed.

At the crest of the dune she saw he had been busy. A fire burned and the smell of something cooking caused her mouth to water. Behind the fire pit, a screen made of poles and large sheets of fabric provided privacy. A blanket and skins were spread about for seating with a view of the setting sun.

The petals led right to the edge of the blanket.

As she came closer, she saw oil lamps burning at the four corners. More flower petals were tossed across the fur pelts. Beside the fire, a low table was set with another candle, Eric's linen napkins, and more flowers.

He stepped out from behind the screen and her heart slowed, promising to stop. She held her breath and burned this image into her mind, to hold the scene dear forever, no matter what happened.

"There you are," he said. His teeth glowed white against his tanned face, and mystery flitted through his eyes. He crossed between the fire and the blanket to take her hand before she could ask why he was so pleased. With the touch of his warm skin against hers, all thoughts of flowers and food disappeared, replaced by her one need, as yet unsated in this world.

Eric.

His eyes promised more mystery, and butterflies filled her stomach. He acted and thought differently than any man of her time. She never knew what to expect, except when they touched.

He pulled her into an embrace, trapping her hand between them. His lips came down to graze her lightly. Her heartbeat warmed with his nearness and she licked her lips with anticipation. "What is all this?" she asked. She waved her hand at his preparations.

"Just man in the age old pursuit of—" He paused and twitched his eyebrows with feigned malice, thrusting against her in mute suggestion. He finished, saying, "—true love."

"Is this what you do for women of your time?" she asked. It was all so magical.

Let him say no, that he has only done this for me.

He held her close and the intensity of his gaze boded a lifetime of heat. "I have *never* done this for anyone," he answered. His nearness and his scent made her head spin. When his breath touched her face, she longed to throw herself down and beg him to take her to that explosion in the heavens …

But she could not. Not yet, for these moments were so precious to her. She fought the sense of impending separation that threatened to swamp her, instead letting her love fire the raging desire and connection she felt with this man. As long as the dream remained unfulfilled, he was here with her, along with this bittersweet anticipation of their destiny.

"Dance with me," he commanded, soft against her neck.

Before she could ask what that meant, he rocked her gently and hummed against her skin, pulling her with him as he took small steps. His breath sent shivers across her shoulders.

He sang in her ear.

She picked up the rhythm of his movement and followed along, swaying in time with his tune, even though she did not understand the meaning.

"Sonny and Cher," he said. "There are many songs just about love. In my time, love is very important." He nibbled her neck and she held him close, lost in his magical spell.

Would they have a future like this in his time?

He stepped back, inviting her into the world he had prepared. "Are you hungry?" he asked. He led her to the table and she sank to the skins. She saw wooden plates and small bowls filled with a yellow liquid.

"What is this?" she asked, sniffing. "It smells delicious." She tapped her finger in the bowl and tasted the liquid when he encouraged her.

"Butter," he said, sitting beside her. "It's made from milk."

"Ah, so that is why you have been haunting my cow pens," she said. "I did not know ye were so interested in food."

He leveled a hot gaze, making her tingle all over. "I am interested in you," he said. He spotted the rippled flesh along her arms and rubbed her for warmth. Leaning close, he sang again in a whisper, "My heart will remember you." He caught her eye, singing more, "Will your heart remember me …"

The brief tune was haunting beyond anything she had ever heard. All songs she knew were either long tales about ancestors, or bawdy words men sang.

Nothing she had ever heard touched her heart like these simple words. While his unspoken message fanned the flames of her fear, she refused to allow her dread to spoil one moment. "My heart will remember you," she returned, singing softly. "Will your heart remember me?"

Suddenly, tears filled his eyes and he turned away, swiping at his face. He stood and busied about, collecting their meal. Using metal tongs and then heavy pads, he removed a large clay pot from the fire. "Careful," he said, setting the pot down in the sand.

"What have you prepared?" she asked. She peeked as he lifted the lid. "I did not know you—"

"I don't, but you seem to inspire me," he said softly. "I hope you like crab," he said. "They are a delicacy in my time."

He placed one on her plate, showing her how to use the little mallet to break open the shell. A second pot came from the fire, this one filled with bread. Soon, they had the crabs opened and were feeding each other pieces of the succulent meat dripping with butter.

She sat back and moaned. "No more, please. I am so full." She sipped lightly from a mug of brew, not wanting to lose a single precious moment. He brought out wet cloths to clean their fingers and she sighed with contentment.

"Do men take care of their women like this in your future?" she asked.

"Some do," he said. "But the way I've heard women complain, I guess it is not common enough." He grinned and kissed her fingertips. "I wanted to say, you were very good the other day with Wolfgar. You have keen negotiating skills under fire."

She shrugged. "There were too many arrows ready to fly. I could not risk your life any further."

He massaged the fingers of first one hand and then the other. "I am sorry to be a problem," he said. "But I had to come with you. I couldn't let you out of my sight. If—"

"Our life here is dangerous, Eric—every day. You have not seen when there is no home, to be cast from all that you love—" She shifted her gaze, not wanting him to see the pain in her eyes. "Is there no such danger in your time?"

"In many places, yes. But for most, life is possible without the violence I expect you face. But life is always dangerous, no matter where or when you live."

"I think your life," she protested, "is a lot safer than ours. It must be so, if you have time to do all of this." She swept her hand around. "No man I know would even imagine this."

She leaned forward to press her point. "Do you carry a weapon? A staff or some length of blade? What weapon do you keep at your side in the future?"

He squirmed, but offered her no answer.

She regretted giving him this discomfort, but she had to make him realize the difference. "In your time, how old do you live?" she asked. "How many long days will you expect to see?"

"That is not a fair comparison, you—" he said.

"How long?"

He pursed his lips and gave her a hard look. "I believe the oldest person on the planet is one hundred fourteen. But the average life span for someone of my health and lifestyle—I should live into my eighties or better."

When he spread all his fingers and pulsed his hands several times, she followed, nodding. "The Druae are known for our good health and long lives. But, by my reckoning, you have close to two of our lifetimes." She looked away and clamped her lips together, fighting the urge to scream that this was not fair.

Two lifetimes of loving.

"If I am not injured," she said, "my life is almost half over—if I am lucky." She looked away and swallowed her pain. *Thank the Goddess,* she thought, *that we see many adventures.*

"But I am lucky," she blurted. She grabbed his hand, not daring to look at his face for fear of opening the gate to her heart and the flood of tears she barely held in check. "I am lucky," she whispered, "for the Goddess has brought you to me."

She pressed his hand to her face and closed her eyes. His warm and beautiful fingers were finally hers to hold. She inhaled the scent of butter and ocean from his skin, and murmured, "Whatever happens—" and sang the beautiful words. "My heart will remember you."

She opened her eyes and the tears began to fall, heedless of her warrior's commands. She closed them in a vain attempt to dam the flood. She held back the sobs, putting her heart into her words. "If you found me in your time, in another life by another name, would you love me again?"

He opened his hand to cup her face, and her tears fell through his fingers like rain. He stroked her head. "Love you again? Dear one, you are my heart, my love, my soul. Without you, there is no life."

His words were a salve to her aching, troubled heart. She cuddled closer to his chest, wishing to draw him into her so that they would always be one.

He held her, cradling her head to his shoulder. "When I first arrived, I thought the power of the stones brought me here. Now I know that it was my love for you, answering the call of your heart song, which drew me through time."

Lifting her face, he gently wiped the tears from her cheeks. "Sweetheart, I have been searching for you ever since the day I was born. There has never been anyone else for me. I have been waiting for you."

He covered her face with soft kisses, drawing her attention from the pain in her heart to his soothing touch. His caress, the gentle lips against her eyelids, her temple, the end of her nose.

Fire, he always brought her fire, and her need for him was a coal longing to be a flame. She also needed his strength, his love, his hope from the future. And she needed him now—for she did not know how long they would have. She wrapped her arms around him and drew on his lips, kissing him deeply.

He broke the kiss and slanted his lips across her cheek. "Marry me, Aydyn. Be my wife, my partner, my lover. Be my woman, the Goddess of my dreams—for what time we have, whatever time we are in."

She leaned her head against his shoulder, dazed by his words and the languor that gripped her body. "I—I do not know. I am free to chose a mate if I desire. But I am devoted to the Goddess, and there is still my duty."

He tilted her head back and kissed along her jaw and down her shoulder, fanning the coals. When he sucked at the sensitive place on her neck, the first flame flickered to life.

"Would you have me?" he breathed into her throat. The fingers of one hand slid beneath her tunic and massaged her back in warm circles. He made her feel fluid, as liquid as the delicious butter.

His hand slid over her ribs and came up to grasp one breast, massaging the round flesh. His warm fingers were so wonderful against her skin. He dipped his head and placed his mouth over her peak, breathing hotly through the tunic. She moaned and arched her back, wishing he would pull the garment out of the way.

He lifted his mouth from her breast, and called softly, "Aydyn?"

She looked at him through hooded eyes, lost in a swirling world of desire. She reached for him and stroked, needing to feel the power—

He grabbed her hand, stopping her. She pulled her gaze to his piercing eyes, and chills swept through her bones. He demanded an answer.

Time will move forward, with or without me.

Dear Goddess, give me the strength, she pleaded. She licked her lips, and said the only possible words. "I will have you, Eric Beck."

A fierce blaze of joy flashed across his face. He pressed her back against the furs and mischief stirred in his eyes. She watched, and her heart began a rapid dance as he tugged at the laces tying her tunic.

Seeing him fumble, she grinned and swallowed her laughter. Because she dearly wanted to feel him touch her bare skin, she took over the job. "Is there something in here you want," she asked. She batted her lashes, teasing him so he would not see her trembling fingers.

He answered her simply. "Yes."

When she had the laces open and her breasts as exposed as the garment would allow, he rose up on his knees and reached for her skirt. Her heart pounded at her ribs as he lifted the brief garment towards her hips.

"I have something I wish to give you," he whispered. "Consider this a promise." He rubbed his cheek into her belly button, his expression clearly honoring her body. "You are so beautiful," he murmured.

He lifted the skirt and pushed aside her loincloth until her womanhood was exposed. She slowly waved her hips, calling him closer. He looked up the length of her body, his eyes again filled with the promise of delights she would live for, and die for.

"I give you this," he said, his voice a command.

Gently, he edged her legs apart with his knee and straddled one leg, putting his bare knee against her moist opening. As soon as he touched her, she moaned and pressed against him. He growled and crushed her with a kiss, plunging deep, bruising her lips against her teeth.

He covered her jaw with kisses, then came back up and feathered her bruised lips with gentle nips and soft whispers. From there, he placed a trail of scorching kisses across her throat and over her collarbone, down to finally take one straining nipple into his mouth.

She cried out. Grabbing his hips, she raised hers, silently begging. He stroked her calf, massaging, reaching her thigh so that she pressed her legs open further until—

His finger stroked her ready opening.

"Ahh, dear Goddess, yes." She sobbed and shivered as he moved against her, opening her, spreading her moisture. Her knees collapsed outward and she moaned, calling him to come deeper.

A heaven of unbearable heat and need swirled around her. She writhed against his finger as he pierced her wet folds, gliding up and down. "Yes," she breathed again as his fingers entered, finally filling her.

"Eric," she called, lost and floating, yet tight, tight enough to—

"I'm here," he whispered. His mouth left her breast and she whimpered. The fingers withdrew and she opened her eyes.

"Look at me," he said.

She focused on him and rubbed against him in mute answer. His fingers slid across her sensitive nub and she sobbed with pleasure.

His voice deepened as he said, "I give you the greatest gift a man can give a woman." He dropped his head to kiss her, ever so gently as his finger rubbed her lightly. She took his kiss, greedily sucking on his tongue, pulling him into her.

Take me. Take me to the heavens, my love.

The piercing sensation that rose from his circling finger was fast taking her home. "Eric," she moaned into his mouth. She could not get him close enough.

His fingers stroked and circled her, then dove within. She pressed her hips, begging him to guide her to the fiery path of completion.

She clenched with the beginning of her release. Every part of her body seemed to open and expand, then contract again, and again. She tensed, coiling tighter and tighter, feeling the sweetness reach for her. She pressed against his hand, more insistent, shifting so that he touched her just so.

She was spinning round and round, drawn deeper and deeper into a swirling vortex of exquisite sensation. He rubbed, faster and faster, then thrust a finger into her, pushing, filling her. He returned to her nub and picked up the pace, circling, rubbing, sending her—

The fire caught and she thrust her hips. Her muscles clenched as she ground against him, taking the power all the way to her crown. She hit her peak and screamed into his mouth as wave after wave of piercing ecstasy consumed her in waves.

She pulled her mouth from his kiss and gasped, her lungs drained. Tears of joy poured down her face, running into her hair. Her womanhood throbbed in final spasms against his hand.

"Easy," he whispered, kissing her cheeks, her eyelids, her forehead. Lastly, he licked the tears that poured down her temples, murmuring his love against her skin. He straightened her skirt and tunic before wrapping her with his arms.

She curled into a ball and he wrapped around her, warming her back. His arm came over her ribs, and she pulled him tight against her. Gradually, her heaving breaths returned to normal.

What he just did to pleasure her was not unknown; the Druae were a free spirited and lusty people. All young girls had their maidenheads pierced when their link with the moon began to insure their enjoyment without pain.

But dear Goddess, she thought, *I did not know life would be every bit as sweet as the dream.*

She smiled and kissed his hand that bore her scent. A sigh of contentment came all the way from her feet and she stretched, pressing her rump into him.

She would not think of the future, of duty, of her people. She would join with this man, and nothing would stop her.

∞

Jarech pulled the Druae iron from its sheath, admiring the razor sharp edge glittering in moonlight. "This will be a surprise," he said. He and Balock, with their men, crouched, hidden in the brush that lined their pasture, waiting for the Kurgan raiders to return.

"They have nothing to fear from us, Father. That is why they linger to rob us dry," Balock whispered. He spit his disgust into the dirt, eyeing his father and the Druae blade.

"Let them fear this," Jarech hissed. "They have taken too much." Over one third of their livestock had been slowly pilfered during these late night raids. "Kurgans," Jarech growled. He spit, adding his contribution. "They will not take another head of our livestock across the river." He raised the blade and bared his teeth. "They will not expect us—or this."

They sank down, waiting as the moon passed across their heads and dipped behind the trees. Thick darkness lay heavy as the late night grew still.

Jarech blinked and rubbed his straining eyes. He had been staring in the dark at the shifting herd until shape no longer had meaning. Since the moon fell behind them, starlight and darkness merged to create phantasms in the night.

A twig broke just in front of him and his heart thudded at the surprise. He had not heard a sound, yet Kurgans loomed in the dark within blade reach.

"Argh," he cried, standing. He thrust the Druae blade at the nearest man, who blocked the strike with a small shield.

Jarech's iron easily pierced the shield and he felt the blade glance off the man's ribs. The wounded Kurgan let go of his pierced shield and stepped back, bringing down his sword. Jarech rushed him, using the discarded shield to hinder the man's strike.

The Kurgan's blade glanced off the shield, leaving an opening for Jarech to bring the Druae iron up under the Kurgan's sword arm. The iron blade cleaved through the Kurgan leather armor and into the shoulder joint with ease. The man fell, mortally wounded.

At Jarech's first cry, the quiet night erupted with the screams of twenty of his men in a chaotic melee of unsheathed blades, heaving curses and crashing cattle.

The surprised Kurgans were overwhelmed and retreated quickly, leaving behind two dead.

"Bring me a light," Jarech commanded. Balock lit a torch and they stared at the two bodies. One had an arrow in the back, and the other was Jarech's kill.

"The blade went through him as if he were no more than a piece of fruit," Jarech said. He wiped the blade on the Kurgan's trouser leg and held the iron edge to the torchlight. His men gathered, seeing the Druae blade for the first time. Jarech grinned, ignoring their whispers and superstitious signs.

"Balock, you are right," he said. "There is no defense against the new metal." Jarech showed the blade to his men. They backed away, none daring to touch the magical iron.

"Fools," Jarech hissed. He held the blade high and proclaimed, "I bear the weapon without harm." The men shuffled their feet and edged closer, muttering hesitant praise over Jarech's prowess in battle.

Balock knelt over the bodies, inspecting the dead Kurgans. "You will need more of that good iron," he called out. He sliced a gold embroidered patch from the leather breastplate of his father's kill. "This one is a member of the royal family."

The men ceased their praise, mouths slapping shut, and stepped away from the Druae blade. Jarech took the gold patch and stared at the body with the neatly severed arm. He swallowed and nodded.

What is done cannot be changed.

He shrugged, seeing Balock watched him. He threw the patch down. "Leave the bodies here. The Kurgans will come for back for them before sunrise."

∞

The Druae party returned from the shore with enough salt to see them through harvest and the winter months. Maisy and the children skipped into the village, blonde streaks in their hair and brown legs flashing.

Now that she was ready, Aydyn rode the fire of awakened passion. She could not get enough of Eric's scent, his voice, the feel of his skin, his flesh touching hers.

"You look like a cat with a mouthful of bird," Eric said. He tugged at her hand and their fingers twined together.

She swung her elbow in a half effort at his ribs, laughing. "If you help them unload the salt, I will talk to Mother about the ceremony." She reached and pulled his head down for a quick kiss. "I will tell her we want this soon," she whispered into his ear, "for I cannot wait any longer." She licked his neck and jumped away when he tried to tickle her. "See to the salt," she cried, laughing.

She found Cayri in her hut. The door was propped open so Aydyn called out from the fire pit. "Mother, we are home."

"Yes, child," Cayri answered. She stepped into the doorway and gave a knowing smile. "You look well. Come in."

Aydyn entered and took her favorite seat on the floor. She sat on a fat cushion and could not stop the smile that filled her face. "Eric and I have come to an agreement. We would like to make a contract. Will you do our ceremony?"

Cayri took Aydyn's hand. "I am so happy for you. I see you have finally realized how Eric is your destiny." She drew the hand to her cheek. "You have always been the strong one. I am proud to call you daughter."

"Did you know, Mother?" Aydyn asked.

"That you would go to the shore and fall in love with a handsome man?" She smiled and released Aydyn's hand. "I can guess that you would like to do this soon? Does this mean you have not—"

"No," Aydyn said, feeling her blush burn to life again. "I had my reasons for waiting, but—"

Cayri leaned close, her face now serious. "Do you feel now is a good time for you to carry a child?"

Aydyn's smile faltered. She tried not to think of the rest of her life. "I have been taking the herbs. We both agree that this not a good time for a child." She pulled her eyes away, adding, "I never really thought I would have children, not with what remains before me."

She glanced around, avoiding Cayri's piercing eye, and noticed the herbs and crystals that covered her mother's worktable. "You have been divining." A chill snaked down her spine, but she refused to let it hold her. She was strong, and she would fulfill her destiny, but first— "Have you seen anything?" she asked.

Cayri shook her head, "No, and I will tell you as soon as I do. Right now, I sense a gathering storm, but I have no clear picture beyond that." She gave Aydyn a direct look as she added, "But I do not think we have a lot of time."

Aydyn nodded. Every Druae lived their life knowing that this prophesied day could come at any moment. Living with this single certainty for countless generations liberated them to live each day completely. "Then we must have a big celebration," she said, smiling eagerly.

The wagon carts of salt rolled into the village, drawing a boisterous crowd. Through the open door she spied Eric's dark head in the crowd.

"This is the time of no moon and I do not wish to wait, so we will have a star ceremony—honoring our birthplace in the heavens."

Cayri stood at Aydyn's side and they heard Eric's voice over the commotion of their return.

"What else may come," Aydyn said, "I will have this time with him."

CHAPTER TWELVE

Aydyn walked with a group of girls. By tradition, the day prior to a woman's ceremony was spent with women of her past as her last day before crossing into a new life with a mate. She laughed, giving full rein to this brief period in her life, without duty to plague her. The afternoon had been filled with a long bath followed by a woman's party with stories, jokes and small gifts.

"We are happy for you, Aydyn. You have pleased the Goddess," Anna said.

"I am fortunate to serve the Goddess in this manner." Aydyn rolled her eyes, indicating her sacrifice, bringing laughter from the girls.

Maisy skipped along ahead of them, but suddenly stopped and pointed to Aydyn's hut. "Eric is here," she cried.

Aydyn came to a stop. Behind her, the girls evaporated in a flurry of snickers and fading giggles. Ahead of her, Eric waited by her fire pit. He was freshly washed with wet hair slicked back. In his hand was another bouquet of flowers. At the sight of him, she brought her fist up to her chest to catch her leaping heart.

I have always been his, and always will be.

"I have been waiting for you," he said. He reached out to kiss her cheek.

She drew in his scent and her knees wobbled with joy. She took the flowers and buried her face in them, inhaling, hiding her delight and the powerful effect he had on her. This force between them was not unlike what she drew from the Mother; the power came alive and sang through her body in his presence.

"Are you ready for tomorrow?" she asked. Her fluttering heart made her words come out breathless. "You have not come to re-negotiate our contract, have you?"

He took the flowers from her and dropped them on the ground. She gasped and reached for them, but he stopped her. He placed his hand at her back and stepped forward, causing her to fall backward, swept helpless into his arms. The ferocity of his gaze warmed her belly. She slipped her arms around his neck.

"I am here," he said, nuzzling her neck, causing shivers to scoot across her shoulders, "to bring you a bride gift." He brought his lips to hers and continued to nuzzle, nipping at her lips.

She laughed as more shivers of delight coursed through her body. His expression warmed her heart with the promise in his eyes. He set her upright, making her head swirl so that she grabbed him.

"Then take me inside," she breathed in a whisper.

While he picked up the discarded flowers, she entered and lit a small brass lamp, using the few moments to gather her wits. She flamed with need and she could already feel the moisture gather. She fanned her face and panted, trying to reclaim her body from his influence.

He ducked through the door. "Do you have a container?" he asked. She nodded towards the clay vase on a side table, a remnant from his first bouquet, and he settled the flowers there. She shook her head as he fussed with the rose stems, arranging them artfully. She loved this funny man more than she could ever say.

"There," he said when he had the bouquet as he wanted. He turned and reached for her hand, pulling her down to sit on the bed. He settled back with a serious look, and she fought to hold her laughter at his somber visage, wondering what could concern him so.

"You understand I have nothing material to bring into this contract," he said. "I have no cattle, sheep, or horses to give you."

She grabbed him, to reassure him she did not care, but he stopped her. She sat back, seeing the mischief in his eye.

"No," he protested, "I am not finished." He reached into his pouch and withdrew one of her mother's carved boxes. She jacked her eyebrows and leaned forward.

"I have carried these a very long way," he said, "to give to you." He opened the box and she gasped.

They are from my dream.

She examined one while he fixed the other to her ear. The workmanship was unique, and the unknown style exotic. The gold was heavy, just as she recalled from her dream. He latched the second earring.

She held up a piece of polished metal and viewed her reflection. "You brought them from your time?"

He chuckled and drew her hair forward to mingle with the gold. "They are yours, and I believe they brought me." He sat back and admired his work, asking, "Do you like them?"

The hope for her pleasure rang in his voice, sending shivers of joy down her spine. "They are special, more than you could ever know," she answered.

Memory of her dream flashed white hot in her mind; the boundaries between her dream world and the real world were becoming mere wisps. She tilted her head and felt the gold warm her flesh, inciting hope.

We will create our own destiny.

∞

"Let's see, August second," Eric said, looking out the open door of Finn's hut. "We have warm and clear skies with a sparkling twilight—a fine day to get married." He pulled at the sleeves of his blue tunic and fussed with his belt.

"Relax, brother. You are not going into battle, ye know."

"No peeking into my head—" Eric waved a finger at him.

"No need," Finn said, grinning. "Ye must have done something right. I saw Aydyn this morning. She was wearing a smile fit to blind—"

Eric ran a hand through his hair and hunched his shoulders against the restraints of his new shirt. "I don't want to disappoint her, Finn. I still don't know about this prophe—"

Finn cut him off, slapping him on the back. "Brother, all you need to know is that ye love her." He peered into Eric's face and asked, "Ye do love her, right?"

Eric froze, frowning.

Just thinking about her makes my heart and belly trade places. I am acutely aware of her every movement in space and time, and cannot bear to have her out of my sight. The idea of her not being in every moment of my life is incomprehensible. She is the Goddess personified, the only woman alive—

"Yes," he said, nodding, "I have that covered."

"Well then, all ye need to do is breathe," Finn said. He rolled his hand, suggesting as much, and Eric gasped.

"Are ye ready?" Finn said. "It is time."

Eric nodded, and they walked the short distance to the main entrance of the henge. Again, the Druae lined up to enter, and Eric and Finn walked to the end of the line through shouts of congratulations, blessings and suggestions for fertility. While all were good-natured, some were exceedingly graphic.

They stood at the end of the line waiting. Suddenly Finn looked up and jabbed Eric soundly. He looked up and gasped.

Aydyn.

Her hair, crowned with a garland of flowers, flowed to her waist. Her eyes were bright and her skin dark, highlighting the copper tattoos. She wore a short, sky blue tunic that bared her chiseled midriff. A brief matching skirt showed off her long brown legs. A necklace of gold links and seashells complimented the tangled loops of gold at her ears.

Eric struggled for air and willed his heart to slow down, lest he collapse in front of everyone.

She stepped up and took his hand, smiling. "You will be fine," she whispered. She twined her fingers in his and the energy flowed into him, instantly spreading a cloak of pale blue light over them.

She was like nothing he had ever known. He remembered to whisper, "Thank you, Goddess."

Aydyn laughed and kissed him on the cheek. "This way," she said as the line moved.

He held her hand and they trailed Finn at a distance. As they got closer to the stones, the power pulled at Eric, tingling his toes and climbing up his calves—making him feel like he was floating. The hair on his arms wafted in the air and the crown of his head sang when the energy spun through him, completing the circuit.

The Druae filed in and manned their bluestones, two people to a stone. By the time he and Aydyn entered, the stones were beginning to glow. Blue light was everywhere, sparking as the energy jumped in a flashing arc to touch each person. Just as the light slowly climbed the stones from the ground up, so did the glow rise to the top of each Druae head.

Aydyn emitted light from head to toe. He watched as her light danced across their hands. The energy coursed through him, taking him to another vibration level, shifting his molecules to a stronger, higher tone.

His heart thudded, feeling as remote as the heartbeat of Mother, deep in the Earth. Gaia, the Goddess herself, reined supreme, commanding him, her child. His breath felt as sharp as pure mountain air, and his eyesight pierced the distance like a bird. Vitality and the desire to live roared through his veins in a molten rush of primal drive.

"Breathe," he commanded. He looked down again, amazed that he was not levitating. Aydyn squeezed his hand and small sparks danced in the air, floating away from their hands.

She pulled him into the inner circle of stones, weaving among the bluestones, touching the Druae with her free hand. First one and another, until all were touched—and with each contact, the power grew.

The energy coursed though his molecules, singing through his bones, reaching for an ultimate pitch, a zenith he prayed he would survive.

Dear Goddess please don't incinerate me before—

They stopped at the altar stone where Cayri waited. They joined hands with her and silent, heavy expectation filled the air. His belly froze, as in that endless moment of pause at the crest of a roller coaster waiting for the fall.

"We give these two to the Goddess," Cayri called out in a strong voice. "We give them with our blessing, seeing the hand of the Goddess herself guiding them along their true path of service." She stepped back and pressed Aydyn's hand into Eric's. Out came a length of crimson red silk rope and she lightly wrapped their hands together in a figure eight.

"This rope shows how you will be held together in this life and in all others. Ye are bound together, now and forever. Honor the Goddess. Honor your love. Never lose your path."

Eric stared at his fierce warrior woman. Her cries from the night before as he brought her to ecstasy still rang in his ears. She gripped his hands and he squeezed back.

A hum started, growing louder. Aydyn looked up and he followed her gaze to the constellation Taurus, clear in the sharp night sky.

She squeezed his hands again, and sparks glittered into the air around them. The hum escalated and she mouthed something he could not hear. His ears were alive with the vibration and keen anticipation filled his belly. She pointed up with her chin.

He followed, staring at a single star that called to his body. He throbbed with recognition. He fixed on the bright light, watching with astonishment as it expanded, and the light exploded into a brilliant stream.

When he gasped, Aydyn clutched his hands in a death grip as the starlight raced across the night sky. The beam came straight at them from across the cosmos, arriving to cloak them in a circle of brilliant white light.

His ears rang and his eyes watered. Aydyn threw her head back, her body as rigid as when she reached her orgasm last night. The blue light traced their hands in an ethereal glow. He watched, and their flesh went beyond joining, overlapping as though bearing no substance. He moved his hand up her arm, and their flesh was transparent.

The power was sweet, as thrilling as the building explosion in his loins. His erection throbbed with the energy of a hyper-dimensional force.

"Eric," Aydyn called. Her lips did not move, yet he heard her voice inside his head. He was aware of her mind.

He stepped in to her and one of his legs crossed hers. Their thighs were clear, fluorescent flesh, passing into the same space. His arm traced around her back and he saw her heart beating against her ribs, a scant palm's width away.

Her arms floated up, circling his neck. She traveled her hand along the same trail to his beating heart before lifting her face, lips parted. He kissed her sweet mouth, his to command into eternity.

Their bodies came together, crossing to merge as one, until finally his heartbeat was indistinguishable from hers. He looked down. Their transparent bodies overlapped to fill the same space until they were one. His joy was ultimate, complete, consuming.

This was the moment his soul sought throughout his lifelong searching.

Two halves, at last making one infinite whole.

The power sang, reaching the pitch of perfection. Stars glittered, brilliant through his transparent hand. He sighed, his joy and relief immeasurable. Tiny pinpoints of light peeled from their translucent bodies, joining to create a spinning sphere above their heads.

Our soul.

"Og arawyn bot wyn," the Druae cried. They raised their fists to the sky and shouted, "Og arawyn bot wyn! Og arawyn bot wyn!"

The sphere of light sped off across the cosmos—going home.

The circle of light around them snapped out. Eric craned his neck to follow the spinning sphere as it telescoped out of his sight into the field of stars. He clutched Aydyn, suddenly wobbly as the hyper-dimensional energy vacated his body. The hum and the light from the bluestones pulsed, fading, leaving his ears to ring.

He shook his head and wavered on his feet, but Aydyn held him steady. The last sparks danced off their hands, released from his tingling fingers. He rubbed his palms on his thighs and struggled with the sensation that his organs still floated. The last of his blue light faded from his fingernail beds.

Aydyn hugged him. She brushed her lips against his neck and whispered, "Was that, as you say, a 'wow?'"

He grinned and swept her into his arms. He smiled into her face, only a breath away. "Yes," he whispered, rubbing his forehead against hers. "That was definitely a *wow.*"

She tugged at his hands, her face as bright as a child's. He looked around as the Druae exploded into a flurry of whistles and bawdy yells. Couples hugged and kissed, moving against each other with obvious abandon and intent. The crowd surged out the side entrance towards the village with cheers and cries of jubilation.

In the village, bonfires blazed in every fire pit. Every lamp the Druae owned was lit and placed on the ground, on tree stumps and tables. Large tables were set up outside the meat house and filled with every delicacy known to the Druae.

He saw platters of whole pig and deer that had been cooking in pits for two days. There were bowls of fresh wild greens with onions, a grain and herb mixture, baskets of flat bread. A large wild bird was stuffed with another deboned foul and carved roulade style. Fresh trout was wrapped in herbs and steamed.

His mouth watered, unable to decide where to begin. Someone shoved a mug of beer in his hand and the music began. A dozen young men brought out drums with various tones and set up an intricate beat. Couples stood and swayed with the rhythm, laughing, kissing and hugging.

He grinned and pulled Aydyn to his side. She laughed with total abandon. Her cheeks glowed rosy in the firelight and the copper of her tattoo sparkled around her eyes. He pulled her hair forward, layering it beneath the gold loops at her ears. She was so beautiful, so magical, so special.

What have I done to deserve her?

Service, whispered the Goddess.

Aydyn pursed her lips and waited for him to speak, tilting her head. Her unabashed faith, her fierce love of her people and dedication to duty—he could not express his admiration even if he had a thousand years to try. He gave himself in to her bright blue gaze, and said, "You are why I want to live."

The tattoos crinkled with her smile. A growl rumbled in his throat and he pulled her to him, proud to be her chosen one. Her long legs snaked around his and their hips came together. She rubbed against him, and his growl erupted as he claimed her parted lips.

They kissed, gently giving. Any concern over how long dissipated in the heat of the moment. Her arms wrapped around his shoulders as she undulated against him, pressing her breasts into his chest. A length of lean bare flesh rose against his leg and his fingers danced across her muscled thigh, reaching the bottom edge of her skirt.

Wild and raucous laughter surrounded them. Finn pulled Eric away just as a group of women took Aydyn and shuttled her off.

"Ye have time to do that later," Finn said. Leering into Eric's face, he thrust a full mug of beer at him. "But first, ye dance."

A circle of about thirty formed. Men and women, young and old, all laughing and calling out a variety of blatantly lewd jokes. Several flute instruments joined the drums and a haunting melody with a primal beat filled the Salisbury plain.

"Come on, now, yer going that way," Finn laughed, giving him a push.

Eric bobbed and weaved, following along. Suddenly the line stopped and Cayri stepped up behind him. She turned and shouted, "Ara meen," and smacked his rear.

He froze.

She threw her head back, howling, "Og arawyn bot wyn." Before he knew what to do, Finn turned him about and pushed him back into line.

He spied Aydyn and saw that the men fell to their knees in

supplication before her and howled, "Og arawyn bot wyn," before rising to spin her about in a dizzy circle. She laughed and crowned the men with her now tattered bouquet before stumbling crazily back into the line.

At last they managed to meet on the side. They cut out of the dance, laughing and gasping. She grabbed for his rear and he countered, reaching for her ribs, dancing across them like a keyboard.

She writhed and twisted in his arms. Facing him, she panted with her fading laughter and leaned against him. Gazing up with a face as innocent as a babe, she brought her foot around his ankle and snatched a leg out from beneath him. They fell in a laughing tumble.

He grabbed her and rolled, bringing her on top. "How long do we have to stay?" he asked.

She sat up and devilish lights danced in her eyes. "Are ye sure you are ready to go?"

He nodded, not knowing what he was in for, but he was ready to dare anything. He stood and pulled her to her feet. "Take me home, honey."

She chuckled and threw her head back. "Ara meen," she shouted, and smacked his butt.

He rubbed his sore rump and whispered, "What's ara meen?"

"It means you are built to deliver many happy nights. Now, fall to your knees and worship me."

A crowd was collecting, drawn by her call. He grinned and dropped to his knees and clutched her leg, shouting, "I am yours to command, night or day."

The crowd whispered, "Aaaahhh. Og arawyn bot wyn," Laughing, they turned and trickled back to the music and their celebration.

His breath landed on her neck and fired gooseflesh to ripple across her shoulder. He turned her towards her hut. "I believe I have something you want," he whispered.

Chapter Thirteen

"Follow me," he whispered, drawing her inside her hut.

Aydyn placed one finger to his lips and this simple touch excited him, spreading warmth from his heart through his bones, to his loins. She laced their hands together, and a power flowed between them. He throbbed.

He slid his hands down her arms, leaving a wake of gooseflesh. She shivered, and he rubbed the bumps away, pulling her close enough to nuzzle her neck. Her hair was like silk, dark, yet full of light. The smell fresh, unlike anything he had ever known—and yet so familiar. A shiver of deja' vu skittered down his back as he pursed his lips—waiting. She squirmed at his hesitation.

He kissed her shoulder, giving in to the ultimate joy of touching her precious flesh. He watched her eyes, tightly scrunched, and when they opened, tears slipped down her face.

"I will be yours forever," she whispered.

"Aydyn," he breathed against her neck. His hands slipped to her waist and he pulled her closer. Carefully, he brushed the hair away from her neck to kiss softly her hair, the tangled loops hanging from her ears, and finally her skin. He sighed and placed his nose against her, sucking in his breath, drawing in her scent.

She turned her head, baring her neck. His lips found the sensitive spot at the base of her throat, wanting to feel her turn liquid at his touch.

He licked. She moaned.

His loving lips and tongue suckled the satin of her skin, and the fire pulsed, alive in his loins. The need to make her his was a raging entity, possessing him. After a lifetime of searching, she was here, igniting a primal power deep within him—the irrepressible drive to seek one's mate.

She whimpered, a small sound of angst deep in her throat, and he plunged into her mouth, trying to slake the thirst that had driven him across time. In a thousand years, he could not get enough.

He took all she gave and demanded more, branding her with a heat that was his alone, bringing the power and the heat full circle. He would take her to the inferno of desire and burn with her in its flames.

She pressed against him, rubbing her breasts hard against his chest. Her breath came in mini blasts of heat against his neck.

Moaning. Was it him … or her?

His hands came to her head, cupping her face, holding her still as he kissed her. He tore his mouth away, gasping for air. He saw a flash of triumph flare in her Druae blue, recognized some epiphany rip through her. Her siren's call surged, a tether running all through his DNA, stirring his atoms, commanding his molecules, directing his soul.

He held her face with both hands and peppered her with little kisses, waiting for her to ask for more. When a groan of pain rumbled in her chest, he knew what she wanted. He moved his mouth to her breast.

"Ahh," she sighed, and the thrill of her pleasure rang through his bones.

She wrapped her legs around his hips, and his hard flesh lifted between them. He gasped, nearly in pain when she wrapped her hand around him and tugged slowly up and down, teasing him.

He pressed her back and took her mouth again, trapping her hand between them until he felt her legs ease open. She released him and he laid a trail down to her belly button. Her hips undulated against him, pressing, pulling, pressing—and her breath was a ragged gasp.

"Thank you, Goddess," he whispered against the taut brown skin between her hipbones.

He could no longer deny the call of her open legs. One hand left her breasts to stroke a firm thigh, then her woman's opening, wet with moisture. She pressed against his fingers, showing him the way to her pleasure, but he wanted to play. He stroked and circled her, teasing her until she writhed and moaned beneath his hands.

Triumph blazed in his heart. He stopped, knowing she would lift her head. She gave him her Druae blue glazed with passion and understanding. He bared his teeth in victory.

Come with me, and we will burn ...

He touched her opening with a finger and she surged against him, but he shook his head. He would love her like no other man— he wanted her to never forget him. She trembled as he probed deeper. He collected her juice and moved up and down, spreading slick against slick.

"Yes, please," she moaned.

Unable to chose the words, and unwilling to trust his voice, he let promise fill his eyes. She gazed back, collected his promise and thrust against him, bringing herself against his thumb. Her head fell back and he felt her tensing muscles surround his finger.

On hands and knees he crouched over her. He traveled the glorious distance back up to her face, caressing her thighs, then dipping and licking at her belly. Her legs sprawled, boneless and open, and he thrust at her, marking each thigh with his wetness.

He lay beside her as his mouth claimed hers and his fingers plunged into her. His tongue impaled her as his fingers played within. She moaned against his mouth and he rubbed his hot length against her hip.

She tore her mouth away. "Please, Eric," she pleaded.

Her need for release filled her eyes, and he knew she could wait no longer. He growled and straddled her legs, his seeking flesh between them, dropping to nick her cleft before springing away.

Watching her writhe was a painful, double-edged sword. He held himself back, waiting until she licked her lips, swollen from his rough kisses, and nodded.

She heaved and bucked against him, and he whispered, "Shh, easy."

She reached behind him with both hands, bringing his hardness to rake across her. She rose on her elbows and panted, watching him with blue fire in her eyes. She, too, was a slave of the Goddess.

He straddled her, pushing her knees gently apart. Her breath filled the hut and roared loud in his ears. He looked at her face while he spread her with one hand. Her head rolled back and her eyes closed.

"Look at me," he commanded.

She lifted her head. He held her open and pressed his hardness into her. He pushed, barely touching her until she said, "Please."

Her hips tilted, guiding him in until she fully encased him. He stopped with a spasm of control, resting on his elbows to keep his weight off her. His ragged breath blew against her cheek, and his legs quivered with restraint. Their sweat poured and mingled, filling the air with raw scent and energy.

He pushed in and drew out. Her muscles clenched and drew him back. He grinned, nose-to-nose, breath-to-breath, and pulled back. She smiled and tightened, drawing him in.

Enough.

"You win," he whispered.

In one wet, sliding stroke, he entered. She sighed, and a wave of energy pierced him with a single command.

Come to me, my love, that we may be one.

He drove into her, at last connected as she moaned and wrapped her legs around him.

He brought his head down and nipped at the skin of her shoulder. She bared her neck, pressing her breasts into him as he marked her shoulder lightly. Grinding his hips into her, they groaned together.

She thrust against his plunging hardness in a dance of seduction. The heat coiled in his belly as their bodies found their common beat—his thrust, her return. Each giving, each taking—with both wanting more.

He growled and quickened the pace. She matched him and whispered, "Yes," against his shoulder.

The power kept building, going further, reaching deeper as he rode the vortex with her. They slammed together, two animals possessed, going faster and faster until nothing could stand in their way. The power of his release burst within and he grimaced with erotic completion, cast through the cosmos once again.

∞

Far to the East, the morning breeze rose, carrying smoke and the cries of women.

"This will seal our fate," Balock sneered. He stared at the dead bodies with regret, but this latest Kurgan attack would drive his father—

He turned away as Jarech strode back and forth. Dead cattle littered the pasture, killed by a piercing blow to the back of the neck. Because the carcasses had not been blooded, the meat was ruined. Flies buzzed in the early morning, drawn to the hardening bodies.

At the first sight of the massacre, Jarech's face turned rigid, yet he said not a word. He stalked through the bodies, his visage growing darker and darker. At one point he stopped and skewered Balock with a threatening look. "This is all your fault," he spit.

Jarech's tone was deadly, chilling the sweat that trickled down Balock's backside. He shifted his stance, preparing to duck and run should his father decide to apply the iron to him. Under the hardening gaze, with nowhere to hide, he withered. He thought of the moon, watching him night after night and cursed the day he set foot in the Druae camp. "Kurgans have been raiding us for years. This is no more—"

Jarech drew his fist back, and Balock stood up, daring his father. A pummeling strike stung his ear.

"If you had not brought the cursed iron—" Jarech hissed. He raised his fist again.

Balock jumped in his father's face. With teeth bared, he snarled, "If the cursed iron had not been in your hand, you would not be alive today." He inhaled and stood his ground, pushing his father.

"The iron is spelled," Jarech insisted, "and now the curse is upon us. This," he waved to the dead cattle, "is all because of your lust for that blue-eyed girl."

Jarech's words were too close to home, and Balock's shrinking scrotum sent a quiver down his legs to rattle his knees. "You lusted for the iron after you killed the Kurgan. I saw it in your face. You were glad enough to have the iron the night your life was saved." He glared back with his most ferocious look.

Jarech brought a quick, hard fist down on Balock's face, knocking him to one knee. "Why, you— I should—" He raised his fist again.

"Father!" Balock cried, bringing his arm up. "Sacrificing me will not change—" His heart hammered and he saw his father considered doing just that. Another punishing blow struck him in the temple and he went full to his knees. Stars danced in his eyes and he raised his arms, trying to cover his head.

"I should have given you to the Kurgans," Jarech hissed. "I should have told them you were the one who killed the boy. But now it is too late. They are gone and—"

He stopped and waved at the slaughter with anger and empty defeat. Turning on Balock's cringing figure, he shouted, "No, you fool, killing you will not change the fact that we—" He unsheathed the Druae blade.

Balock lowered his arms and faced his father's rage. He would not die like a frightened little girl.

"Killing you will not change the fact," Jarech finished, "that we are all dead now." The heat sizzled out of his words and he threw the iron to the ground at Balock's feet. He slumped and sat next to him. "With no cattle," Jarech said, "we will not live through the winter. The Kurgans have killed us without raising a battle cry."

Balock watched the flies grow thicker. Slow starvation through the cold season was a cruel death. "We must go to the Druae," he said.

"And do what, Balock?" Jarech sneered.

"We will take their iron and kill them," Balock said. "What else can we do, Father? If we stay here, we will starve." For the first time he shuddered with fear at the path the Druae iron had cast for him.

Jarech growled and kicked at a bloated body, filling the air with an angry cloud of flies. "There are more of them—"

"We will surprise them in the middle of the night," Balock said. "Take their iron, sell off the men, keep the women and children."

"And see some of us killed in the process," Jarech growled.

"Or stay here and starve," Balock said. "Unless you have another idea."

Jarech ran a hand through his hair. For long moments, he dug his heel into the dirt and stabbed the ground with the point of the Druae blade. A snarling tirade of curses and spitting contempt for Kurgans filled the air, disturbing the flies.

He fell silent and inhaled a ragged breath. With a half-hearted wave, he said, "These fields are tired and the pasture is thin. We have been here long enough." A hard exhalation followed. He wiped the dirt from the iron, and sheathed it. "We will harvest and then pack," he said, standing. "We must be settled well before the first cold blows. Tell the women to prepare."

∞

Eric watched as his wife of two weeks skipped across the village compound on her way to oversee the storage of newly harvested grain. There was a spark in her easy laughter that was becoming, even at a distance.

He smiled. His searching was finally at peace.

But how do I keep what I have found?

"I wouldna think that to be yer problem," Finn said.

Eric turned and clapped his brother-in-law on the back, protecting his ribs from the familiar elbow. "Finn, you sneaky dog. Don't you have anything better to do than poke around in my thoughts? What are you about this morning?" They clasped hands in the Druae shake and Eric saw that Finn held something behind him. "What are you hiding?" he asked, trying to peek around Finn's shoulders.

Finn laughed. "Now that ye are family," he said, "ye must have an iron blade." He presented a sheathed sword.

Eric froze.

Finn held the blade Eric had found buried in the brick wall of the chamber. The hammered-copper, silver chased hilt gleamed shiny and deadly in the soft morning light. A chill tingled in his fingertips and he hesitated to touch the gift. Something important eluded him, slipping through his mind before he could—

"Ye do not like it," Finn said. He frowned and peered at Eric. "This blade is one of my finest pieces, ye know." When Eric still did not take the offering, he pulled back. "Ye can have yer pick of any in my smith, but I can see ye have some trouble."

"No, I—" Eric stuttered. He took the sword and removed the sheath. "This is what I found buried in the wall," he said, "above the chamber. I pushed this, like so—and the stone floor beneath me rolled away, dropping me into the chamber with the crystal."

Something terribly important skittered through Eric's mind, firing trepidation in his heart. He kneeled and sketched in the dirt. "Here was the chamber, and the stone floor above." He slashed the diagram in the dirt, even as a chill sprouted at the base of his neck. "There was a false hill above the stone floor. The walls of the hill were made of a crumbling brick. And hidden in the wall was this—acting as a lever."

He stood and mimed the scene for Finn, needing him to know how it was, for if it had not been exactly right, he would not have—

—*come here.*

He stopped, stunned. What would happen to him, and Aydyn and the Druae, if he had not arrived? Panic ripped through his heart and he grabbed Finn by the shoulders. "This is carved into the rock at the base of a stone seat." He drew his initials and 62108 in the dirt. "Look at this," he cried. "The hill here, and the stone seat here. These marks—put them in your memory," he said, stabbing at the ground.

"These markings must be in place." He stopped, panting, and stared at the ground.

"But, Eric, ye have arrived now," Finn said softly. "This has already happened." His face crinkled in concern and he cocked his head, looking to see if Eric understood. "And there is no hill above the chamber."

"Yes, but—" Eric waved his hands with frustration at Finn's logic. "A hill does exist in my time, so you must arrange this just so in your future." He panted, having trouble keeping time travel straight in his own head, much less trying to explain it to Finn. "Just remember these marks. Put them in your memory.

Finn brought his brows together in skepticism, but Eric shook his head. "Promise me," he demanded. "Promise me you will remember those marks."

Finn gave his nod and they shook hands, making a contract. Eric exhaled his relief. He took the sheathed blade and held it carefully; he didn't know how time travel worked. Would the lever be there in another future, a future he has now changed by being here?

A pain throbbed in the base of his skull and he rubbed his neck. Missing his entry to this time was too scary to even consider. He would keep the iron safe, just in case.

∞

"Wow," Eric said.

He stood with Aydyn in a storage hut specially designed to keep foodstuffs ventilated, yet inaccessible to animals and insects.

The walls were lined with shelves holding hundreds of clay pitchers filled with dried fish and seaweed that they brought back from the shore.

Rows and rows of empty thatched baskets would soon hold a winter's supply of dried fruits, nuts and spices, harvested and thrashed grains, and dried meats. A vast pharmacopoeia of herbs and medicinal plants already dried in the rafters.

They stepped out and Aydyn closed the door. He had watched her fastidiously attend to each detail: the specially treated linen cloth covering all of the windows, exact record keeping of every item, the careful organization.

"You take care of everything," he said, grasping her hand. She smiled and the color of her eyes was a pool he begged to drown in every night and day of his life.

"This is my duty," she said. She tugged on his hand, drawing him closer. "Just as taking care of you is my duty." She reached up and planted a quick kiss on his neck.

He grabbed her by the waist and nuzzled her hair. He loved to watch the procession of gooseflesh that trailed over her shoulders when he kissed her neck. "About that duty," he said. He pulled her to stand hip to hip as his seeking flesh hardened, apparently never at peace in its journey to find her. He reached behind his back and opened the door of the shed. As quiet as a pair of mice, they slipped back inside.

She chuckled and moved against him, enticing what didn't need enticing. He wrapped his arms around her and claimed her mouth, wanting the soft touch of her lips. He teased her gently, coaxing her response until she opened and their tongues met. He delved deep, never able to slake his thirst for her, worshipping her with his tongue, his hands, his—

The heat was quick, always so close to the surface, never cooling, never less in intensity. Fire caught in his loins and surged through him. He rubbed against her and she moaned deep in her throat.

You are mine, his heart exclaimed. He took her mouth roughly, holding her head so that he could claim all of her. Infinity would not give him his fill of this woman.

He pulled back to see her face. Her eyes were molten, like blue star-fire, and her lips were swollen from his rough kiss. The thrill of knowing she was his ran through him.

She dropped her lids at his perusal and pulled a pout, rocking her hips—sending the power to surge through him, her force filling him long before he filled her.

Her power eclipses everything.

The mystery of what would happen to them was a shadow he lived with. Only this living energy between them had the power to obliterate his doubts and fears. She was a force to be reckoned with and she was his, just as he was hers.

Together, we become an infinite force.

He slipped his hand up to hold her beautiful face. He would have all of her, and if they burned this house down, he didn't care. "Love me, Aydyn," he whispered, stroking the fine line of her jaw. "Love me like there is no tomorrow."

She closed her eyes and a single tear emerged from the corner of one eye, but when she opened them, there was only heat and need.

She kissed him, gentle, hesitant, her tongue darting across his lips to reach his mouth. He felt as though his entire body swelled on some universal tide. He eased his linen pants down to his hips, letting him spring free. Her cool hands on his hot flesh were an ecstasy of pain.

I need you.

"I know," she whispered. "I need you, too."

He turned and saw an ample stack of empty grain sacks. He nodded, "Over there." She grinned and pulled her tunic off, her breasts bounding free. He fell back on the sacks with his legs caught up in his pants. Landing on his rear, he laughed, grunting, "Oof."

She chuckled and shimmied out of her leggings to stand before him, naked and proud. She was the Goddess of Life surrounded by her bounty. Cupping her breasts with both hands, she offered them, and he saw the subtle blue spark of the Goddess in her eyes.

He propped up on his elbows and she walked to stand over him, straddling him.

"Take them off," she said, motioning to his clothing. She planted her hands on her hips and tapped an impatient foot, humor sparkling in her face.

In a flurry, he shucked out of his shirt and tangled pants, tossing them aside. Running his hands up her long shapely legs, he cupped her buttocks and kissed her thighs, brushing the top of her womanhood with his head. As always, he was a supplicant honoring the Goddess.

He smiled, enjoying the pain of denying himself while he took another pleasure. He licked her nub and they moaned together.

"You cannot do that while I am standing," she gasped.

He felt her clench. "I can, and so can you," he murmured. He brought one hand forward and held her, licking. She was wet, and he easily slipped two fingers into her.

In and out he stroked as she rocked her sex against him. Her thrusts became more insistent as her need increased, and he sucked harder.

"Eric," she called, her knees quivering. She pushed him back and squatted so she grazed the top of him. He strained towards her, but she shook her head. She pointed to her breasts, tight and hard.

Needing no further encouragement, he filled his mouth with

one glorious globe. He massaged her other breast, then pushed his throbbing head against her wet opening.

"Oh, dear Goddess," she moaned. She held on to his shoulders with both hands and small spasms rocked her hips as he stroked her. She sank down on her haunches and he impaled her.

She bobbed on her feet, pulling him into her. With her legs threatening to collapse, she pushed him back and sat with a satisfied smirk.

He gasped. Her wet, scalding heat covered him. She worked him from the inside with her muscles, calling for his orgasm. Back and forward she rocked, allowing him to slide out only a small distance before she ground her hips back into him.

Hot, wet, sliding—he pushed back, adding to her friction. The first tingling of orgasm flitted through his belly and he clenched, driving deeper. He reached up and grabbed her hips to bring on the rhythm that would take them home.

She dropped her hands to the floor by his head and shifted her hips, pressing and sliding back, driving him in a horizontal direction. He lifted his head and caught one of her breasts in his mouth. She grunted in little whimpers and arched her back, pressing into his mouth.

She spread her knees a little further so that she splayed flat against him. In a flash, the sweet fire ignited in his belly. Again and again he thrust, rabid with intent as the pulse of his orgasm fired through him. She gripped him tightly inside with her climax as he exploded, crying out, "Aydyn!"

The tension poured from her and she sagged, collapsing on his chest, her eyes closed. The mutual pounding of their hearts was so loud that he lifted his head to gaze around, half expecting to see paramedics peeking in through the cloth-covered windows. "Good Goddess," he gasped, and dropped his head to the floor.

She was an inert mass splashed across him. He pulled the hair from her face and watched as she recovered from 'the little death'. Her eyes fluttered open and she struggled to focus. When she saw him, she smiled, and softly gasped, "Wow."

He brushed more hair from her sweated face and kissed her forehead. Her Goddess power still held him within her, keeping him swollen even after his release.

"I love you," he said, stroking the back of her head.

Their hearts and breath returned to normal and she stirred, sitting up. "I have a surprise for you," she said. She waved her eyebrows in comic invitation and reached out to pinch his ribs. He flinched, but she reached past him and picked up the leather bag she carried. She sat up and peeked into the bag, enticing him. He peeked with her.

Two gold rings.

"Aydyn," he said. He picked out the larger one and whistled through his teeth. "Sweetheart, this is stunning."

Emotion erupted from his heart and filled his throat. He coughed, feeling that familiar and painful flood of joy she inspired rush through him. He examined the heavy gold band through a wash of tears and wiped his eyes. Finn's unmistakable wandering vine traced the outside, and on the inside was a tiny endless knot.

"The knot is my design," she said. "Do you like—?"

"This is beautiful," he said. "Just as you are."

"I want us to be as it is in your life as much as possible," she said. She took both rings and placed them in his hand. "Will you say the words?"

When she asked how couples joined in his time, he had no idea why she inquired. She was picking up his speech and asking about life in the twenty-first century with an almost fanatical fervor. In the heat of her curiosity, his old academic fear of changing the future melted and ran. He could not deny her.

"Without you, my heart does not exist, my life has no value, no completion," Eric said. Powerful emotion crowded his throat, compressing the words. He took her left hand and slipped the smaller ring on her finger. "With this ring, I thee wed." He kissed her fingers and gave her the other ring. "Your turn," he said.

She took the ring with somber intent. "You have no idea how much this means to me," she whispered. Her face softened and she picked up his hand. "With this ring, I thee wed." She slipped the ring on his finger and kissed the back of his hand.

"Now we kiss, yes?" she asked.

He pulled her to him, his heart singing for hers. He admired his wedding band. The workmanship in the solid gold was exquisite, but in his mind nothing material could compare with the experience of crossing dimensions to share the same space as this wild woman of nature.

"Kiss," she said. Her lips pursed, waiting, and he captured them.

Slow, deep and steady, he told her of his love with his tongue and lips. He kissed her nose, her eyes, her forehead.

She hugged him tight and whispered in his ear. "I would bind you to me, for all of time—past, present and future."

The shadow slid through his mind, bringing a chill to his neck. *Gold*, he thought, *is what brought me here*. He stared at the ring on his hand and the haunting precipice opened before him, daring his heart to jump—

He pulled back and clutched her even tighter.

Never, never will I let you go.

"I am yours," he whispered, "for all time."

She jumped to her feet and pulled him up. "Come, I want to show our rings to Cayri," she said.

They dressed and exited the shed. She glowed with childlike glee as she pulled the door shut, checking to see that all was securely latched. They walked down the steps, admiring their new rings.

She stopped cold.

He crashed into her and fought to keep from knocking her over. "What—" he cried. He peeked over her shoulder. Her face was ashen, big-eyed with nostrils flared as she stared at her mother's hut.

A chill shot down his spine. He followed her gaze, holding his breath, waiting for her to reveal whatever danger she had detected.

Without a word she sprinted off, leaving him behind.

Chapter Fourteen

Please, dear Goddess, not yet, her heart cried.

Aydyn ran the short distance to her mother's hut. Her stomach was sick with fear but she kept her eyes on the door. Someone was here with her mother—someone who brought the end of her people.

At Cayri's hut she heard low voices—her mother and a man. She held her face in a calm expression and called out, "Mother? May I come in?"

"Yes, child," Cayri answered.

Aydyn's heart did a flip when she heard Cayri's tone. She stepped through the door and smelled him before her eyes adjusted to the dim light. "Wolfgar?"

"He has brought us news, Aydyn. Come hear what he has to say," Cayri said, motioning her to approach.

Aydyn nodded to Wolfgar and sank to the floor in her usual corner. He returned to his seat and Cayri settled, giving him the nod.

"We have been up the coast since I last saw you," Wolfgar said, "doing—what we do." He shrugged in small apology before continuing. "As we approached the pass that begins the cold sea, we saw a congregation on the coast. Men, women, children and livestock waited while boats are built."

He paused to give them a direct look. "Being a man of curious nature, I went down the coast and back ashore to see the nature of their—"

"Stock," Aydyn stated. She smiled at him and tried to keep her heart in check. She was certain he carried the news they expected. In these moments of waiting, she fought to keep the angst of her emotions from clouding the air, for Cayri would be reading him for intent. The big men of the north were known to be pranksters, and one could not always take them at their word, even if they were family by contract.

She watched for long seconds, breathless, and when Cayri reached for the water skin, she knew that what he told them was authentic. Cayri passed the skin, asking, "And what did you learn?"

"We watched their camp," he said, "for some time. While the quality of their stock was interesting, we could see they did not have enough to keep them through the winter. Because of this, we did not take any."

He sipped from the skin and cast his eye to Aydyn. Her heart continued to race, but she motioned for him to continue.

"I hear you have taken a mate, Aydyn," he said. "Our congratulations to you from the north. When we see you in the spring, Loryn will have a life-gift for you."

Aydyn nodded, murmuring her thanks, but inside her heart was near to bursting. He played with her, and there was no way to stop him. She smiled and watched, disinterested.

"Your happy news," he continued, "may be a disappointment to someone in this camp of travelers we found."

His gaze was flinty and Aydyn clenched her belly. "And why is that?" she asked, nonchalant as she tucked one trembling hand under a fur.

"Because the people we saw on the coast are Tarans, Balock's tribe," he said. "And I believe they are coming your way—to stay."

"Balock?" Aydyn asked. She frowned, remembering the oaf who had tried to court her last Beltane. She also recalled how he accosted her when she rejected his offer. "You saw Balock?" she asked, uncertain how to understand this news.

"Aye," he nodded, "The one from last spring, at Beltane, when he—"

"You are certain of this?" Cayri asked.

"I am certain of who I saw. And I will tell you these people are desperate—this I could sense." He shrugged his great shoulders, suddenly claiming to be unconcerned. "They are preparing a large boat. Mayhap they are not coming here after all. They could sail south."

Aydyn shot a look at Cayri and the calm acceptance in her mother's eyes was a sword thrust.

Balock is our destruction, and he is coming because of me.

She rocked back, leaning against the wall, her heart and mind in a chaotic tumble. Wolfgar rose and she struggled to her feet, standing mute while her mother saw him to the door.

"I could not go home without telling you this. If Loryn found out from my men I knew something and did not forewarn you—" He shook his head, portending the worst. "If you need our help, you will ask, yes?" He paused at the door.

Aydyn and Cayri passed silent glances. "We will bring Donnye to you in the spring," Aydyn said. "Perhaps you can keep him for the summer—" Her voice sounded distant to her own ears.

"How long before they arrive?" Cayri asked.

Wolfgar clasped Cayri's arm and bent to peer into her face. "We are family by contract. If there is trouble you will—"

"There are several Druae contracts among your people," Cayri said. "You will soon see the Druae arm of those families move to your camp. Take that word back to your people, so that the families may prepare homes."

"Do you wish them to travel with me now?" he asked. "I can make room for—"

Cayri smiled and shook her head.

He shrugged, his offer clearly stated. "You have until after the new moon," he said. "It will take them that long to make their boat seaworthy." He clasped his fist to his chest and bowed to Cayri. "You have but to say the words and we are here for you."

Again Cayri shook her head. "You are kind to offer, but we have known about this event for some time."

Aydyn could not muster her mother's encouragement. Still, she stepped from the shadows. "I will see you in the spring," she said. "You owe me ewes and lambs."

"Women," he cried. He laughed and stepped out the door, admiring the new construction. "Your Goddess ways are soft, yet you survive. Such strength defeats the sword. It is a strength men fear." He waved in final salute and crossed the village, heading for the river.

Aydyn watched him go and knew the weight of the great stones in her chest. "It is my fault after all," she said. She clenched her lips tight, daring them to not tremble, and fought back her tears. "I was so stupid, thinking Eric was the cause, and all along I am—" The words spilled with heart-breaking guilt all through her. "Mother?" she pleaded.

"Do not fret yourself over this destiny," Cayri admonished. "We are not at this junction because you rejected Balock. Think, Aydyn, what you have learned. You did the right thing to reject Balock, for you were meant to be with Eric."

She grabbed Aydyn's arm and squeezed hard, commanding her attention. "Balock desired you, the iron, and the power of the henge long before you rejected him. Do not blame yourself any more than you blamed Eric when he first arrived."

Aydyn panted and clutched her mother, needing her calm strength and faith. "What now, Mother? What happens now?" So much was going through her mind, she felt suddenly as if her life was out of control.

"We will ask Eric," Cayri said with a steady look. "He must fulfill his part of the prophecy for us to proceed."

Eric. What will I do with you, my love?

She rubbed her eyes and fought the desire to wail when so much depended on her.

"Do not worry," Cayri said. "Everything will be right for you and Eric. I have seen your happiness, child, remember that." She smiled, casting a light on Aydyn's aching heart.

"How are you always so certain, Mother?" Aydyn asked. She stood and threw her shoulders back with little conviction. "How can I do this alone? There is so much before me. I—"

"You are not alone," Cayri said. "You have your family and the Goddess with you, and you have Eric—"

Eric!

"Send him back," Aydyn said.

With all of this loss, Goddess, *please let me save him.*

She grabbed her mother and begged, "Promise me you will send him back."

"He must fulfill—" Cayri protested.

"Yes, but afterwards, I want you to send him back. You told me this was possible." She had to see Eric safe before she could finish her duty.

Cayri opened her mouth to argue, but Aydyn held her hands up. "Balock will kill Eric if he finds him. Whatever you require of me, Mother," she demanded, "do not ask me to bear that."

She felt tears brimming her eyes and dashed a hand across her face, lest they pour down her cheeks. She had to guarantee Eric's survival, just as she had to see the destruction of the stones.

Cayri's response took an eternity to come.

"As you wish," she said finally.

The air whooshed out of Aydyn in a gasp, but she rushed on. "You will send him back to his time," she said. "To where he was when he came here."

Cayri's scrutiny for this request was intense. Aydyn dropped her gaze. The chill of her grief was a terrible burden, but she would see this done. "Tell me, Mother, what is the point of having this power?"

She held her hand out and made a fist while her crying soul called the force straight from her heart. She opened the fist, and sparks burst from her palm. "I will serve the Goddess and honor Aradwyn's contract with the Star Children," she declared. "And then when my duty is done, I will serve my desire."

Cayri nodded at last, saying, "If you are sure, I will send him back when the prophecy is met."

Aydyn closed her hand, snatching at the sparks. "We will not mention this to him," she said.

The two women locked eyes and clasped hands, sealing the agreement.

∞

"I don't like it," Eric said. He paced outside Finn's hut, watching Cayri's door. "Wolfgar has gone laughing on his way. So what are they talking about?"

Finn sat on the ground, idly sharpening a blade as though tomorrow was opening day at the fair. He offered no answer. Eric wanted to shake him by the shoulders and scream.

"Now, what good would that do?" Finn said.

Eric growled. He continued pacing. "In my time, when two women get together like this, you can bet trouble is close behind."

Finn looked up with his perpetual happy smile. "Ye really must calm down, brother. This canna be good for ye."

Eric rolled his eyes heavenward. "Oh, good Lord, who's gonna—" Rubbing his face, he asked, "Finn, please. Do you know what's going on?"

Finn stood and brushed his legs off. "I think we are about to find out," he said, motioning.

Cayri stepped out her door and began swinging a brass bell. As the pure tones rang across the compound, Aydyn walked towards them.

Her strides were long-legged and filled with business. Eric saw her closed face and shielded Druae blue, and his heart stuttered. When she arrived, he grabbed her. "Aydyn—"

She took his hand and squeezed. Smiling, she pulled him close, making his heart flip. "Cayri is calling a meeting. She will explain everything."

A thousand questions filled his head, but there was no time to ask. The Druae were answering Cayri's bell, following as she walked towards the henge.

"Come on, brother," Finn said, clapping him on the back.

Aydyn tugged his hand for them to go, but he planted his feet, shaking his head. He did not want to hear what Cayri would say. His world was going to be turned upsidedown. Again. Just when he was getting his feet under him.

"No," he said.

Aydyn faced him and took his other hand, trouble and grief filling her eyes.

It is time, he thought, *to stop and make a stand. I have been pushed around just about enough.*

He stared into her eyes, begging for the pool to take him, but she remained distant. He shuddered. If his fierce and beautiful warrior woman was afraid, then he was terrified—terrified he would lose her again. He remembered her declaration of this fear the night she cried in his arms, and now he understood.

Believe, whispered the Goddess. *Your love is your strength.*

He shuddered again, torn in too many directions. After long seconds he noticed the pleading in her face—and realized how much she needed him.

I cannot disappoint her.

He looked down and called for the strength to rise from his heart and fill his limbs. He closed his eyes.

Help me, he begged—and was startled when the tingling moved through his feet. It climbed up his legs and danced along his spine, reaching for his fingertips, shooting fire through their clenched hands. He opened his eyes and a cloud of tiny colored fireworks burst all around them.

Aydyn cocked her head. "You did this?"

He grinned. The power came when he called, and surged now through him, tingling.

Tears glittered in her eyes as she gazed at the force surrounding them. Her face turned soft with wonder and she whispered, "What have you done, Eric?" She squeezed his hand and more sparks filled the air.

Her face was at once soft and sweet, yet terribly sad. He thought he saw something hiding in her blue depths, but she nodded to the crowd trickling towards the henge. "Shall we go?"

He opened his hand, one finger at a time. The power rippled and sparks flowed off his fingers like silver fireflies. He did not want to let go of the power, just as he did not want to let go of her. His fear of loosing her welled inside his chest, suffocating him.

"Will you stay with me?" he asked.

His words were sharp. His heart pounded too hard and too fast, as if aware of something beyond him. The carousel tilted and his belly swooped. The precipice appeared, reaching for him, threatening, daring him to jump. He pulled back, terrified, his breath stalled in his throat. The abyss receded, leaving the taste of terror to soil his mouth.

"Eric," Aydyn called. She smiled and squeezed his hand, sending waves of her energy to mix with his. "We will go together."

He nodded, no longer afraid, even though her response answered his question but not his heart. Surrounded by a glittering cloud of energy, they turned and walked to the henge.

A calm silence awaited them. The Druae filled the bluestone horseshoe, sitting on the ground, on the altar stone, or hugging their favorite bluestones. Cayri and Talie stood together in the center, waiting or them to arrive. Aydyn stopped to sit several yards from Cayri, pulling Eric to a place beside her. She held his hand in her lap.

Eric squirmed. His heart pounded so hard he felt like everyone could hear the drumming in the silence. Aydyn squeezed his hand and whispered, "Breathe."

"My brothers," Cayri called out, sweeping her hand and turning to encompass every member of the tribe. "We are fortunate to live in such important times, for we are the honored chosen."

A murmur rolled through the crowd as people nodded and smiled, clapping each other on the back. A look of joyous exaltation lit their faces.

"Since Eric arrived," Cayri said, "you have known the prophecy would be finished in your lifetime."

She waved graciously towards him, the Druae smiled, and Aydyn hugged his shoulders.

"Today we have learned of a threat," Cayri said.

The murmur rippled quickly, then died as the Druae gave Cayri their full attention. Aydyn squeezed his hand tighter, mashing his fingers together as she pulled him closer.

"The threat is not a concern," Cayri called, "but I have seen this is, indeed, our time to fulfill our destiny."

The crowd jumped to their feet and roared with jubilation, shouting, "Og arawyn bot wyn! Og arawyn bot wyn!"

Eric gaped his mouth and stared, confused. He looked at Aydyn and she smiled with sad eyes. "We are privileged to perform this duty," she said.

Cayri walked through the crowd, touching each one as she passed. "Now, only the prophecy is important. You each have your duties to see that the Star Children contract is honored, and so we begin today."

The murmur became a cacophony and Cayri clapped her hands. "We will have another moon ceremony, and there is much to do."

"What about the stones—and our future?" a female voice called out. "When do we learn that, Cayri?"

Dead-silence descended as every pair of eyes turned to Eric. The back of his neck prickled, and in Aydyn's lap, his mashed fingers tingled, numb and disconnected.

He peeked sideways.

She still watched him—as they all did.

He did not know what to say. He scrunched his face and rubbed his free palm into his eyeballs—but no magic words of wisdom appeared. He opened his mouth.

Everyone leaned towards him.

All I have to do is destroy the stones and give them their future.

His throat closed up and nothing came out. He clapped his mouth shut, and a sigh whispered through the crowd as the bodies leaned back in a wave.

"Believe," Cayri cried. "Believe, and the future will be."

Eric hid his face in his hands. He wanted so desperately to help them, but the words would not come. Aydyn hugged him close, burying her face in his neck.

All around them, the Druae rose and left them alone with the stones. They sat for a long time, waiting for everyone to leave.

"Tell me exactly what the prophecy says," he said.

"A traveler across time will arrive, bringing the means to silence the stones. Seek him for your future." She sat back and peered gently into his face. The sun came from over his back and caught her full in the eye. Turquoise and copper sparkled, while her lips dared him to smile.

"How can you smile, when this is the end of your world?" he asked.

"This is the beginning of a new world, one you will show us. I have faith in you," she said.

He moaned and ran a hand through his hair, staring at the distance beyond the outer circle. "What is the duty Cayri spoke of, for each Druae?"

"We have made plans for our immediate future. Each Druae woman who marries an outlander is prepared to take her relatives. This is written in every contract. We all have a place to go when we leave here."

"Where will you go?" he asked.

"Finn and I go with Cayri to Alba, a wild mountainous country on the northern-most end of this land. It is our father's home."

Inside, Eric cringed. What she didn't say left a cold hollow in his chest.

What about me?

"And what is your duty, Aydyn?"

She inhaled and sighed, pushing a heavy breath. "My duty is to see everything Druae is removed from the stone circle. Those of us who share this duty will live in the forest until we have removed all mark of Druae from this land."

He shook his head, unable to laugh at their crossed purposes.

This is why I found so little trace of them.

"This is a part of Aradwyn's contract?" he asked.

"Yes, these are the Star Children terms. We are allowed to use the henge, but no one else. The power is entrusted only to the Druae, and when we are gone, because we are the keepers of the power, our legacy must die."

"Why do you not fight?" he argued. "Fight for your home and your life?"

"Because the prophecy tells us this is the time to—" He opened his mouth to protest, but she silenced him. "To move on to a new life. But first, you have to show us how to stop the stones from making their power. We cannot leave until they are silenced."

At last, the moment he hoped to avoid was here.

He shouted in pitiful laughter. He scrubbed his face and held his head, but his duty remained.

Service, whispered the Goddess.

He pressed her hand to his face while stabbing tears pierced his eyes. Silent, he stood and pulled her with him, wrapping his arms around her so they could stand together against the forces of time. She put her arms around him and buried her face in his neck, and for just a moment, he could pretend everything was all right.

At last, he pushed her to arm's length. "I expect you have a great deal to do," he said. His voice was busted gravel, tearing at his throat. She nodded mutely, her lips pressed together.

If she sobs, I'm gonna lose it.

He turned her around and said, "Go, begin your duty while I figure out something."

She gave a brief glance over her shoulder, but walked away without a word. He turned immediately to stare resolutely at the stones he was tasked with silencing.

There was not much time, and destruction was not his forte.

∞

Aydyn fell into bed, exhausted. After leaving Eric in the circle, she was caught up in the whirlwind of activity in the village. She had not seen him all afternoon, and her heart and body ached for his touch. She refused to think about the life she planned without him, focusing instead on each moment they had remaining. His absence today seemed a lifetime.

The early evening was cool and she burrowed down into her covers. The village was settling down, and she sensed many Druae collapsing into their beds this evening. The soft sounds of life embracing each passing moment soothed her weary body, mind and spirit. She closed her eyes and a sigh of utter release escaped from her lips.

She reached with her toes and the fox fur slid along her legs. A sense of contentment rose, filling her heart with a sweet melody of peace. She drew her hand in a lazy path along her warm belly, across her ribs and up over her breasts. Arching her back, she stretched like a fat cat on a warm hearth.

A hand slipped to her waist, following the same recently traveled path to her breast. There, the calloused palm cupped her full flesh, and the long fingers tugged at her nipples. She pressed her rump back until firm flesh bobbed for her warmth, bringing another promise.

"Aydyn," he whispered.

A rash of bumps sped across her shoulder. "I missed you," she said, pressing into him with insistence.

"I see," he responded, nuzzling her neck below her ear.

One hand slipped between her legs and stroked her, pulling her heat down. Easy, she rode his hand, back and forth, drawing the escalating tension into her loins. His hard flesh replaced his fingers, slipping into her.

Her need for him was a fire burning in her soul. Panic fueled the need into a quick blaze. She couldn't take him deep enough, could not burn hot enough—could not keep him by her side.

The fire was close now, so very close. Her body cried out, *take me now, make me yours*. She squeezed him tight, quickening the pace and sparking the sweet fire, taking her home to the stars.

She crested, hanging suspended beyond time, while her heart stuttered with joy and pain as one.

He strained with a grimace of ecstasy, pouring his release into her. He collapsed against her neck, his breath a roar in her ear.

She pushed the hair from his eyes and he kissed her neck, licking her dampened skin. Inside, he pulsed against her. She held him inside, unwilling to let him go. With his blanket of love surrounding her, she knew she would make it though the coming days until—

What once was—will be again.

With that thought to guide and comfort her, she was gone.

∞

In this dream, she was both participant and spectator.

There was a lake filled with swans gliding in pairs. She frowned when a single golden swan moved into the center of the lake. "Eric," she called, but the swan turned away, neither seeing nor hearing her. The golden one slid gracefully into the crowd of pairs, searching.

Panic tripped her heart. She had to help him find—her. She rose, but she was tethered, bound by chains. She pulled and pulled on the iron fetters, when suddenly she was standing on the altar stone of the great circle.

"I must go to him," she cried. She pulled against her restraints, but the harder she fought, the tighter she was bound. Tears ran down her cheeks; the golden swan was slipping away.

Believe in the strength of your love *whispered her heart.*

She turned to the lake, but the swans were gone. Her heart stopped cold. She shrieked, "No!" rattling the very heavens. Golden tears fell from the sky, splashing her cheeks with grief.

Believe!

The scene shifted and she blinked. A woman walked with Eric. They wore fine, strange clothing of bright colors and fabrics sweeping the floor. She blinked again and the couple changed, yet she knew they were still Eric and the same woman. Again, the couple changed, and again, now going so fast they became a blur. Aydyn gasped and the scene stopped.

Eric and the woman walked past the stone circle, now tumbled down. Tears pricked Aydyn's eyes as she followed them, her heart racing. The woman lifted her hand to his face, caressing him, and Aydyn was blinded by a glint of gold. She pressed forward, wanting to see who would touch her love with such gentle care. She strained to see and recognized the woman as herself.

She shaded her eyes and the scene became the lake, again filled with swans in pairs. She opened her mouth to protest, when the swans parted to reveal the golden one's return, this time with his mate. A delicate silver chain wrapped around each slender neck, binding them eternally. The golden swans rose side-by-side, gracefully spiraling up until they disappeared into the stars.

"Ahh," Aydyn sighed as the scene dissipated like mist driven before the sun.

She curled towards the warm body beside her and entwined her legs with his. She pulled him close and pressed her face into his warm back, skin to skin, inhaling.

The Goddess had shown her the way.

The sleepy tatters of the dream were still alive in her mind when she opened her eyes. Eric's face was inches from hers, his hooded green eyes watching intently.

Dear Goddess, how I love him.

"I love you, too," he said.

"Are you reading my mind, now?" she asked.

"Yes," he smiled. "But that was an easy read."

He turned her over, planting quick kisses across her face and neck. She shivered and threw her head back, eyes closed as he stroked and massaged her body. His hands were so strong, so compelling in the way he worked her flesh, seeming to know things that were secret, even to her.

"I dreamed about swans last night," he said, breathing the words into her belly.

His voice was soft and his revelation startling, but she held her reaction, for his splayed fingers were tense across her ribs, warning her. Half asleep, she was unprepared for a challenge. She hooded her eyes and stared mutely as his words chilled her.

"I will not be separated from you," he said, delivering a kiss to her flesh with each word. He looked up, and the challenge burned clear in his hard green eyes. "There will be no argument."

The threat poured like honey from his voice. Her soul shivered, but she held her gaze soft. She kept her lips pressed together and let him speak while her heart stumbled painfully.

"I have the answer to the stones—" he said. "But before I show you how to silence them, you must promise me—" He stopped and stared straight into her eyes with scorching intent. "Promise me you will not send me back."

Chapter Fifteen

Aydyn lay still as stone, except for the brutal pounding of her heart. At this distance, with him lying on top of her, there was little she could hide. She blinked to shutter her Druae blue. "I have not decided what to do with you."

"You actually consider sending me back?" he asked.

He spit the words, and her resolve shriveled in the face of his accusation. She exhaled, a deep breath held too long, before answering. "You would be safer."

His fingertips tightened against the skin over her ribs. In his eyes, a blaze ignited. Through tense lips, he asked, "Was my safety considered before I was pulled through time?"

She heaved him off and jumped from the bed just as he leaped to his feet. They glared at each other. "Eric, it will no longer be safe for you here."

"And you expect me to go on my way, and leave you here to face the danger?"

"I am better equipped to live here under the coming conditions," she said, breathless. Her heart was a mad animal flailing against her ribs. She did not know whether to scream or cry. "No, you cannot stay. I want you to go back to your life where—"

He strode around the bed and grabbed her arms. When he pulled her close, she tensed, expecting him to shout. Instead, soft words stabbed like a knife into her soul. "Don't ask me to do this."

She closed her eyes against the pleading in his voice. She could not think with his lips so close his breath fanned her face.

"I will stand by your side and we will face this together," he said. "Whatever happens, I will not leave you."

She dropped her forehead to his and sighed. She had no need to slip into his mind. His intent was clear.

And so was hers.

She pushed away, peeling her arms from his grip. She gulped several breaths and walked away from the bed, to where there was room to move, to where a simple oak staff lay propped against the wall.

She turned to argue reason. "We will live in the forest, without any comforts. We will live on cold food, sleeping in the trees while Balock likely hunts for us." Challenging, she added, "Men will be looking to kill you."

He came to face her, standing tall enough to look down into her eyes. "I can take care of myself," he said.

She hooked his foot and yanked. As he fell flat on his back, she snatched up the staff and brought the oak down in a killing strike to his temple. She stopped an inch from his face as she placed her foot on his throat.

He gazed up at her, big-eyed and grunting from the sudden impact with the floor. She snarled. "No, you cannot take care of yourself."

She pulled her weapon back and stepped away. The look on his face made her belly crawl with snakes, but she had to make him see how futile it was for him to stay here and die. She stood back while he rose.

"If I have to force you, I will," he said. He crossed his arms and planted his feet, his glorious hips thrust at her in defiance. "If you will not promise because you love me, then do so to secure my end of the prophecy."

There is was—his ultimatum. Her throat swelled with the need to cry.

If you only knew what I would do for our love.

She swallowed and clenched her jaws to stave off the impending tears. "This is the only way you will silence the stones?" she asked.

He nodded mutely, his green eyes as hard as the tiny pieces of glass that washed up on the shore. She looked down and slowly counted her bare toes. When she looked up, her face was wiped clear of turmoil. "I promise," she said.

"Say all of it," he demanded.

"I promise," she said with a long exhale, "not to send you back."

∞

Eric paced in front of Finn's hut, throwing his hands in the air.

Unintelligible noises crawled from his growling throat.

He ran a hand through his hair, then pierced Finn with a look of disbelief. "Did you know anything about what she was planning?"

Finn sat on the ground working an intricate braid using pieces of cowhide, linen and horsehair. "I know things, brother, ye do not want to hear about," he said quietly. "But I dinna know of this."

Eric's anger fizzled and he slumped to the ground next to Finn. He admired the unique and intricate weave Finn produced, a design he had never seen before. To imagine this knowledge and art form lost for all time was like witnessing the passing of a species. His heart tore apart at the prospect of such loss. He fingered the tail of the braid, and asked, "What will happen to you, Finn?"

Finn completed his braid. He tied the bottom off in a complex endless knot, trimming the ends and hiding them inside the weave. He peeked at Eric at last, and the old mischievous smile played across his face. His elbow whipped out, tagging Eric in the ribs. "I dinna know that part, brother, for we are still waiting for yer tale. Tonight we have our last moon ceremony. Ye know the people will expect to hear their future."

Eric stared across the plain at the magnificent stones.

I will destroy the henge, the most heinous act I could possibly imagine. If only—

"After the henge is destroyed—" he started.

Finn gave him a sharp glance, stopping him. "If ye love her, then ye must have faith in all she does, for without that, yer love is worthless." He grasped Eric's hand in the Druae way and squeezed. "Believe, brother—or be lost."

∞

"He will silence the stones?" Cayri asked.

Aydyn paced in front of her mother's worktable, taking several long strides. The sick feeling over her betrayal twisted in her stomach, but she ignored the pain. "Aye, he has promised to silence the stones, and I have promised not to send him back."

"You promised him—" Cayri said, frowning.

"Yes, but we did not—"

"—contract," Cayri said.

"Exactly," Aydyn said. Her stomach continued to roll, but the swans from her dream were like a beacon of strength in her mind. She stopped pacing and glanced at her mother. The two women nodded silently.

"We will not mention this again," Aydyn said.

Cayri searched Aydyn's face. "Are you sure this is what—"

"This is best, Mother. As you taught me, what once was—"

"Will be again," Cayri answered.

∞

Balock sweated in the hot sun, tying the knots that held the smaller boat together. "Why do we waste our time building a second boat?" he said, nodding to the larger vessel, "when we do not need it until later. We are wasting our time hiding behind this great boat." He stopped and flexed his fingers, cramped from tying the rope.

Jarech checked the knots and clapped Balock on the shoulder. "A fine job," he said. He bent low, busy with a knot, and whispered into Balock's ear. "Two plans, Balock. One for all to see, one hidden. Thus, if someone watches, they will not know your plan."

He stood back and admired the smaller boat, fit to carry twenty armed men. "We will soak this one in the water tonight, to swell the wood and tighten the knots." He looked at the sky and rubbed his chin. "Tonight is the full moon. We will have this boat ready and make our crossing on a dark night."

Balock sucked in a gasp and hissed, "Cross the water during the dark of the night?" He froze, uncertain as the tactical advantage of his father's plan warred with his fear of crossing in the dark. "They will never see us," he said at last, nodding hesitantly at his father's genius. "Yes," he confirmed. He crossed his arms and grinned back at Jarech, swelled with sudden confidence. "We will take them in the dark without their cursed moon to watch."

∞

Eric walked among the giant stones. Twilight mourned the passing of the sun with a violet hued sky. A preternatural silence hung over the henge, as though the energy waited, prepared as the Druae were, for this fateful moment.

Have I done this before, he thought, *as the Druae believe? Will I be faced with time travel again, in a never-ending time loop? Or will this silencing of the stones trap me here, breaking the cycle? Dear Goddess, guide me*, he prayed.

He looked down and the hair on his arm wafted in the air. His bare feet tingled with each contact of the ground, ringing with the harmony of Mother Earth.

All energy flows in a current. And all currents are subject to disruption.

He saw the first bobbing heads as the Druae approached for their last moon ceremony in the henge. He smiled, hearing their laughter and jesting. Someone sang a gay tune for this special, joyous occasion—all because they believed. And from such faith came an unwavering strength and commitment to their honor, sustaining their hearts through unparalleled upheaval.

He was a part of this event due to forces, he believed, that were beyond him. If changes occurred in history because of what he was about to do, then let those forces in charge be responsible to the piper. He was just the messenger, and these people deserved to live.

He took his place at the altar stone, waiting for Aydyn's arrival. He knew she was close, for the ground hummed and the energy surged, seeking to join with her one last time. He saw her approach with Finn, Cayri and Taliesin, and the blue light in their eyes sparked as they passed into the inner circle of bluestones.

The Druae touched their stones, old friends greeting, and more sparks flew. At first they were tiny sparklers, but as more Druae claimed their bluestones and more of the circuit was established, the sparks grew into bold arcs. The power built, filling the air with crackling static and mini flashes of lightning.

Aydyn approached and sparks jumped between them as she reached for his hand. She touched him with one finger, and the power shot through him. Eric threw his head back and the power sang through him, and when Aydyn finally grasped his other hand, a skin of energy lifted him from the ground.

Oh, the power of the Goddess.

He grinned with a joyous display of teeth, throwing his head back and presenting his ecstatic face to the heavens. Taurus, guiding the way to man's mysterious other home in the night sky, winked in glorious understanding.

The murmur began, a humming that came from nowhere and everywhere. Eric's teeth and fingernails thrummed with a fine vibration. He looked at his hands, joined with Aydyn's, and the skin of energy under his feet rose up his legs and became a blue light surrounding them.

Cayri stepped onto the altar stone. Eric stared in awe as she lifted her hands and drew the vibration up. One by one, the bluestones flickered on like dancing neon signs.

"Druae," Cayri called.

"Druae! Druae! Druae!" they shouted, shooting their fists to the heavens. The bluestones followed suit, casting their full light into the night sky.

"We are the chosen," Cayri called out.

Cries of honor erupted, and Eric joined in the cacophony, shouting with Aydyn, "For the honor of Aradwyn, Aradwyn!" he cried.

Cayri lowered her hands to calm the crowd. The shouts quickly broke down into whispers as they leaned forward. "The time is now," she said, "to honor the contract Aradwyn made with the Star Children long ago. Tonight, we will begin our duty."

More murmurs flowed, with the men nodding their conviction. "And what of tomorrow," challenged a female voice. Several good-natured chuckles followed, and more shouts of "Tomorrow!" filled the air.

"Tomorrow," Cayri said, "we embark on a new adventure, one planned for us long ago." She turned, spreading her arms, and her long robe opened like the wings of a great bird. The bluestones shone brighter and the air crackled with static charge. Eric watched her, and a rash of prickles rose up on his scalp when she leveled her gaze at him. He returned a subtle nod.

"Tonight, for this last full moon, we have a ceremony of the future," she said, her voice rising to carry over the moving forces of nature, "for our future awaits."

An excited rustle flitted through the crowd.

Eric's belly clenched. Aydyn squeezed his hand, sending the power into his chest, surrounding his heart and filling him with the strength of her indomitable faith. He inhaled, and felt as though his chest and shoulders drew three feet across. She made him feel invulnerable—and eternal.

He released her hands and rose. The power was his now, under his command. He walked to Cayri and the altar stone. His pounding heart filled his throat and he swallowed hard, clearing the way for the words he hoped would provide a future.

All eyes were on him, like pairs of blue fireflies. The energy field surged and the vibration peaked, going beyond his perception, leaving his ears tingling with the memory of its presence. Light from the bluestones pulsed around each person and beamed into the night sky.

Sweet hope filled his heart and fueled his words.

"Your sons and daughters," he said, calling out loudly so all could hear, "will be revered in my time." At his first words, all breaths stopped. The sound of so many hearts beating in time was an echoing drumbeat, throbbing all the way to the heavens.

He turned to sweep his gaze across the crowd. "Your beauty will be legend," he said. The collective breath escaped with a single sigh, "Ahh." They leaned towards him, and he knew he was blessed to be a part of these proud people at this moment in time.

He pointed to Doyle, wearing a leather armband decorated with fish and a weaving vine. "Your art will live to enchant the heart and mind for thousands of years." Doyle grinned and lifted his arm to show off the band.

The crowd scooted closer, and Eric gave them time as they collected around him. He glanced at Aydyn, sitting with Finn and Cayri, and the love in her eyes was his gateway to the universe.

On top of the altar stone, he squatted, bringing his voice and words closer. "From this small group," he said, waving over their heads, "will arise one of the mightiest people who walked the earth."

As one, they waited.

He looked at Taliesin. "Your wisdom, Talie, will create a group of powerful wise men whose work is drawn from nature and the Mother. The tradition of these men exists, far into the future. They still perform their ceremonies in my time among these very stones."

The crowd turned to whisper and point. Talie stroked his braided beard and nodded his approval. Beside him, Aydyn lifted a hand and blew Eric a kiss.

"Caryi," Eric said. "Your powers over nature and time will carry forward, to mystify and marvel the scholars, especially me."

Cayri nodded and a flurry of gold and silver lights glittered in the air around her, rising to disperse overhead.

"Finn," Eric called. "The legacy of your iron will begin an entire new age, altering the path of mankind."

Finn stood and bowed to the crowd. When a female voice called out, "What of his other legacy?" Finn thumped his chest with one hand. "Aye, I am a lover, what can I say?" he said. Laughter rang through the crowd.

Eric sat on the altar stone with his feet hanging over the edge, now just a little above the seated crowd. He pointed east. "You will populate a vast land, extending from the cold north, all the way to the warm waters in the south." He swept his hand and they followed his movement with childish glee, laughing and clapping backs, gouging ribs.

"Your design, the endless knot, will be recognized and appreciated all over the world," he said.

The women in the front, Anna, Cat, and Moiré lifted their fists, showing the unique knot designs that decorated their leather wristbands. Cheers and more raised arms came up in waves from the rest of the crowd.

Eric paused to let them settle. His heart felt too large for his body and his ears still rang with the force field. But the words were coming easy now, because he knew he spoke the truth.

When he leaned out, as though to whisper, the silence was instant. He captured every eye, taking the time to reach each and every one, pointing to those in the back. "You will challenge two of the mightiest nations ever to exist." He paused, glancing about, and drew in their hearts with his eye.

"Of these great people you will challenge," he said, sending his voice across the rapt audience, "one is known for their strength and power, the other revered for their freedom, art and beauty. Both will learn to honor you and your fierce courage with great respect."

As his words echoed off the stones, the back of the crowd jumped to their feet, shouting a mix of jubilation and war cries. Their energy carried to the front and every Druae stood, jacking their fists into the night.

The power was intense. Lightning sparked and flowed through the crowd, and a hot metal scent scorched Eric's nose. He held his hands out, easing them back down before someone got incinerated.

When all faces turned his way, he said, "After Aradwyn's contract is fulfilled, the Druae will be no more." The faces nodded to one another before turning back. He waited, giving them time to hear. "But the beauty and the wisdom, the strength and the life of the people will continue, in another place, in another time—by another name."

Maisy jumped from Anna's arms and tugged on Eric's pant leg. "Who will we be?" she asked. Her tiny voice was carried across the energy, and Eric saw the rear of the crowd lean forward. A hundred and fifty pair of keen eyes pierced him, waiting.

He paused to let his breath catch up with his heart. He had no doubt about whom the Druae would become, but the irony of the moment begged his attention.

No one had ever been sure where the term "Celt" originated.

He tucked his head and smiled.

Remember, you are just the messenger.

He put his hand on Maisy's head. "You will be called the Celts, Maisy. But the Druae name will not disappear. The wise men will be called Druids."

"Celt," she said, flaring her pudgy lips around the new word. "Celt," she said again. She placed her little fist across her chest, and declared, "Celt!" in her childish voice. She thumped her chest, as though implanting the word in her body, and turned to the crowd. They were rising to follow her.

"Celt," ran the whisper to the back and to the front again. They looked at each other as they pronounced the word and laughed at the funny new sound. Finally they turned to Eric and Maisy, shouting, "Celt!"

The cry echoed off the stone circle, firing a new vibration. The bluestones hummed with a sweet tone and the blue light pulsed into the sky as though sending the new name to the heavens.

"Celt! Celt! Celt!" came the cry as they gave their fists to the heavens.

Maisy clambered up on the altar stone to give Eric a hug. Her little arms wrapped around him and the cries of the new Celtic people rang in his ears. He glanced at Aydyn, standing with her family, rejoicing in the hope they held for a new future. The love shone in her eyes, and he knew he would do it all again and again, just for her.

Maisy jumped down from the altar stone and ran through the crowd. "I am the first," she cried. "I am the first Celt." Anna stepped next to Eric. "I think you have given her something to do with her mouth other than wear out her thumb." She gave him a quick hug, whispering, "Thank you for giving my daughter a future."

Aydyn and Cayri came to Eric, while Finn and Talie carried on a raucous debate over whose legacy would see the most glory. Eric shook his head, praying he had not created a monster. In the background, he could see Maisy still running to tell everyone that she was the first of the new tribe. He cringed.

Who gave me this job?

"You could not have done better," Aydyn whispered. She grabbed his arm and hugged him close. Behind her, even though the people were dispersing, the bluestones continued to glow. Eric frowned and cocked his head, wondering at this new anomaly.

Aydyn answered before he could ask. "They are waiting for you to speak the words of their destruction. It is part of the contract."

Cayri nodded to Finn and Talie as they joined them. "Eric is just telling us—" she said.

All eyes were on him. Words of encouragement were one thing, but destroying a star gate was all together different. He turned and faced the outer ring of trilithons while the four Celts stood at his back, waiting.

He said, "We will burn them." He turned and met four frowns of bewilderment. "Bring wood and water."

Aydyn's eyebrows lifted, but when he gave no other word, she jabbed Finn in the ribs and the two took off at a lope. He watched them go, feeling Cayri's eyes on him.

"Stone, fire, air, water. Such is a simple plan," she said.

He smiled with more confidence than he felt. "It worked for Hannibal."

Pray, he thought, *we have the time to make it work.*

∞

Eric watched the preparation, refusing to think beyond the urgency of the moment. Sweat dampened his palms and he wiped his hands on his pants. Would fire and water really be enough?

They brought wood as he asked, along with water tainted with the acidic soil from beneath the great oaks. Dozens of ladders and chisels were brought, and a hundred torches lit, even though the bright full moon watched them from a clear sky.

"What was his name, brother?" Finn asked. "The man with the elephants—ye called them, these great creatures from another land. Why was he taking such animals over the mountains?"

Eric rubbed his face. "Hannibal went to make war, and the

animals were a part of his army—"

The chisels pealed like church bells until one by one, they drove finite cracks into the lintel crosspieces. Eric flinched at the damning smack of iron hammer against chisel. "Hannibal," he said, "had to break a road through the mountain rocks. "This technique worked for him."

Behind the men with hammer and chisel came women with kindling to set the fire base. A second wave of men followed, supplying the solid ingots to build a hot fire.

Finally, every lintel was chiseled and laid with wood. The moon was long gone and the sun approached, daring to put the light of day on their deeds.

Aydyn came with two torches. She nodded to her brother and passed one of the torches to Eric. "I will help you light the outer ring," she said. She motioned to Finn. "You, Cayri and the others will light the center fires."

Finn bowed with his fist crossed over his chest. Before he sprinted away, he winked at Eric and said, "Celt?" He turned on his heel without waiting for a response, and was gone.

Eric's hand holding the torch shook. He looked at Aydyn and her eyes were steady and calm. He wondered how she could face this moment with such peace and clarity.

"Because you have given us a new path," she said.

She stroked his face, pushing his hair back, and for one precious second he closed his eyes and let her cool touch sooth the heat of doubt that flared in his heart. He pressed her hand to his cheek and kissed her strong, warrior's fingers.

"We are ready," she said.

He nodded.

"Climb here, light each fire, and I will meet you there," she said, pointing to the stones behind the center horseshoe.

He saw Finn and a group of men standing ready to climb ladders and light the fires laid on the five great trilithons. In the east, the sun peeked over the top of the forest. Its rays cut soft shadows through the stones.

He nodded to Aydyn and she climbed ahead of him. Everyone stood atop the stones and waited for his signal. He held his torch by the first pyre, and when he saw the sun's rays touch the altar stone, he torched the kindling.

The fires roared to life as sunlight bathed the altar stone. He ran along the circle to set the next fire and the next, leaping from lintel to lintel. He reached the end with Aydyn, and they clambered down a ladder.

Thirty-five fires scorched the crown of Stonehenge. Sickness welled in Eric's heart. His shoulders fell and he rubbed his forehead; exhaustion consumed him. "They must tend the fires," he said, motioning to the men with their ladders and great piles of wood.

Aydyn nodded and he exhaled with a heavy burst. "Keep them hot—all day," he said. "We will test one tonight."

He took her hand. Her amazing strength flowed into him, right when his knees threatened to give. She accepted what needed to be with such total unwavering and fierce determination that he feared he must certainly disappoint her.

She pulled him close and placed her forehead to his, just as he had seen her do with Donnye and Rowan. He relaxed, and her soothing energy washed over him. She hummed a tune, familiar, yet not—and he sagged against her. Inside his mind, he turned to her, needing her calm energy to soothe his grieving heart.

I am so proud of you. I know how difficult this was.

Her thought slipped into his mind as clear as his own. "You are?" he whispered.

She nodded against his forehead, and her unflagging strength sizzled down his spine. "You could never disappoint me," she said.

Believe, came the Goddess.

He realized how much she believed in him. Once again, she had made him feel invincible—and eternal. He sighed with relief and pushed his shoulders back, ready for anything as long as she was by his side.

∞

Aydyn and Cayri walked, watching the men as they prepared to pour the tainted water over the heated stones again.

"You are certain of this?" Cayri asked.

"Rowan went directly there. We saw the second boat drying," Aydyn said, "—hidden behind a larger vessel."

"Tomorrow there is no moon," Cayri said, "and I fear what may come in such darkness." She gripped Aydyn's arm and her eyes glazed, reaching for a vision. Aydyn closed her eyes—and took her mother to the smaller boat.

They watched the boat in the fabric of time. Cayri waved her hand across the vision, and the fabric rippled, changing, revealing the future of the boat—its passage across the water, bringing armed men to their shore.

Together they blinked and their eyes returned to focus.

Aydyn gasped. "We must hurry—" she said. "We have no way of knowing when—"

Behind them, a loud crack came amid shouts from the men. They watched as the first lintel stone split and slowly tilted to one side, screaming as rock ground against rock.

Another crack came, and another. All around the circle, the lintels gave way and sagged with great clouds of stinking steam as the acid solution hit the scorched stones.

Aydyn shuddered with the screaming stones. Beneath her feet, the ground trembled when the first great stones fell. She looked at the smaller bluestones and felt their power wink out.

My duty begins now.

She threw her shoulders back. "Bring Eric's clothes and prepare the chamber. We will meet you there. And bring Finn, he will want—"

"So soon? Would you not take another night?" Cayri protested.

"No," Aydyn spit. Her eyes burned and air refused to move through her gaping chest. Her future loomed dark and lonely, but at least Eric would be safe—and that was all that mattered.

"Go now," she demanded, "before I change my mind."

∞

Aydyn found Eric commanding the men in their last efforts to finish the remaining stones. When he looked up and saw her, his eyes lit with relief and joy—and her resolve was a rope around her neck. She smiled and waved, begging the Goddess to help him understand.

My love, please believe in me.

He ran to her, breathless. "It's working," he panted, "they're coming down, just as I—" He caught her expression and stopped, peering into her face. "What?"

She drew on all her abilities, for this would be the test of her life. She was a warrior, an Ovate of divinity, and a sister to the stars.

I am a woman trying to save my man.

"I went with Rowan last night, to see—" She paused to watch

as another stone cracked and tumbled with a fierce grinding. She smiled with sadness and frowned. Her world would never be the same, but her destiny would be fulfilled.

All I have now is the future.

"They are close, Eric. Closer than we thought. They could be here any moment," she said.

"Then we must go," he said. He waved to the smoldering ruins of the great circle. "I think this will satisfy the Star Children's contract. Whatever circuit was created there is broken."

She tore her eyes away from the fallen stones. "Cayri has asked for you to help in the chamber. Can you come now?" She wiped the fear and grief from her heart and looked at him with innocent eyes.

He dusted his hands on his pants and nodded. "My work is done here," he said. He stared at the ruin he had wrought on Stonehenge and shook his head. "The boys seem to have the nature of it, but I need to tell—"

"Cayri's request is urgent," she said. "What you have to say can wait. We will be right back." She tugged on his hand, pulling him away from the stones. Her stomach was slowly turning to rock and she needed to have this done before her resolve shattered, just like the great stones. "Come."

They ran all the way, reaching the chamber winded and thirsty. She stopped so they could catch their breath, and passed her water bag. She watched as he took a long drink.

Believe in me.

He wiped his mouth and handed her the bag. She took it and let it drop to the ground. She stared, taking in every bit of him. The particular green of his eyes, the tiny quirk his lips make when he smiles, the timber of his voice when he said—

"I love you."

Her throat seized and she looked down. She remembered the swans in her dream and the vision of their many lives together. She gathered the strength of the Goddess, and sang his beautiful words. "My heart will remember you."

His knees gave and he took a wobbling step. He rubbed his temple and looked at her, frowning as he slowly wavered to the ground.

She caught him, lowering him gently. She kissed him, and sang, "Will your heart remember me?"

"Aydyn—" he struggled.

She knew he was alert and only temporarily paralyzed. She gripped his face, finally able to put her heart into her eyes. She let the tears pour, blinding her as they rained onto his cheeks.

"Believe—believe in me. Believe in the strength of our love," she choked.

She looked up. Finn and her mother stood waiting. She nodded and swiped the tears from her face. Taking a deep breath, she clutched his hand as if she would never let go.

And yet—

She smelled the smoke, could see the fallen stones.

There is no going back, only forward.

She kissed him gently. His eyes pleaded, frantic, but she held on. She placed her finger to his lips. "Shh," she said, halting his silent tirade.

His eyes changed, and she knew he stopped fighting.

She poured all her love into her Celtic blue. "Know that we will love many lifetimes. I have seen this." His eyes softened and she nearly burst. "Stop looking for me in the past," she commanded. "Look to the future, for I will find you—and love you again."

Chapter Sixteen

Eric couldn't stop the silent flood of tears that followed him through time. A drop beginning in 1600 BCE ran down his face, mingled with Aydyn's tears, and dropped from his chin three-and-a-half thousand years later.

All I wanted was to live my life with the woman I love.

His heart and soul cried, *Aydyn.*

After her last words, Finn carried him to the chamber and dressed him in his modern clothes. "Brother, ye canna fight wi' women when they know what they are doing," he said. He propped Eric's boneless body against the wall beneath the carving of a Star Child in a bio-space suit.

"Remember, have faith in her," Finn said. "She is the heart of the Druae, as are ye." He leaned down and whispered in Eric's ear, "Believe and anything is possible. Dinna ye learn that from her?"

He rose and planted his fist across his chest. "Thank ye, brother, for all ye have done. We will remember your words." He threw his head back and cried, "Og awawyn bot wyn," and thumped his chest before bowing out of the chamber.

Then the crystals came alive, but this time, Eric couldn't scream. He knew dark oblivion and pain before materializing in the original chamber he discovered. The last tremor of time travel rippled through his bones and he opened his mouth for another soundless scream. The silence he produced gave no echo, and wrapped around him, as empty as his heart.

All that was left to him was his pain and his tears.

The drug was quickly wearing off and he pushed himself upright.

The chamber appeared untouched, even the lantern was still lit. His mangled hat lay at his feet, as though he had just this moment tripped over it and fell.

He glanced at his watch, now unfamiliar on his wrist, and saw the hands moving perfectly. He worked his jaws and sucked on his tongue for saliva. "Tuh—two o'clock," he stuttered.

At 1:45 he had returned to the hole after lunch. Then he sat on the stone and found his initials, stood, fell, and broke through the wall. He looked about. His hand was inches short of making that plunging discovery again.

A chill peppered his scalp and he raked his fingers over his head. "Take this nice and easy," he said. He turned to where the initials should be, but was afraid to look.

Did Finn remember his instructions? The rock formation waited, daring his faith. "Have events been changed?" he croaked. His heart thudded with insistence, the jungle drumbeat stirring. He heard her last words. "Look for me in the future, for I will find you and love you again. "

"Aydyn, what have you done?" he whispered.

He crawled to the stone perch and stared at the place where the initials should be buried. He wanted so badly to believe in her words.

"We will love many lifetimes."

Alone in the 21st century, he didn't have the luxury of her faith and her visions. All he had was the clawing ache of her loss. *Aydyn*, his heart cried. He stood on shaky legs and sagged against the stone seat. He sat and held his head in his hands, staring once again at his boots, just as he did that day. Fresh tears filled his eyes.

One, two, three, they fell to the dirt.

If the initials were gone, would the wall also be void of the iron lever? He was afraid to know if the portal between their times was forever closed, afraid to feel so cut off from her. He shivered, hearing her voice so clearly.

"They are not there, you know."

He rubbed his face and frowned. "You've really lost it, old boy," he muttered. He hung his head, his eyes wrung out and gritty. The pain of missing her rippled through him, and he brought a fist to his forehead. Breath was meaningless in his rigid chest.

"Mr. Beck, you need to breathe."

"Aaghh!" he yelped. He stood up and lurched, catching his feet in his hat. He pirouetted and went down like a sack of sand, plopping to his butt with a distinct lack of grace. As he landed, his hand flew out and plunged through the fragile wall.

He glared at the figure climbing down his rope ladder. His heart hammered with deja' vu. He stuttered, "Who are you? What …what do you—" His fingers trembled and he brushed the pulverized earth from his arm. He looked at the ruined wall where the lever should be.

"You won't find anything there," she said.

He shook his head and wondered what world he had fallen into. The woman's voice was so familiar. And how did she know?

"What you are looking for?" she repeated. "Because I know." She stepped off the last rung of the ladder and turned towards him. A small beam of afternoon sunlight poured in from the opening to backlight her form.

He eyed her shadowed presence and his heart did a flip-flop—his old friend, the salmon on the bank. His palms sweated and he wiped his hands on his pants. He remembered the earrings, and patted his empty pockets.

She kept the earrings.

"Thank you, Goddess," he whispered.

"Excuse me?" the woman asked. She stepped closer and extended her hand. "I am Lily, Mr. Beck, Cedric's friend. I came to see you last night, but you had already left."

He wondered if he had suffered some physiological impairment on his last pass through time. His belly swooped and the carousel careened. His traveling companion, the precipice opened wide. He stopped breathing.

Believe.

"Eric, breathe."

Her voice pulled him back from the edge, and air flooded his lungs with a hiccup. The voice was Aydyn's. He strained for a glimpse of her face, but she remained in the shadows. He closed his eyes and opened his heart, begging for a spark of the Goddess to guide him.

She reached for the lantern, and where her hand passed in the darkness, he saw her flesh outlined with a flickering blue glow. The yellow lantern light dispelled the blue glow, but illuminated her ring. *Gold.*

He lifted his left hand; the ring Aydyn gave him in marriage shone in the dim light. He clenched his fist and brought the precious gold to his chest, willing to hope, daring to believe. With his right hand, he touched Lily's fingers.

A tiny cloud of sparkles danced above their hands.

Her fingers were strong and cool, the hand callused.

Her scent came to him, fresh and subtly familiar. A tingling thrill shot through him and he leaned closer, wanting her face.

Dear Goddess, can this be possible?

"How do you know what's there?" he stammered, waving at the ruined wall.

"I know a great deal, Mr. Beck." She pulled her hand from his and her gold ring flashed.

The insistent beating in his chest drove him forward. He glimpsed long dark hair, firing impossible hope. "Tell me what you know."

She stepped into the lantern light. He sucked in a gasp, unable to speak.

"I know who you are," she said. She took off her ring and tugged his from his left hand. She held the twin gold pieces to the light, comparing the identical endless knots on the inside. Aydyn's knot.

His heart was sweeping out of control, making him fear he would pass out and find her gone when he woke. He grabbed her and pulled her into the light.

Eyes the color of a Caribbean pool begged him to dive in. The copper was gone, but gold earrings lay against her neck in tangled loops.

Believe, his heart cried.

He knew her being here was fantastic, utterly impossible. He trembled, finally understanding the precipice that had plagued him relentlessly—all this time waiting for him to believe.

Believe!

Did he dare hope in the depth of Aydyn's faith and power she had known what she was doing? Since finding her, hadn't his life been filled with miracles utterly fantastic and impossible? He stopped, uncertain, when the abyss challenged him for his heart's greatest hope.

Believe in the power of—

"Our love," she said. She pursed her lips and sang in a soft whisper, "My heart will remember you."

The tune sliced through him, iron against simple flesh, laying him bare to the abyss. He sighed and released his heart with a burst of joy. "Will your heart remember me?" he responded.

A tear filled one of her eyes, but she kept singing. "Will your heart remember me?"

The tear escaped and he caught the drop on a fingertip. "My heart will remember you," he sang. He smiled and pulled her close, needing to feel the beat of her heart next to his. He held her so until he felt their heartbeats merge into one.

They had at last, come home. He bent to kiss her precious lips. His goddess had found him.

∞

The red falcon cruised the updrafts, searching the ground far below. Small game had already returned to the stone ruins, and a rabbit teased at her attention.

Two men stood among the stones and the falcon watched. Even though they were as tiny as insects, their voices carried on the breeze, bringing their anger to the sky. The bird dove, swooping over their heads as one man struck the other to the ground. Again and again he struck, then turned and left the fallen man where he lay.

The bird turned to leave, but the command came, *wait*. She went back, watching as the stricken man rose and limped after the other. She followed their long journey to the beach.

They reached the shore and claimed a boat that waited with a group of armed men. The falcon dove the beach, scattering the placid sea birds and shrieking at the men as they launched the boat. Again and again she dove at their heads, driving them into their boat, off the beach, and back to their land.

The men shouted at her and raised their fists, but the surf quickly sucked them away. When the swell lifted to take the boat, a big man stood and cast an object back to shore. The metal piece fell to the sand, its silver gleaming blood red in the warm morning sun.

The falcon screamed a final time at the intruders before climbing to tremendous height on the powerful ocean air currents. She circled, watching the boat grow smaller and smaller. At last, when they were gone from her keen sight, she turned inland.

As wild and free as the wind, she flew back to the forest, ready for a new home and a new adventure—ready for the future.

∞

DANA LYONS

Dana Lyons lives in the mountains of western North Carolina with her husband, Randy, four cats and two horses. She loves to travel and cook, try new wines, study quantum physics, and discover new mysteries of the heart and mind. Says Lyons, "If you believe enough, if you love enough, you can draw upon a power to create the life and love of your dreams. Love is a force that comes from within, yet steers the course of your life as if from the faraway stars."

Two more paranormal romances you might love!

Sofia never believed the words on the parchment to be more than myth. Until one winter morning changes everything. Now the breathtaking man who haunts her waking hours is the very soul whose immortal curse she must put an end to - one way or another.

ISBN: 978-0-9793252-2-9

Deep in a box of used books, counselor Tory Sasser comes across a novel without an ending: Heatherfield. She reads the story of scarred war veteran, Jake Benjamin, a fictional character in a fictional town. Or is he? Tory is desperate to find her way back home to reality. Yet what is more real than true love? No, Heatherfield isn't all it seems ... not at all.

ISBN: 978-0-9793252-8-1

www.ingramcontent.com/pod-product-compliance
Lightning Source LLC
Chambersburg PA
CBHW020321260626
47156CB00004B/1318